Carolina Grace

Southern Breeze Series, Book 3

Regina Rudd Merrick

Scrivenings
PRESS
Quench your thirst for story.
www.ScriveningsPress.com

To my husband, Todd Wayne Merrick. You're the reason I can write about a girl finding "the one."

ACKNOWLEDGMENTS

There are always many people to thank when a book is finished. For the first one, you want to include everyone who had anything to do with the process or getting you to that point, but for the third?

For the third, you really know who to thank.

First, I want to thank my husband, Todd, for putting up with a writer's capricious moods and extended silences. I'm not mad, I'm just thinking.

Next, my daughters, Emily and Ellen, who encourage me every step of the way.

My parents and in-laws, for their excitement and wonder at this thing called being an author. It helps keep ME excited!

For my church family and my friends, I thank you for your encouragement, your prayers, and your understanding. I can't do it all, and when I try, you tell me I'm being hard on myself. That's a blessing.

To Mantle Rock Publishing, thank you for taking a chance on a local girl and sticking with me through an entire series (and beyond!). You've made such a difference in my life. Jerry, Kathy, Pam, Diane, I wouldn't be the writer I am without you!

And to my Lord and Savior, Jesus Christ, who saved me forever, I praise you, for I have been fearfully and wonderfully made. May You receive honor and glory from anything coming from my fingers and my mind.

For you are saved by grace through faith, and this is not from yourselves; it is God's gift—not from works, so that no one can boast. [Eph. 2:8-9] NKJV

Amazing grace! How sweet the sound
That saved a wretch like me!
I once was lost, but now am found;
Was blind, but now I see.

CHAPTER ONE

Charlotte Livingston's head shot up when the elevator opened. The hollow sound echoed in the hallway of the hospital adjacent to the Emergency Services waiting room.

The breath she held left her in a sigh when she saw the doors close behind two nurses with a cart. The late hour meant no visitors, but for those waiting for word, the wide-open lobby felt cold and claustrophobic in its loneliness.

"How many times, Lord, will I have to sit here and wait to find out if the ones I love are okay?" She got up and stretched, walking around the familiar room, her heels tapping on the shiny tiles. Not much to see that she hadn't seen before: three-month-old hunting and decorating magazines, various health-related pamphlets for conditions she hoped she never had to face, and a Gideon Bible. When she sat back down, she leaned forward, covering her face with her hands.

Her nerves were taut, the long day taking its toll on her as she worried and waited for word. Magazines exhausted, phone almost dead and charging at an outlet, she began to pray silently. Maybe that would hurry things along.

Her phone buzzed: Anything?? Her best friend, Lydia, was chomping at the bit, which was typical.

Charly sighed and tapped her reply. Nope. I'll keep you posted.

As she was settling in to repeat the Lord's Prayer as a last resort to keep her mind busy, the elevator doors opened, and she heard footsteps rushing toward her.

"Finally. I thought you would never get here." She stood and put her hands on her hips in frustration.

"Sorry, it takes longer to get out of the house these days." Jared Benton carried a portable car seat holding a newborn, setting it gently on a coffee table and covering the sleeping infant carefully with a soft blanket.

Sarah Benton went straight to Charly and hugged her. "Charly. Where's your mom? Have you heard anything?"

"She's in with them, and no, nothing. I'm going crazy out here."

"I'll go to the nurses' station and see if we can get a little info." Sarah looked at her husband and motioned for him to stay with Charly.

Jared nodded. "Since you recently had the prettiest baby in the county in this hospital, I think you should have a little pull." He grabbed her hand for a second, before letting go.

"Handsomest. I'll be right back. Don't worry."

"Do you think they're okay?" She covered her face with her hands and closed her eyes. "I will never forgive myself if something happens."

Jared sighed. "Charly, don't beat yourself up about this." He looked up. "Here's Sarah."

She looked up to see a worried frown on her face. "Sarah? What's wrong?"

Sarah cleared her expression. "I'm not sure. They're going to let me go back there."

"Are you sure you're up to it?" Jared looked concerned.

"Lucy asked for me."

Charly shook her head in frustration. "Something's wrong. I just know it."

"We don't know anything." Sarah checked on the baby, still sleeping. "Keep an eye on Beau Alexander."

"You know we will." When she rushed toward the swinging doors, Jared shook his head and looked at his best friend's little sister. "Like we can't be trusted."

Sarah paused. "I heard that. I'll be back as soon as I know anything."

Sarah went back to the nurses' station and a nurse came out from behind the counter to escort her to the double doors.

A tiny squeak emanated from the baby and both Jared and Charly jumped.

"He makes that little noise all the time."

"What?"

"Squeak in his sleep. Don't know if he's dreaming or what. Must be carrying on lots of conversations in those dreams."

Charly grinned slightly. "Do you guys sit and watch him all the time?"

Jared's smile grew. "Pretty much."

"He's a keeper, for sure." Charly looked in wonder at the baby, his tiny hand held up in sleep as if propped up, holding his fingers out reminiscent of a high-five.

EMMALINE QUINCE TOOK A DEEP BREATH. Most days, her job as a wedding planner in Pawley's Island, South Carolina was rewarding, fun, and carefree. And then there were days like this.

When Lucy Dixon Livingston became her business partner, she thought her troubles were over and then this.

Yes, it was a blessing, but four weeks early? Come on. Really?

Okay, it had to be the frustration talking.

She walked up to the bride and her mother, who were bickering about which step the bridesmaids needed to stand on, the pastor cracking jokes with the groomsmen, and the groom standing there looking like death warmed over.

Nothing she couldn't handle, but with Lucy by her side, she felt more confident, especially as she felt herself getting older and the brides seemed to get younger and more opinionated.

She walked up to Christy, her bride, and her mother, Barbara. "What's the problem, ladies?"

"Mom is convinced someone is going to fall off the steps if they're too close, and I've assured her they'll be fine and that they've been walking, talking and standing for several years now, and if they think they're fine, they're fine." The bride practically had steam coming out her ears with her last "fine" and never took her eyes off her mother, who was getting teary-eyed.

"Barbara, let's take a walk for a second." Emma finally caught the pastor's eye and said, "Everyone, relax and take five. We'll be right back."

She led the emotional mom down the aisle and handed her a tissue. She kept a little packet in her pocket for rehearsals and weddings.

Her mama always said, "a lady always has a tissue," and she'd finally learned the lesson. She still rebelled, inside, every time she thought about it.

"I'm fine. Really, I am." The mother of the bride was trying to convince herself.

Emma pulled her friend in for a hug. "Now, Barbara, I know better."

"I'm happy," she said and then began to boo-hoo loudly enough for the bridal party in front of the auditorium to look back in concern.

"Shhh. It'll be okay. This is perfectly normal."

"But she's leaving me, and then she yelled at me." The blubbering answer would have been humorous if it hadn't been slightly pathetic.

"Barbara, look at me." Time to get stern. Ain't nobody got time for this.

The red-rimmed eyes of Barbara Turnbow looked at her, a loud sniff accompanying the quivering chin.

When pressed for time, Emma's southern accent came out in full force. "Barbara, these kids are gettin' married tomorrow. Christy needs her mama, and she needs you to be strong for her, or she'll be the one busting into tears. Do you want those pictures tomorrow to be of y'all cryin' and carryin' on? Or do you want those pictures to be the illustration of one of the happiest days of your life?"

"She's the one gettin' married, not me."

"Yes and how long have you prayed for that boy up there?"

Sniff. "Since she was born."

"Alrighty, then, your prayers have been answered. Did you do anything to answer your prayer?"

Head shaking in the negative. "No, it was all God."

"Right. If it's a gift from God, why are you tryin' to take over and nit-pick?"

Barbara lifted her eyes to Emma, her lips twisted in a damp grin.

"Now, mama, look up there at those kids. Don't they look nice on those steps?"

She smiled through her tears. "They look wonderful. And with the dresses it will be perfect."

"If we spread them out any more, it'll be uneven, so I think you need to give Christy this one, okay?"

Barbara heaved a loud sigh. "Okay. I'll try to keep my cool."

Emma patted her on the back. "It's all right, honey. If you're going to lose your cool, now is the time to do it."

"I miss her already."

"I know. Remember, you're not losing a daughter . . ."

Barbara blew her nose loudly and chuckled. "I know. I'm gaining a son."

"Ready to do this thing?"

The mother of the bride straightened her spine, stretched her eyes open to minimize the puffiness (it never works, by the way), strode up the aisle, and took her place on the second pew, left side, Emma following at a fast pace behind.

"All right, Pastor, I think we've got a plan, and the girls and guys look perfect where they are. You may proceed to the vows portion of the ceremony."

RANCE BUTLER PICKED up the clipboard off the desk at the nurses' station. The way his eyes kept crossing, if he didn't get some sleep soon, he wouldn't only be seeing blurry lines; he'd be seeing two of everything.

Go to medical school, they said. Be a doctor, they said. You'll make lots of money, they said. It'll be fun, they said.

At twenty-eight, in his third year of residency at Georgetown General Hospital, he was close enough to the end to push back the burnout, but this rotation in the "high risk obstetrics" elective had been more than he bargained for.

"Young man, you need to get some rest." Jackie Warren, the nurse on duty, was his mother-hen.

He grinned at her and leaned both elbows on the counter. "Tell me something I don't already know." Resting his chin on his hands, he closed his eyes for a second.

"Don't you be sleeping here on my desk. Find your own." She twisted her lips and placed another clipboard on the counter next to him. "Got a present, especially for you."

He heaved a sigh and raised himself up to look at the medical records in front of her. "Ah, what I always wanted. A last-minute admission with Doctor Price."

"He'll be in here as soon as he can get in from his garden." She chuckled. "I hear she was in his office this morning and he told her it would be several days. I guess he didn't give the Livingston baby one of those free wall calendars."

Scanning the paper, he twisted his lips in a frown. "Not due for four weeks." He read on. "I'll go in and check. Something's not right here."

Adrenalin kicked in, and the bounce was back in his step. When he approached the swinging double doors, he glanced over at the young woman with long, blonde hair and a dark-haired man in the waiting room, smiling over a baby-carrier. He lifted the left side of his mouth in a slight grin. Something inside him bloomed. Nice little family.

He stopped short when a darker-haired woman he didn't know rushed out the doors and to the waiting room.

"Charly, we need you!"

CHAPTER TWO

Charly entered the birthing room with trepidation. What had she done, asking her sister-in-law to come to the school to help her with a problem student? As soon as she walked in the door of the classroom, she knew something wasn't right. Lucy Livingston seemed to have more energy than usual, but she seemed, well, puffy, for want of a better word.

Tom Livingston, Charly's older brother, knelt next to Lucy's head, looking so pale she was worried he would pass out. It wasn't out of the question, after all. He might be the county sheriff, but when it came to his wife, he was a big, stuffed ball of goo.

Lucy saw her and reached out for her other hand. "Charly, I need to tell you something." She paused and strained, her jaw clenched in pain. "Wait a minute. And get out from between me and the tissue box. It's my focal point."

Tom smiled wanly. "I learned the hard way." He showed her the bruise on his arm. "This was from the first time I got in her way."

Lucy relaxed. "That was a big one."

"Oh, Lucy, what happened? Was it coming out to the school? Did you fall?"

Lucy waved a tired hand. "Honey, I came to the school after my appointment with Dr. Price. He told me it would be several days before I delivered. Now, if he doesn't hurry, he'll be the LATE Dr. Price when I get hold of him."

The hospital resident came in. "Mr. and Mrs. Livingston?"

Tom rose and shook his hand. "I'm Tom, and this is my wife, Lucy." He looked over at the others in the room. "My mother, Mrs. Livingston, and my sister, Charlotte."

He nodded, acknowledging Charly and Mary Ann. His eyes flickered a little when he saw Charly. "Hello, I'm Dr. Butler. I've been told Dr. Price will be here as soon as he can get out of his garden." His lips quirked up in a brief smile.

"It's getting closer." Tom settled back within reach of his wife.

"That's what I hear." He checked the chart and the monitors. "You're being awfully quiet."

Lucy glared at him. "Not my first rodeo."

Charly was still worried, but she couldn't help noticing the concerned young intern. Were his eyes truly such an intense blue? She switched her attention back to Lucy when she spoke.

"Charly, the reason I asked for you was that I wanted you to be here for the birth."

"Really?" A smile broke out on her face.

Lucy nodded. "When Hayes was born, we thought you were too young, and you're a grown-up lady now." Lucy closed her eyes. "Here it comes again." She squeezed Tom's hand until his fingers were turning blue. His slight grimace was the only indication it hurt.

Charly grimaced in sympathy and glanced at Dr. Butler. She was surprised at his quick grin when their eyes met. She grinned back before she thought.

The door swung open, and a nurse, following the obstetrician, rushed to the doctor to help him on with his delivery gown and mask.

"Do you want covers for those shoes?" She laughed and pointed down at the muddy garden shoes he still wore so he could rush to the hospital. "Might get 'em dirty."

Dr. Price chuckled and turned to the resident. "You're in for a treat, Dr. Butler." He looked over his glasses and into the face of the delivering mother. "You told me you thought it would be sooner, didn't you?"

Lucy glared at him. Uncharacteristic for her, but highly characteristic for a woman giving birth. "I hope you're happy now. You got here in time to play catch."

He laughed as the nurses put her in position. "I'm glad I got the tomato plants in the ground before they called me. Almost ready, looks like."

After a few intense contractions, things moved swiftly. How was Lucy living through this? Charly had watched videos of birth but seeing someone you love in this much pain was almost more than she could bear. She couldn't help wondering if she would ever have the nerve to go through it herself.

"Bless you, baby. Bless you, baby." The doctor prayed as the baby was delivered.

Charly was silent, watching the miracle of birth before her eyes. Tears gathered as she saw her nephew being born. When Lucy relaxed for a moment, she was happy. Now the recovery could begin.

The baby, handed over to the nurse, began to cry lustily. Why didn't they give the baby to Lucy? Was something wrong? Wait. Lucy was still having contractions.

The doctor resumed his position and began praying again. "Bless you, baby number two. Bless you, baby."

Charly lifted her hands to her face in awe. She went to stand next to her mother sitting in a chair out of the fray. "Did you know they were having twins this time?"

Mary Ann Livingston's sightless eyes were filled with tears, a smile on her face. "No, sweetheart, I didn't know either. What a blessing."

Baby number two was born, a niece this time. Dr. Price handed the baby to Dr. Butler who took the screaming young lady to be weighed, measured, and have her APGAR score checked while the nurses helped Lucy.

"A boy and a girl." Lucy pulled her hand from Tom's and touched his face with a tired smile. "We did it."

He leaned over to kiss her. "You did it. I can't believe it happened so fast."

"Second births generally go faster." The doctor came to them, carrying both babies. He looked down at each little face. "I've prayed over deliveries for over thirty years." He looked up at Tom and Lucy. "It never gets old." He handed them both to Lucy, Tom helping to support her in the bed. "Little master weighs six pounds, three ounces, eighteen and a half inches long, and little miss weighs in at five pounds, nine ounces, and eighteen inches long. APGAR scores are excellent for thirty-six weeks. I don't think you would have made it much longer if your water hadn't broken."

"I can assure you they had outgrown their space." Lucy beamed down at them. "I can't wait for Hayes to see them." She looked over at her sister-in-law and mother-in-law. "Charly, bring Mom over.

Charly took Mary Ann's hand and guided her to the bedside, where Tom took each hand and put them on a baby. "Two more grandbabies for you to love, Mom."

Tears fell from her eyes. "I wish I could see them. I know they are blessed babies. When did you find out they were twins?"

Tom laughed down at his wife and children and then looked up at Charly and his mom. "At about three months. They thought they could hear a second heartbeat, but we weren't sure until the ultrasound."

The nurse came and took one of the babies from Lucy. "I need to check your blood pressure. Mr. Livingston, would you like to hold your son?"

"I thought you'd never ask." He took his infant son, shaking his head in wonder. "When can Jared and Sarah come in?"

The nurse looked at her watch, calculating Lucy's blood pressure readings. "I'll go get them now. I think we can overlook the age restriction for little Beau this time." She wrote down her readings and winked. "I'll be right back."

"Have you picked names? I think I'm still in shock. I can't believe you didn't tell anyone." Charly paused. She narrowed her eyes and tilted her head. "Wait. Is that why you said you didn't know if it was a boy or girl, so you'd get a little bit of both at your shower?"

"Busted. And why we have a gender-neutral nursery this time." Lucy reached out for Charly's hand. "You have no idea how hard it was not to talk about it."

"We kept the second baby bed hidden in the closet of our room. I'll have to put it together when we get home, and they can sleep in the same bed for a few weeks." Tom couldn't take his eyes off his babies.

Sarah walked in, her jaw hanging in shock. "How did this happen?" She stopped, her face infused with red, when laughter erupted in the room. "Okay, not how did this happen, but how could you not tell me you were having twins?"

Lucy handed her baby girl to Tom, who stood holding both babies with pride. Then she reached out for a hug from Sarah. "It was murder not telling you; especially since we were pregnant at the same time."

"I thought you were bigger because you were shorter, but my goodness! These babies are as big as Beau."

Charly couldn't stand it anymore. "All right. We've waited

long enough. What are their names? We can't go on calling them 'baby boy' and 'baby girl,' now can we? If I don't text Lydia the info soon, she'll be down here beating down the door."

Tom and Lucy looked at one another and nodded in unison. Tom gazed upon his new babies. "This young man is Evan Atwood Livingston, and this young lady is MariAnne Dixon Livingston."

Mary Ann put her hand to her mouth. "Oh. Bless you, are you sure?"

Lucy smiled. "Mama, we're sure. We wanted to name them after my daddy and our mama. You've been the best mother a girl could ask for, and you've helped me so much, since my mama isn't here."

"You're an answer to prayer. How could I not mother you along with my own chicks?" Mary Ann leaned in to hug Lucy. "Three grandbabies in five years. I am blessed beyond measure."

At forty, Emma couldn't believe how much older she felt than her partner, Lucy, and yet here Lucy was, at thirty-five, giving birth, and she was the mom of a teenager.

When she got to the hospital, the excitement was just beginning. The waiting room was empty, and the nurse at the desk beamed. "Hi, Emmaline. You're in time to join the party. We're pretty empty right now, so if you want to go on back, you can."

She entered and waved to a room full of people, but her focus went straight to the babies. Sarah had her baby in the carrier. This baby, she knew. Then she looked at Lucy and Tom. They were each holding a baby. Wait. Each?

"Twins?" The question squeaked out of her. "This explains so much!"

A tired Lucy laughed. "Didn't we do a great job keeping these guys a secret?"

"Too good. Girl, I would have made you sit down and take it a lot easier had I known."

Lucy waved her hand. "I was fine. How did the rehearsal go?" Lucy wrinkled her nose. "Sorry to bail on you."

"Only one mother-of-the-bride meltdown this time, and I took care of it. I can't believe I'm now working with parents who went to high school with me."

"Huh, by the time my kids get married, my classmates will be grandparents, so don't even."

Emma tucked her auburn hair behind her ear and looked at the babies, remembering a tiny, squirming infant named Sophie. Fifteen years. Where had the time gone? What would it be like to be in charge of a tiny person now, after all this time?

"Meet Evan and MariAnne."

"They're perfect." Emma couldn't take her eyes off them. They surely were. "Sophie will be over the moon."

Charly walked over and put her arm through Emma's. "She'll have to fight me for baby-sitting dates."

Emma hugged her arm to her. "With double the pleasure, you may have to tag-team it sometimes."

"Especially when you throw Hayes into the mix." Charly chuckled.

Sarah walked over to them, baby Beau in her arms. "These guys will be the best of friends, I know."

Lucy laughed. "They won't have a choice, because they'll be together all the time."

CHAPTER THREE

*R*ance took a deep breath. He let it out. A successful birth. He was glad he wasn't specializing in obstetrics, but it was satisfying to be in on a twin birth without complications.

It was also good to know there were families out there that hung together. Something he'd never known. It was a lonely way to grow up, without siblings, aunts and uncles.

When he reached his apartment for a long-overdue sleep, he stretched his taut muscles and eyed the weights in the corner of his bedroom. He'd neglected his weight-lifting. He needed the endorphins to relax him and help him sleep. Right now, he was too tired, and rest was the only thing on his agenda. If he could sleep.

Sleep eluded him. When he did fall asleep, he slept like the dead. But getting there? There were only so many sheep you could count, and only so many poems you could recite. He was beginning to hate the thought of wearing wool or eating lamb chops ever again. Maybe if he started counting items he didn't like?

After a soothing shower and fresh shorts and tee, he lay on

his bed and started thinking, as usual. He reviewed the day. It started out easy enough. He made rounds with Dr. Price on the obstetrics floor; he helped send home a new mother and instructed another on how to use the fiber-optic phototherapy blanket at home for her slightly jaundiced newborn. When an accident occurred on the bridge over the Waccamaw River, three patients were brought into the Emergency Room, so he stepped in to help out. One was admitted with a fractured ankle and the other two, treated and released.

When night fell, he thought he'd get a break. That was when the last patient came in, in active labor, after her water broke at home. It was also when he saw the blonde. He assumed she was the mother of the baby in the waiting room, wife of the well-dressed man. But she wasn't.

He felt his face relax into a smile. Eyes wide open, he stared up at the ceiling and thought about her in the birthing room. She was the aunt. Young and no ring on her finger. He didn't think he would forget her soon.

With that thought, his eyes began to close, and the only thing he saw as he fell asleep was a curtain of long, blonde, silky hair.

DURING THE DRIVE home from the hospital with her mother, Charly was quiet and couldn't quite put her finger on why. The miracle of birth still overwhelmed her, she supposed.

"Sweetheart, are you all right?"

She missed her mother scrutinizing her when she knew something was wrong. Maybe that was the reason it had gotten easier to deny there was ever anything amiss in her life. She kept it to herself and thought out her problems on her own.

"I'm fine, Mama."

They were heading across the bridges of the Waccamaw and

Pee Dee Rivers, the two rivers separating the city of Georgetown from the Pawley's Island zip code.

"Mama?"

"Yes, Charlotte?"

Charly grinned. Her mother refused to corrupt her name by calling her anything other than "Charlotte," and she didn't mind. "Have you ever felt as if you were in a rut?"

Her mother laughed out loud. "You're talking to the number-one rut-maker, here. I can put myself in a rut quicker than anybody I know."

"Oh, Mama, you're a tough lady."

"I've had to be, but it doesn't mean I am inside. I give up now and then, like after your daddy died and when my eyesight started going. I wanted to sit down and die." She was quiet for a minute. "Sometimes I still get melancholy, but I try to let it go when I realize what's happening. What's troubling you?"

"I'm not sure."

"Everything all right at school? You haven't said much about it lately."

"Yes, school is great." As they entered the lighted boulevard through Litchfield Beach, she saw the Food Lion sign. "Do we need anything from the store?"

"I can't think of anything. Still got plenty of eggs and milk?"

"Yes." To be honest, Charly would know better what they needed than her mother. Another thing that made her sad.

"How's Lydia? I haven't seen her in a while. I miss that girl."

Charly chuckled. "She's fine, just super-busy. Besides working at the shop and supplying all their handmade souvenirs, she's taken a job as a barista at the coffee shop in the hospital."

Mary Ann chuckled. "She doesn't have time to be in a rut, does she?"

"No." She sighed before she thought.

"Charlotte, have you ever thought about moving out and getting your own place?"

Charly felt her eyes go wide at her mother's question. Where had this come from? It came from being a discerning mother.

"Not really. I mean, you need me at home. Don't you?"

Her mother laughed. "Oh, darlin', I need you always, but I can make it living by myself in the smaller house. Have you noticed I've picked up more of the cleaning lately?"

"I wondered why I couldn't see where I'd been vacuuming." She laughed along with her mother. "Are you trying to push me out of the nest?"

"No, sweetheart. You never say anything, but I think you may have missed out, not living away at college like Tom was able to do."

"It was my idea, if you will recall. Besides, Lydia needed to commute, too, so we decided it would be more practical to live at home and save the money."

"Yes, and that was five years ago, and none of us had come to terms with my blindness. Lydia aside, we have now, and I think it would be good for both of us to be a little more independent. Don't you?"

"Tom would flip his lid."

"You leave Tom to me. You wouldn't be far, and he's not far either. I have lots of people I can call on. After all, you're gone all day and I'm fine."

"I'm afraid you'll be lonely." And could she live by herself? It was a foreign concept, although one that had niggled in the back of her mind for a while. Maybe if she had a roommate.

"Maybe I will. And then again, maybe I won't."

They had pulled into the garage of the little ranch house that had belonged to Tom in his bachelor days. It had been a blessing when he decided he wanted to raise his family in the old homestead. Their mother needed a smaller, simpler house, and little did he know a big, rambling farmhouse was the house he would need within the next five years.

"I'll think about it. It wasn't something I was considering for a while."

"Maybe finding your own place would help you with the rut you're talking about?"

"Maybe."

"And maybe if you didn't have me to take care of, you'd spend more time finding Mr. Right." Mary Ann Livingston smiled at her daughter. "I'm not trying to rush you."

Charly laughed as she put the car into gear and started gathering her things. "I know. You want more grandchildren, don't you? Well, I'm doing my best. Apparently Mr. Right hasn't shown up yet."

"You never know. He might be right under your nose and you never even saw him."

CHAPTER FOUR

When Charly got to the hospital the next morning with Hayes, her four-year-old nephew, she couldn't help looking for a pair of intense blue eyes. It was a passing thought, in between keeping Hayes from touching everything between the door and his mother's room.

When they reached the door, Dr. Price was coming out. "I know this young man. How are you, Master Hayes?"

The tow-headed youngster frowned. "I'm not a master."

"No, you are a big brother, aren't you?"

"Yep. I come to play with my brother."

Hayes was squirming, Charly trying her best to hold on to his hand.

She knelt down and looked into his face. "Hayes, we talked about this. He's too little to play yet. You know how Beau mainly sleeps?"

Hayes nodded and looked at her with wide, solemn eyes. "And poops."

Dr. Price laughed. "Yes, they poop a lot."

Charly laughed and shook her head. "For a while, it will be like it is with Beau. In a few months, you'll have lots of fun."

The doctor patted the young boy on the back. "Now remember, we have a strict 'no returns' policy." He winked at Charly and went on his way.

She opened the door to see the sun streaming into the room, and both babies in their mother's arms. Lucy's eyes lit up when she saw her firstborn son.

"Hey, buddy!"

"Hi, Mama." He hesitated.

Tom came across the room and hoisted Hayes up in his arms. "We have a surprise for you. I know you were expecting one baby, and guess what?"

He eyed the two blankets. "What?"

"We got two."

"Like two Beaus?"

Lucy giggled from her bed. "Not exactly." She beckoned him to her.

Tom brought him over to sit on the bed next to his mother. "See? We've got a baby brother and a baby sister. This is Evan, and this is MariAnne."

Hayes's brown eyes grew large with wonder. "You had two babies in your tummy?"

"I did."

Charly watched with bated breath as he stared at each baby. She thought she had been surprised, but this little boy was in awe.

Lucy kissed the top of his head. "You can touch their little hands. They like to grab hold of things."

He stroked MariAnne's hand and looked wide-eyed up at his mother when she grabbed his finger and squeezed. "She's got me, Mama."

Tom looked at Charly and grinned, then turned back to his son. "It's the way it is with little sisters, bud. Once they get hold of you, you're hooked for life."

A mist of tears filled her eyes as she beheld the happy family.

"I'm going to leave you five alone. I'll be back in a few minutes."

She turned to go, stopping when Lucy called out. "Thank you, Charly. You're a good little sister."

She grinned. "You're a good big sister, Lucy."

IT WAS CLOSE TO LUNCHTIME. Nurses and aides were bustling around with carts laden with lunch trays, and the smell, contrary to common supposition about hospital food, was amazing. She wandered down to the gift shop and browsed for baby items, then saw the coffee shop next door, wondering if Lydia was on duty.

Coffee. That was what she needed. Her Saturday had started differently than the usual Saturday during the school year. She was up early to make sure she was ready to take Hayes to visit the hospital, so the benefits of her first cup of coffee were long gone.

Café Mocha. Yum. Waiting in a rather long line, she looked at the mostly filled café tables in Café George. She strained around the people in front of her, looking for her best friend. Lydia had proven herself adept at yet another task, making the perfect café mocha. She caught a glimpse of the purple streak in her hair.

The man in front of her wore scrubs with a lab coat over them. A hospital employee.

When he turned, as she did, to survey the lack of seating, he sighed. That's when she realized who he was. Dr. Butler. He turned a little further and recognition registered in his eyes. He remembered her.

"Hi. Weren't you here for the twin birth last night?"

"I was. You're Dr. Butler?"

"Yes, and you're . . . Charlotte?"

She smiled. He did remember. "Yes. Charlotte Livingston. Most people call me Charly. I answer to either."

He gave her a dazzling smile, and she felt a little dizzy. Wow. She didn't think she had reacted so to a smile since about ninth grade. She looked past him and saw Lydia watching them with a comical smirk on her face.

"Charly. Nice." He turned to check the line in front of him then back to her. "I'm Rance, by the way."

"Hi, Rance, nice to meet you."

"Likewise, Charly."

She noticed the depleting line in front of him. "Um, I think you're up." She stifled a giggle.

"May I help you, Dr. Butler?" Lydia was milking it for all it was worth. Glancing between the two of them, she was cheesing it up, big time.

"Hi Lydia." He turned to the counter, studying the menu. "I'll have a double shot espresso on ice, please, with a shot of syrup."

"Coming right up. Busy day today?"

"Always." He grinned at the barista as he paid his bill and turned back to see Charly glancing at the tables. "I see one table over there. If it's still there when we get our drinks, would you join me?"

This was unexpected and a little exciting. "Sure." She looked at her watch. "I don't have long. I brought my nephew to see his new siblings and thought I'd leave the family unit alone for a bit. I don't want to leave him too long."

"No worries. I don't have long either. I'm on a half-hour break, and I think ten minutes of it is already gone." He paid for his drink and moved to the side to wait for his beverage.

Charly moved up to the counter, twisting her lips in a smile.

"Good morning, ma'am, and how may I be of service today?" After the official greeting, Lydia leaned closer and whispered, "You know him? Oh my goodness, oh my goodness." Her eyebrows were almost at her hairline.

Charly looked around to make sure they weren't being over-heard. "I'll have a café mocha, skim, with whipped cream." Then she whispered. "He helped deliver the twins last night. Have you seen them?"

"They are perfect. I ran up to see them before my shift started. But back to Dr. Butler." Lydia rang her up and took her money. "What's the scoop?"

"No scoop, simply an accidental meeting for coffee." Charly winked at her friend. "I miss you, and we need to talk."

She glanced at the good-looking doctor waiting for his drink. "I'll call you when I get off work."

"Gotcha."

Charly wasn't sure, but she sensed his eyes on her. She smiled at Lydia as she received her change and moved over next to Rance. Awkward.

"Rance?" The barista called his name and handed him the beverage and straw.

"Thanks." He turned to her. "I'll go grab a table before someone else does."

She nodded. "Be there in a minute." She could see Lydia craning her neck to see where they were going to end up.

Cup in hand, face warm, she made her way through the mix of hospital employees and people visiting loved ones. When she sat down, she noticed his drink was half empty.

"You're almost finished." She took a tentative sip of her hot beverage and opened the lid to stir it a bit. "One reason I always let them put whipped cream is to cool it down. I learned the hard way."

"Don't you hate burning your tongue on something you love? Pizza is the worst."

"Pizza. Yes. The cheese on the roof of your mouth. Ouch." She laughed and looked into his intense blue eyes. Whoa.

"I guess that's why I started getting them iced. I can down

one of these in a few minutes. It's one step away from intra-venous coffee infusion."

When he smiled, his whole face lit up, and his eyes crinkled into slits.

"Are you from around here?" Charly took a sip and tilted her head, looking at him. She felt as if she should know him but didn't know how.

He twisted his lips. "Charleston. Grew up in Mount Pleasant and graduated from high school there, I'm sure a little ahead of you." He grinned. She was surprised when he gave her his graduation date, five years ahead of her.

"A little bit." She grinned back. "I went to Waccamaw. Where did you go to college?"

"Clemson, then USC Greenville for medical school."

"Ah."

"What?"

"My big brother was determined for me to go to Clemson, like him." She swirled the cup in her hand, trying to keep the chocolate from settling to the bottom. "Good school."

"Where did you end up?"

"Coastal Carolina."

"Also a good school."

She shrugged. "It was. I didn't live on campus, but I loved being part of the school. Lydia and I commuted together."

"I like her. She's good."

"She's a whiz at anything she tries." She shook her head in disgust as he laughed.

"What did you study?"

He didn't take his eyes off her face, which was a little disconcerting.

"Special education. I teach at Georgetown Middle School, across the way."

"Career woman." He smiled and then startled when his pager

started buzzing. "Here we go." He looked at it then up at her. "Duty calls."

"I need to get back to Lucy's room anyway." They stood up, discarded their empty cups, and went to the hallway. "It was nice talking to you."

"It was." He looked away then back at her. "Walk you back to the obstetrics floor?"

"I'd like that." She fluttered her fingers at a staring Lydia and led the way to the elevators.

THEY PARTED WAYS AT THE NURSES' station, and Charly made her way back to Lucy's room. Rance Butler. What a name. A little older than she thought. Still, he was in his residency, and medical school was a protracted affair, it would seem.

She felt the grin on her face as she knocked on the hospital room door. Who had time for the opposite sex when there was so much life to be found in this room? As she peeked in, she saw Tom sitting at the foot of the bed, Hayes sitting next to his mother holding Evan, and Lucy holding MariAnne. Her heart melted into a puddle of goo. Her big brother was the luckiest guy in the world.

"Can I please take a picture of this?"

"I've been afraid to move lest we lose this picture." Lucy chuckled and looked down at her brood with contentment. "I always knew I wanted kids, but I never thought it would be so satisfying to simply sit and hold them." Her sigh brought tears to Charly's eyes.

She finagled Tom into the shot and took the picture. "Perfect." She showed them the image. "Sorry I was so long. I ran into someone in the coffee shop."

"Friend or family?"

Tom would be the one to ask, wouldn't he? He would never

stop being "big brother," and truly, she didn't want him to stop most of the time.

"Both. Lydia, of course, because she works there, and Dr. Butler. We were in line together, and he remembered me from these guys." She reached in to scoop up her niece, hiding her face in the perfection of new-baby smell.

"I see." Lucy stared at her until she looked up. She could feel her face heat.

"What?" Charly gave Lucy a dirty look and then turned her attention to the baby. "Mommy is getting nosy, isn't she? Yes, she is, and someday she'll be asking you questions about every male you come in contact with."

"I can tell you right now her Mommy won't be the only one." Tom laughed.

"You're both practicing on me, huh?"

"Of course we are." Lucy's smirk said it all. "Dr. Butler is cute, isn't he?"

Charly's lips twisted, trying hard not to smile. "He is. I was surprised he remembered me. There was a lot going on."

"Pu-leeze. What red-blooded American male wouldn't notice you? You're cute, you're blonde, and you have a smile plastered on your face all the time."

Tom tilted his head and looked at his wife. "I think you described yourself, Luce."

"Maybe I did, but it applies to Charly too."

"We can't help it if we're two of a kind, now can we?" Charly batted her eyelashes at her brother and winked at Lucy.

Lucy looked over at Charly holding the baby. "And it's looking as if Miss MariAnne will fit right into our mold, doesn't it?"

"It does. Her hair is almost white, isn't it?" Charly fingered the downy bit of hair, marveling at the miracle that, once again, here were children with parts of the same DNA as she.

Hayes started squirming with the sleeping baby in his lap. "I'm thirsty."

"Trade?" Charly handed her niece to Lucy and took little Evan into her arms as Hayes slid from the bed and went straight to his dad.

Tom swung him up into his arms and held him, eye-to-eye. "How about we go for a walk? Maybe get some juice?"

"Yeah. And maybe a cookie?" Hayes giggled as his dad tickled his ribs.

"We'll see." He turned to Lucy. "Get you anything?"

"I've got all I need right here. Love you, boys."

"Love you too, Mommy!" Hayes waved as they went out the door.

"Okay, they're gone. What did you talk about with the irresistible Dr. Butler?"

"Oh, you. Quit trying to drum up business. We talked about where we went to school. Basic stuff. He is from Charleston, went to Clemson."

"Hmmm. I wonder if Tom or Jared knew him and didn't realize it?"

"He's about five years older than me, so right between me and them. Clemson is a big school."

"Are you going to see him again?"

Charly laughed out loud. "Luce, we met by accident in line for coffee. It wasn't exactly a date."

"Relationships have started with less. Your brother and I met on a fix-up date looking at furniture."

"True. It seems like a lifetime ago, doesn't it?" Charly sat on the edge of the bed and reached out to take Lucy's hand in a brief squeeze.

"Three lifetimes ago. Namely the lives of Hayes, Evan, and MariAnne Livingston." Lucy's smile was infectious, and her sister-in-law's abounding confidence in Charly finding her Prince Charming was enough to build hope within her as well.

CHAPTER FIVE

*R*ance squealed his tires leaving the parking lot of the hospital. The top was down on the Jaguar. Finally. A long weekend. All he wanted to do was sleep, but he hadn't seen his mom in a while. His dad, either, which was fine with him. Things had been tense between them for a while. Today he would enjoy the fresh air and sunshine. There had been little time on the beach or golf course for this doctor candidate.

He touched "Mom" on his phone, and it rang twice before Anna Butler answered. "Hey, Mom."

"Hey, Son, how are you?"

"I'm fine. Thought I'd come down for the night, if it's okay with you and Dad?" Maybe Dad was out of town. He could hope.

"I'm sure it will be. Your father has a meeting this afternoon at the Citadel. He said he'd be home for supper, and I'm cooking Chicken Parmesan. Sound good to you? Or we could go out, if you'd rather?" Her voice sounded nervous. An only child, Rance was used to tuning in to his mother's moods. Something his father never seemed to care enough to do.

"Chicken Parm sounds great. I'm ready for some of your cooking. I should be there in about an hour, and don't make a fuss. I need a night away from the hospital."

"That'll be nice. I'm sure your father hasn't made any plans. Maybe the two of you could go fishing tomorrow. A father-son outing?"

Fishing? With Dad? It had happened about three times in his lifetime as he recalled. Ashton Butler, a federal probation officer, had always seemed to have more time for the deadbeats and criminals he worked with than for his own son. He didn't realize it at the time, but it was why he tried to push his buttons as a teen. He was constantly trying to get a rise out of him. And boy did he. Dad never got physical in his punishment, but the cold shoulder was worse. He dictated terms and left him to his own devices.

Rance never let his grades suffer though. Academics was the one thing he had going for him. He was smart. He knew the only way to get out from under his dad's thumb was to outsmart him, to be a success in ways he never could. The Academic Magnet High School he attended was a surprise to his dad. He didn't think he could hack it. But he did. He hacked it well for a kid who wanted to put his fist through a wall on a daily basis.

And then there was Mom. Mom was a peach. A little over-protective, he didn't let her in on the more dangerous of his adventures. She would be scared out of her mind.

Driving from Georgetown to Mount Pleasant was a long, flat, straight stretch of road. Once you left Georgetown, you couldn't see the ocean from Highway 17. It was a lot of pine tree farms, Francis Marion National Forest, little houses, leftover hurricane damage from five years ago, little ladies with their woven basket stands, and churches. Why so many churches on this one stretch of road?

Fresh, hot air, which was summer in the South. What did he

expect? He cranked up the radio and set out to enjoy the ride, courtesy of the Rolling Stones.

MOM MUST HAVE BEEN WATCHING for him. She came out the front door as he was grabbing his bag from the back seat.

"There's my boy!" She reached out and pulled him into her arms. "I've missed having you around."

"Mom, I've been gone pretty much the last six years."

"I know, and you're busier now and don't get to come home as much. It gets lonely without you."

"I'll try to call more." He kissed her on the cheek and looked into her face. Was her hair a little grayer than last time he was home? She had colored her hair since he was in middle school, so it was getting harder to remember what her natural color was. She seemed a little washed-out. Maybe she was tired. "You doing okay?"

She swatted his chest and looked down. "I'm fine." She looked up at him and shook her head. "Now you get yourself in the house, and I'll pour your tea. Sound good?"

"Sounds like heaven." He gave her a half-grin and picked up his bag on the floor. He put his arm around her shoulders and led her in.

"You'll be in your old room. I put clean sheets on there, so it should be nice and fresh."

"Mom, you didn't have to go to any trouble. I can sleep anywhere these days. Having the opportunity to sleep is what matters."

"I know, and that's why I wanted to make it extra-nice for you." She opened the oven door to check on her meal, and the smell of chicken and marinara sauce tickled his nose and his taste buds.

"Something smells wonderful." He winked at his mother and

looked around, spying another favorite. Chocolate pie. "How did you have time to make a chocolate pie?"

"Hon, you know I can whip up one of those in less than a half-hour." She pulled a glass from the cabinet and walked to the refrigerator to get ice. "Now you go get your stuff put up, and I'll have a glass of tea waiting when you get back. I want to hear all about your adventures in the hospital."

"Noted. Be right back."

He grabbed his gear and walked through the house and up the stairs to his room. The stairway was lined with pictures, the majority featuring him, and a few sprinkled in of the family, including his grandparents, and a few great-aunts and uncles. He came from an uncommonly small family, it seemed to him. His mother's parents had both died when he was small, so he had no memories of them. He spent time with his father's parents and never felt as though he knew them.

He dropped his duffle on the chair in his old room and stood there, looking around. The deep, cleansing breath he took reminded him his room still smelled like his room. He felt himself smile and relax. Coming home made all the drama that had gone before worth it.

He jogged down the stairs and back to the kitchen, where his glass of iced tea and a plate of cookies awaited him. "You didn't have to go to so much trouble." He spoke with his mouth full of cookie.

His mother laughed. "I know, but I like to spoil you when you're here with me. I don't see enough of you."

"I'll bet Dad doesn't share your opinion."

She shook her head. "Oh, you shouldn't say that. He was asking the other day when I thought you might come home again. He misses you. It's not his way to show his feelings."

He munched on another cookie, relishing the gooey chocolate and caramel. "He could have called me or come up to see me."

"He never knows when you're going to be in the middle of something, and he doesn't want to interrupt."

"Mom, he's never called me. At least not since I've been in Georgetown. I may as well have dropped off the face of the earth. Maybe I should have taken the residency in Alaska."

His mother's laugh bubbled to the surface. "You, without sunshine and ocean breezes?"

"I could handle it." He grinned at her. "In the summertime, anyway, when it's sunny twenty-four hours a day."

"Your daddy's a private person, that's all." She glanced over at him as she spread butter on the loaf of Italian bread that would become garlic toast. "I guess I am, too, to a certain extent."

"Is everything okay? You seem worried." He'd noticed the little line between her eyebrows. It was her "worry line," and he had watched as she made herself relax her face and try to smile.

"There is something I've wanted to talk to you about but haven't known how to do it."

Okay, now he was worried. Mom was always one who could put things on the back burner, and she seemed to think this couldn't be put off. At least no longer than it already had been. "Mom, are you sick? Is Dad sick?"

"I should wait until Ashton comes home." She wiped her hands on a towel and put it on the counter. "But I'd rather tell you before he gets home. Then we can discuss it with him." It was as if she were coaching herself.

She sat down next to him at the counter and turned to face him, her face set. "I've told you how I met your dad, haven't I?"

"You met him when you moved to Charleston after your mother died."

"Right. I went to work in his company, and before long we were dating. It was quite the whirlwind."

Rance snorted. His mother liked to tell how his father swept her off her feet and didn't give her a choice. She simply had to marry him.

She hesitated, looking down at her hands, studying her wedding and engagement rings. "There are a few things I never told you." She shook her head slowly, her eyes closed in pain. "Oh, Rance, you're going to be angry, I know it."

He felt his heart begin to beat harder. He was focused on his mother. "Mom, what is it? And whatever it is, you're my mother, and I couldn't be angry with you."

She looked into his eyes and shook her head. "Dear, dear boy." She touched his cheek with her hand, tears forming in her eyes. "I never told you I was married before your father."

He was taken aback. Of all the things it could have been, this wasn't what he expected. Why would this information make him angry? "What happened?"

"I left. Plain and simple. I had had enough, and I left." She stared into his eyes. It was as if she were staring at him from a long way off. "I left my husband, and I left my son."

He sat and stared at her. What could he say? He had a brother. All his life, he had wanted a brother or sister, and his mother would laugh and wave him off, telling him he had no idea how lucky he was not to have to share her. And somewhere out there, he had a brother, and he had been kept from him.

His eyes narrowed. The line between his brows matched his mother's. "I don't understand." He didn't want to start talking until he understood the situation.

"I know you don't. You have no idea how many times I wanted to tell you, and then I would put it in the back of my mind and try to forget what I had done. Rance, I left my husband and little boy, and I don't know if you can ever forgive me." She reached for his hand. "Can you?"

He looked down at her hand grasping his. Could he? "Why did you do it?"

She squeezed and let go. "Clifton and I married right out of college. We were barely twenty-two, and it wasn't long before

Sam came along." She closed her eyes as tears filled them. "I'm sorry. I haven't talked about this in a long time."

"Take your time."

"No, I've started, and I want it out before Ashton comes home." She blew her nose and straightened her back, glancing at the clock on the wall beyond him. "Clifton's family was part of the Georgetown County elite and owned J.H. Watson Paper Mill. My mama and daddy were so proud when I landed a Watson. They knew I'd be set for life. I had doubts, but it was so flattering to be courted by Clifton Watson. I was young, and he was charming. It's the only excuse I have."

He narrowed his eyes, still confused. This was his mother, and she was telling him things he couldn't even imagine. "Go on."

"Things weren't good. We lived on the family estate, in the guesthouse adjacent to the pool. Our first mistake was not going out on our own. Then there was Clifton. The happy-go-lucky college student started turning into his father, a workaholic who spent more time at his office than at home." She stopped to wipe her eyes and after a moment looked up at her son. "I thought once Sam came, everything would be all right. It wasn't. I spent five years trying to make it work, trying to be whatever he wanted me to be. It came to the point I had to leave. When his family got involved, the only way they would let me go was for me to leave Sam with them." She gave him a sad smile. "He was a Watson, after all."

"Mom, couldn't you have fought it? Filed for joint custody or visitation rights at least?"

She shook her head furiously. "Giving up Sam was part of the deal. Well, with J. H. anyway. J. H. was Clifton's father." Sadness clouded her features. "I guess you could say I made a deal with the devil."

"What kind of grandfather makes a deal like that about his grandson?" This was insane. Was this story true? Had his mother had a breakdown? Once again, he stared at her. "Why are you telling me this now?"

When she looked back up at him, he saw not his mother but a haggard woman with nothing left to lose. "Two reasons. I was pregnant when I left, but didn't know it, and because the devil is dead, and he was your grandfather."

CHAPTER SIX

Sophie was bouncing in the seat next to her mother. "I can't wait to see them!"

Emma laughed. "They're pretty amazing." She sighed as she turned at the light down the street from the Highway 17 bridge.

"What's the matter, Mom?" Sophie and she had been a pair, the two of them, for the past thirteen years.

She smiled over at her raven-haired daughter. So much like her dad. "Sometimes I get a little sad that you never had any brothers or sisters."

"It's not too late, you know."

Emma arched an eyebrow at her daughter. "Um, do you know something I don't know?"

"I'm just saying, you're not too old to have a baby. All we need to do is find you a husband."

"I had a husband, and one was enough."

"Mom, Dad died thirteen years ago. I don't even remember him. Have you ever thought about dating?"

She pulled into the parking lot and unbuckled her seatbelt. "I did, and it wasn't worth it."

"Really? When?"

"You were little, and it was a mistake. I decided then and there, being alone was not the worst thing that could happen to me."

Sophie looked at her mother soberly. "That's true. I mean, the apostle Paul made it look like a good option."

"You're wise beyond your years." She grinned at her offspring.

"You're a wedding planner, Mom. Don't you want to plan your own wedding?"

"Wise and nosy. Sweetie, right now I wouldn't have time to go on dates. Especially now, with Lucy out of commission."

"Easy out, Mom. I may start praying for you a boyfriend." When she saw her mother's dirty look, she laughed. "Okay, man-friend."

"You pray all you want, and God will do what He wants. You know, I'll be praying too."

Sophie shook her head in disgust. "This could get interesting, me praying for a step-dad, and you praying for alone-ness. Who even does that?"

"A lady who doesn't want to go there, however is pleased as punch when the rest of the community wants to get married and hires me to help them. That's who." She got out of the car and locked the doors. "Now let's go visit those twins before they're teenagers like you."

"Yes, ma'am."

CHARLY ROLLED the window down on the passenger side of her car. If she rolled them both down, hair went everywhere, mainly into her face. This was the best of both worlds. It had been a rainy March, and now coastal South Carolina could enjoy days on end of warmth and sunshine.

She pulled into the parking lot of the hospital, glad to see the number of visitors decreased throughout the day, leaving plenty of parking for after-work visitors like her. She took off her sunglasses and slipped her phone into her purse, along with her keys.

Why did it feel so good to be in the warmth and sunshine after a day at work? She looked around, admiring the landscape featuring azaleas in full bloom backed by the later-blooming crepe myrtle. Naturalized daffodils and tulips were a pop of color in what would, in any other climate, be a sterile, municipal building. Benches were placed along the sidewalk, giving patients and employees a beautiful place to relax on a beautiful day.

She noticed an employee sitting, sunglasses on, and head back on his laced fingers. A smile stretched her lips as she recognized Rance Butler. There was no reason to think he would remember her, so she decided not to bother him. Chances were that his eyes were closed anyway. Let him rest. He was tired. Besides, she was here to see her niece and nephew.

The automatic door to the entrance of the hospital was just ahead when she heard her name. She turned to see Rance at her elbow.

"Hi." She felt flustered. Was her face heating up? It wasn't that warm.

"Hey. Here to see the twins?" He squinted when he took off his sunglasses. He looked tired. And his eyes. There was a quality there she hadn't noticed beyond the fact they were the most vivid blue she had ever seen.

"Yes. I think they're going home tomorrow. At least I hope so. I think their big brother is ready to be back at his own house with his mom and dad."

"And their entourage." They both laughed, and Rance's eyes crinkled, emphasizing his ready smile.

"Bless his heart, he doesn't know what's about to hit him. It's something I never had to deal with. My brother is twelve years older than me, and I always wanted younger siblings. What about you?"

It was as if a shutter closed on his face. The smile was gone, and she couldn't describe the look on his face. Anger? Pain? "I'm sorry . . . I didn't mean to get too personal."

He shook his head. "No. Don't apologize." He gazed into her eyes for a moment and then put the smile back on his face. "Only child. Always wanted an older brother or sister."

"Well, for me it was like having a third parent. He'll always see me as his 'kid sister.'"

"Don't knock it. You seem to have a great family and group of friends."

"I do."

He gestured for her to precede him into the building. "My break is over, so it's back to the grindstone."

"I understand. I may be a teacher, but when school is out for the day I feel like a kid again, especially in spring."

"We're lucky. Spring starts early here."

"Ah, we're not lucky, we're blessed." She crinkled her nose at him. "Better get to the maternity wing. Nice seeing you."

"Nice to see you too." He hesitated at the doorway, looking at her, hands stuffed in his pockets. "You know, we've already done the 'have coffee' thing."

"We have." Her smile grew as his expression softened.

"Would you be interested in going out sometime?"

She tilted her head. It wasn't as if a handsome man had never asked her on a date before. This felt different.

"I could be persuaded." She grinned when his eyebrows shot up.

"Saturday? Dinner? I've heard Alfresco Bistro is good, if you like Italian."

"I love Italian, and I've only ever eaten lunch there, so it's a date."

"It's a date, then." He gave her a brilliant smile. He pulled a notepad out of his pocket. "Give me your number, and I'll call you later in the week. You never know what can happen around here."

She wrote down her number and handed the pad back to him. "I know. And if something comes up, I understand. At least in education there aren't many 'teaching emergencies' on the weekend. Your line of work, on the other hand . . ."

"Exactly." He looked down at her clear penmanship and grinned. "Teachers have much better handwriting too."

She laughed. "I had to re-learn how to print when I started my student-teaching." She looked at her watch and looked up at him in surprise, noting the passage of time. "I'd better get up there before visiting hours are over."

"Yeah, I think I stretched my fifteen-minute break a little bit." He walked closer to the door and sighed as he let it open for them. "So, unless I see you before then, I'll see you on Saturday."

A QUICK GLANCE into the hospital nursery told her Evan and MariAnne were in the room with their mother. She was glad, and she hoped there were no other visitors so she could hog those beautiful babies. There was a little guilt niggling at the back of her mind. She should have brought her mother, but it was much quicker to swing by here after school rather than go all the way back across the rivers to Litchfield Beach and back. She justified her actions by reminding herself the babies would be home tomorrow, and Mom could spend all day with them if she wished.

When she got to room 206, there they were, Tom, Lucy, Evan, and MariAnne, all snoozing, the television playing, volume turned down to silent. It must have been a busy day.

As she tiptoed over to the bassinets next to the bed, she was glad they had put a pink cap on one and a blue cap on the other. At this point, they looked identical to her. Mr. Evan decided to choose that moment to stretch his little hand up, fist balled, and scrunch up his face. Now was her chance. She put her hand on his little tummy, and he stilled. There was nothing like a sleeping baby and the sense of accomplishment when you soothed whatever was troubling them.

Her gloating was short-lived. He shifted a little, stretching out one leg at a time from his previous position of having both legs drawn up and folded together. It was amazing how newborn babies found their pre-birth positions even after birth. He was waking up, and the way his face was working, he was about to let it rip. Did she dare pick him up? She looked over at Lucy, then at Tom, then at sweet MariAnne as she still slept. She dared.

She wrapped the blanket around the tiny infant and picked him up, careful to support the armful of baby. Finding herself swaying without thought, she felt a jolt of maternal instinct as she never had before. What would it be like to have your own child? As a teen she had held a newborn Hayes and more recently Beau Alexander, Sarah and Jared's baby. This was part of her family, and she had watched as he came into the world. It was different.

When her mother was her age, she had Tom. The idea startled her a little. Tom was thirty before he married, and she assumed she would be older, as well. Maybe she would be. It wasn't what she wanted. She wanted a family. A husband. Staring down at the infant in her arms, she began to tremble at the thought. Tears were close to the surface when she heard a soft "hey" from the bed. Lucy was awake.

"Hey, yourself." Charly made herself relax and smile at her sister-in-law. "Lots of company today?"

"You know it. I think half of the sheriff's office and half the church was here today. Emma and Sophie left not too long ago."

Lucy pushed herself up and adjusted the bed to a higher sitting position. "I see you got little mister quiet. I didn't hear you come in, but as soon as he squeaked, I started waking up."

"You do have mom-antennae, don't you?" Charly laughed and looked down once again at the sleeping infant. "I could do this all day. What did Sophie think about them?"

"She fell in love immediately, which is common with these two, it seems." Lucy giggled. "As for holding them all day, we may be calling you to do it all night in a few weeks." Lucy peered over at her sleeping daughter. "I'm so glad I have a girl now. I love my amazing boys, but I love hair, makeup, and shoes, and it's not the same with boys. They grow to resent it."

"Especially the makeup part." Tom's voice surprised the ladies. "Hayes, Evan, and I will be glad for you to experiment with makeup on MariAnne instead of us."

"Oh, hush, you." Lucy's laugh tinkled through the room and woke the sleeping princess. "Here, Charly, hand Evan to me, and you get Miss Priss."

"Happy to do it." She went over to the bassinet, wrapped the baby up as tight as she had Evan, and picked her up, staring into her beautiful eyes. The baby couldn't seem to be able to decide whether she wanted to cry or coo, so Charly started singing softly, which quieted the infant. Her eyes never leaving Mari-Anne's, she spoke, in a sing-song voice. "Are they hungry?"

"What do you think?" Lucy raised her eyebrow and twisted her lips in a smirk. "They are, but jaundiced babies have a hard time. They want to sleep, and as soon as they start eating, they get all comfy and you have to make them stay awake."

Lucy began nursing Evan, and sure enough, he began dozing as soon as he began to eat. "It's easier to feed them one at a time, since I have to flick their cheeks or do something to keep them awake. Later on, when they've gained a little more weight, I'll be able to feed them at the same time."

"Are you going to bottle feed?"

"Occasionally. I want other people to be able to feed them, in case of emergency. You never know, something could come up, and then where would they be? Traumatized. They say it's not a thing, but I did the same with Hayes, and look at him. He's perfect."

Charly's face lit up. "He is, isn't he?"

"Active, but perfect." Lucy looked up when Evan began eating in earnest. "So, what's going on with you? School go okay today?"

"Pretty good. I'm glad the school year's winding down. As much as I love it, I can't imagine doing this twelve months out of the year."

"I know. I loved my kids, but all teachers need a break. It's so intense at the end of the school year. Spring fever."

Tom laughed. "The sap is rising."

"You bet. As soon as the first pretty day comes, all eyes are on the windows, and all thoughts are at the beach or the ball field." Charly shook her head. "Our problem student is doing better. Thanks for your advice."

"No problem. I'll send you a bill for my usual consultant fee."

Charly laughed. "Babysitting?"

"You bet. And as you can see, I've raised my rates." She gestured to the two infants.

"Perfectly fair rates, if you ask me." MariAnne began to squirm. "I think this one is ready for tea time."

Tom rose from the chair and took his sleeping son, putting him on his shoulder to burp.

"Hand her to me. We've got this routine down." She snuggled her daughter and kissed the top of her head before feeding her. "They both smell so good, don't they?"

"Nothing like new-baby smell." Tom flipped up the footrest on the recliner and leaned back, Evan sleeping soundly after a burp that would put a man to shame. Within minutes, both Livingston men were asleep.

Lucy glanced over at her boys and grinned. "I saw Dr. Butler this morning."

Charly felt her face flush and refused to meet Lucy's eyes. "Did you?"

"He came in with Dr. Price on his rounds."

"How nice." The heat from her face and down her neck threatened to make her fan herself. The awkward thing about fair skin.

Lucy laughed out loud, causing her daughter to startle and begin eating again. "Your face is beet-red."

"It is not."

"Is, too. Are you going to tell me, or what?"

"Tell you what?"

"When you're going out."

Charly stared at her. "How did you—"

"I'm a mom, remember, and you're my little sister now."

Charly twisted her lips in embarrassment. "Okay, I'll tell you. I saw Rance outside before I came in. He was on break, sitting outside on one of the benches."

"He's stunning, isn't he?"

"Oh my goodness, yes." Charly fanned her hands to cool her face and laughed quietly. "Anyway, he suggested, since we'd already done the 'have coffee' thing, maybe we could go out for dinner."

"You mean an actual date?"

"Yes, an actual date. We're going out Saturday night."

"And?"

She shrugged. "And nothing. We're going on a date. Dinner. We'll see where it leads."

"I see." Lucy arched a brow and grinned. "Well, I'll be praying for you. And for Rance."

Charly sighed. "Thanks, Sis. Who knows? It may not go

anywhere. I know nothing about him except he's amazingly handsome, grew up in Charleston, and has these piercing blue eyes."

Lucy winked. "And sometimes that's enough."

Charly looked up from scrubbing a sticky place on the kitchen floor. The doorbell. Who would be coming by the house on a Saturday morning?

She was trying her best to stay busy, and to keep her mind off her impending date. Saturday had dawned bright and clear, and the level of nervous energy she was expending was bound to crash. Hopefully not until she got home tonight.

She heard her mother go to the door. "Mom? Who is it?" She wasn't company-ready by any means. She had this awful, unreasonable fear of Rance showing up at any time, her looking like this, and he would cancel the date and cross the street to the other side the next time he saw her.

"It's just Tom. He called my cell phone from the driveway to let me know it was him."

She heard the front door open and Tom's voice coming from the living room. "Just Tom? I represent that." He stuck his head in the kitchen door. "Are you keeping my floors spotless?"

"I'm trying. We dripped Coke on the floor, and when I vacuumed, it left a dark spot on the white tile. Why anybody would put white tile on a kitchen floor is beyond me." She gave him an accusing look.

"Hey, when I lived here, I kept Clorox wipes under the sink for such an occasion. Never had a problem."

When Tom and Mary Ann had struck the bargain to trade houses—his cozy and convenient ranch for the sprawling, ancestral farmhouse—Charly was thrilled at the change to a house with so little upkeep. Keeping it up to Tom's standards was another thing altogether.

"I'll put them on my list. We ran out of the stockpile you left in the pantry." She twisted her lips in a smile and laughed at the sheepish look on her brother's face.

"Good idea. I can pick some up for you when I go on my next diaper run." He turned to his mother. "Mom, how would you like to ride over to the house with me and spend the day with us and the kids?"

"Are you sure? I wouldn't want to be in the way."

"Believe me, you won't be. Maybe if you're there I can get Lucy to lie down and rest. Besides, I brought the car."

"The T-bird?"

"You bet."

Mary Ann clapped her hands. "Wonderful. When I felt the soft spring air this morning I thought it would be a wonderful day to be in a convertible."

"I guess today's your lucky day then." Tom chuckled, one eyebrow raised at his sister. "And I hear you have a big date tonight."

"It's only dinner." Charly waved her hand in dismissal and felt heat in her cheeks.

"Maybe I should be here to meet your young man?" Mary Ann looked torn.

Charly rolled her eyes, a look lost on their unseeing mother but not on Tom. "First of all, you've met him. Mom, I'm twenty-three years old. Almost twenty-four. I think I can get ready for a date and leave without supervision."

"She'll be fine, Mom. I did a background check on him." He winked at Charly.

"You didn't." She was mortified. What if Rance found out? She could never face him.

"Just the basics. Traffic citations, check to see if he has a criminal record. He's pretty clean, except for some pretty hefty speeding tickets."

"Oh good grief."

"Relax. He helped deliver my children. How bad a guy could he be?"

She continued shaking her head. "Will I ever be free of the 'little sister' curse?"

"Nope. You'll always be my baby sister, and you'll always be Mom's baby. Get used to it. Enjoy it while you can, before somebody's calling YOU Mom."

"Fine. You didn't bug his car or put a tracking device on it, did you?"

"Huh. I'll keep it in mind for the future, when MariAnne starts dating."

"All right, you two. Let me get my purse and my scarf, and I'll be ready to go."

"Your chariot awaits." Tom waited until his mother was out of earshot. "I did a little checking."

"Tom!" Her ire was heating up, and she sent him a glare meant to wither, which it did not.

Tom stood his ground as he faced her, his brows furrowing. "He's a bit of a daredevil, Sis. So be aware. I'm sure you're right, and he has it all out of his system, but he's been pretty reckless in the past."

She crossed her arms in defiance. "Do you remember Donny McHale?"

He looked surprised. "Yes. Why?"

"He was in my Sunday school class from preschool on. Everybody thought he was the picture of responsibility."

"I know. His wild streak surprised everyone once he got away from home."

"Maybe Rance is the opposite. Maybe once he got away from home, he became more responsible." She couldn't help feeling a little superior at the moment.

Tom's half-grin/half-smirk always irritated her when he knew he was right and sure she was wrong. "Maybe. And maybe he's two different people. One at work and another at play. I'm only saying be careful."

Mom came in the room, stopping the conversation. Why did he have to interfere? When would he let her live her own life and make her own decisions? She was glad he and Mom were leaving so she could let out the building steam of her temper. She didn't want to worry her mother, but she'd love to let loose on both of them. She was an adult.

"I guess we'd better go then. Tell Rance I said hello." Mom hugged her and kissed her on the cheek as if she were going on a long trip.

"Mom, I'll be home this evening."

"I know. Can't a mother hug her baby girl goodbye?" Her eyebrow quirked in humor. "I may be blind, but this is a small house, and I'm not deaf. You're stiff as a board. Relax before Rance gets here, or you'll scare him off."

"Mother."

"Have fun, sweetheart. You deserve it."

"Hug the babies for me?" Charly felt the anger seep out at her mother's calm voice and demeanor.

"You know I will. Tom? Are we ready? Tell your sister you're sorry, and then we'll go."

He tilted his head at his sister, then took his Mom's hand and tucked it into the crook of his arm. "Charly, I'll butt out, okay?"

She nodded, her arms still crossed. "I accept your apology. And I'll prove you wrong."

He sighed and shook his head as his mother chuckled. "Right this way, m'lady."

"Livingston women are tough, and you, my dear, are outnumbered."

"Tell me about it. Lucy worries about being outnumbered at home, and then I add you two, and I'm sunk."

RANCE PULLED up to the neat brick ranch and felt a smile crinkle his face for the first time since he'd seen Charly earlier in the week. Something about her intrigued him. She was a beautiful woman, and she didn't go out of her way to attract men. A unique characteristic in the circles he ran in. Not that he had time to run in a "circle" these days. He let out a sigh and forced himself to relax.

In the hours he wasn't working or sleeping, he had to choose what he thought he could get done. He finally figured out that he could do three things per evening, and usually those three things included studying lecture and rotation notes, eating a fast-food meal, and sleeping. Exercising, watching a ballgame, going out for a nice dinner? None of those things just happened.

Tonight, however, he had planned nothing other than time with Charly. He unfolded his lean frame from the low-slung Jag, folding his sunglasses and placing them in the pocket of his linen blazer. How long since he'd been on an actual date? The first year of his residency here he had gone out with a few nurses and interns, but the longer the residency lasted, the less time he had for a social life. He hadn't been "wowed" in a while. But Charly? It would be interesting to find out what made her tick.

"THAT ONE."

Lydia lay on her stomach across Charly's bed which was strewn with the four outfits she had proposed for this first date.

With a critical eye, Charly took one last look at herself in the full-view mirror. Her sleek blonde hair had been pulled up in a carefully contrived messy bun, and the swingy, blue floral shift dress was the color that garnered compliments every time she wore it. Feminine, and with the platform sandals, demure without broadcasting the fact she was a school teacher.

She nodded at herself in approval. "I agree."

She wasn't out to "snag her a man," but then again, she was a little proud that her long, lean legs lent themselves well to this style of dress. First-date jitters aside, she felt pretty good about herself. "I guess I clean up pretty well, after all."

"Uh, yes, says the purple-haired midget."

"You're not a midget, you're a sprite."

Lydia's eyes sparkled. "That's nice. If I were blonde, I could be Tinkerbell."

"No, you would make a terrible blonde. Way too smart."

"True." Her laugh rang out only to stop short when the doorbell rang.

"He's here. Want me to get the door?" She wiggled her eyebrows.

"No way. He might like you better, and then this outfit would be wasted."

"Very funny. Fine. I'll follow you to the door like a puppy."

Charly shook her head and took a deep breath to calm her nerves before opening the door. She had to laugh when Rance's eyebrows shot up and his smile widened at the sight of her. Nice.

"Come in for a minute?" She held the door open wider, gesturing for him to enter.

"Sure." He looked around. "Oh, hi, Lydia."

Lydia gave him a quick wave. "Hi, Rance, I'm not here as a barista but a fashion consultant."

"And now she has to go, right, Lyd?" Charly's words were slow and even.

Lydia's eyes rounded in comprehension. "Right. I have a weaving project to finish up tonight. An artist's work is never done, you know." She scooted between Rance and the door. "Have fun, you two."

He laughed at the look Charly shot her friend. "Nice place."

"Thanks. Mom and I have lived here for about five years." Charly felt awkward suddenly.

"Lydia's a hoot."

"She can be." She lifted one eyebrow.

"And yes, I remember your mom from the hospital." He winked, causing her blood pressure to increase. "Is she here? I'd love to say hello."

What could she do with her hands? Purse. She needed to get her purse.

"No, my brother picked her up a little while ago to take her for quality grandchildren time. She never turns down an opportunity." She tucked a stray lock of hair behind her ear. "Would you like to sit down?"

"If you're ready, we can head out." He paused and looked down then up at her with a smile. "I made reservations for seven. Thought we might take a stroll along the waterfront while we wait."

"Sounds nice. I'll get my purse, and we can be on our way."

So far, he hadn't tried to entice her into any daredevil schemes as her brother feared. A chuckle made its way out as she locked the door behind her.

"Penny for your thoughts. They must be humorous." He raised his eyebrows as he opened the passenger door of the Jaguar.

"Something my brother said earlier. He thinks he is the authority on everything. Big brother and all."

"Yeah, well, I never had one, so I'll take your word for it."

His face darkened. Had she said something? After maneuvering the winding residential streets of her neighborhood, he made it back out to Highway 17, where he was able to pick up speed. They rode in silence for a few minutes, and then he seemed to shake himself out of his thoughts.

"You teach middle school?"

She laughed. "Yes, special education. Which basically could cover most middle-school aged kids. It's an interesting time of life."

"I sure wouldn't go back." He turned to her with a grin as he stopped at the light before crossing the bridges to Georgetown.

"I don't think anybody would. I love it though. There are so many kids struggling on so many levels. It's a great age to be able to make a difference in a teen's life."

He nodded. "That's what good teachers do. They make a difference."

"I hope so. Sometimes you think it's never enough."

Rance whipped the sports car into a parking spot along the Harbor Walk in the historic district of Georgetown. He jumped out to open her door before she could get to it. She could feel her face heat when he reached down to help her out of the car. "Thank you."

"You are more than welcome." He looked at his watch. "Looks like we have about a half-hour before our reservation. Would you care to poke around the shops?"

"Sounds like fun. I've been down here a few times during the day, but it's pretty with the lights along the boardwalk."

They strolled down the street. Some shops closed early, but a few were open. The closed shops had beautiful displays in the lighted windows, enticing you to come back and shop the next day.

"You'd think, since I grew up on the coast, coastal art wouldn't draw me, but it does. I guess since my best friend is an artist on the coast, what else would I know?" She had stopped to look at an impressionist-style painting of the shore, its blues and greens fighting for attention with the sand and sun. It was a small painting, barely eight-by-ten, and it fascinated her.

Rance leaned closer. "It is nice." He stared at it for a minute. "Looking at the ocean makes me forget what's going on when I turn back toward land." He was quiet.

Charly tilted her head and smiled at him. "You described what happens any time I stand and look at the water."

"Maybe if more people spent more time gazing at the horizon, they wouldn't get caught in so much junk on land. Me? Sometimes I'd like to get on a boat and sail away, never coming back."

He wasn't smiling. He wasn't kidding.

"It sounds nice, but I'd have to come back and see my family."

He nodded. "Well, you have good reason. Twins notwithstanding."

He seemed to shake himself out of his thoughts. He looked at his watch. "Five minutes until our reservation. Want to stroll that way and see if they're ready for us?"

RANCE WAS MUCH BETTER at first dates than this one. He could always pull charm out of his hat at a moment's notice. For reasons he couldn't explain, with Charly he was his real self, and it happened without thought. Maybe he wasn't being pretentious because she wasn't.

He could have kicked himself for asking her if she wanted some wine. She smiled and mentioned she didn't drink, so he ordered the non-alcoholic limonita with her. He loved it when she blushed.

"I've heard the pasta here is wonderful." Charly was poring over the menu in the dim light.

He chuckled. "I've had the veal. It's amazing too."

She put her menu down and looked at him with a smile. "It sounds good, but I think I'll go with pasta."

"Always a good choice." He looked up at the waitress as she delivered their drinks.

"Are you ready to order, or do you need a minute? Do you have any questions about the menu?" The girl's light brown hair was pulled back in a low ponytail, revealing a generous helping of freckles on her face. She pulled out her order pad.

"I'm ready. Charly?"

"Yes. I'll have the scallops and risotto. Does this come with a salad?" Charly looked up in question.

"Salad or soup." When Charly opened the menu again, she pointed to the array of salads and soups.

"Oh, I have to try the Crab Jalapeño Tomato Bisque. How spicy is it?"

"Do you like Jalapeño Poppers?"

"Love them, even with seeds."

"Then it's not too hot." The waitress laughed and recorded her order. "And for you, sir?"

"I'll have the Veal Marsala, medium rare, with an arugula salad." He closed the menu.

The waitress took their menus. "I'll be back in a minute with your soup and salad."

As she walked away, Rance laughed. "Jalapeño seeds? You're more of a risk-taker than I thought."

"I'm on a date with you, aren't I?"

He leaned on his elbows on the cloth-covered table, looking into her eyes. Her eyes were a mix of blue and green, unflinching, honest. He could get lost in them.

"That you are. I like you, Charly Livingston."

"I like you, Rance Butler." After a few minutes, her eyes skittered away, embarrassed.

As their server arrived, Charly looked down, away from him, her full concentration in placing the linen napkin on her lap. In the ambient light of the restaurant, he could see pink infusing her neck and face. He kept looking at her, feeling his cares flow away and yet feeling his heart beat faster.

CHAPTER EIGHT

This couldn't be happening. She had dated a few guys since high school, but this? This was different. When they sat there at the table, staring into one another's eyes, it was unlike any encounter she had ever had. There was something, maybe it was chemistry. Whatever it was, something drew them to one another.

Rance walked her to the front door, not offering to kiss her, instead taking both her hands in his and telling her he had enjoyed the evening. After he left, she went inside. Leaning on the door, she wasn't ready to talk to her mother. Maybe she wasn't home yet. No, the television in her mother's room was on. She might not be able to see, but the Secondary Audio Programming setting on the television had been a blessing to Mom.

She stood there, eyes closed, and began to pray.

"Okay, Lord, I'm so unsure here. I've committed to dating the man You want. Could it be Rance?"

"Charly? Is that you?"

"Yes, Mom, I just got in." She put her purse on the hall table, took off her sandals, and carried them to her mother's room, and then crawled up on her bed with her. "It was a nice evening."

"I'm glad."

"He said to tell you hello, and to enjoy the babies he helped deliver."

Mom laughed. "Oh, and I did. They're growin' so fast." She sighed. "Tell me about your date." She clicked the television off and put the remote on her bedside table.

"We went to the Harbor Walk in Georgetown, did some window shopping, and then ate at Alfresco Bistro." She would share the bare bones. It was all her mother needed to know, at this point anyway.

"Sounds nice. What did you order?"

Safe topic. "I had the Crab Jalapeño Tomato Bisque and scallops with risotto. Oh, Mom, it was so good. You would love the bisque. It was hot but not too hot."

"Says you. You got your daddy's tolerance for heat, for sure."

They laughed together. Charly leaned her head on her mother's shoulder. "We had a good time."

"Are you going to see him again?"

"I don't know. We didn't plan anything, and with his schedule at the hospital, it's hard to plan very far in advance." Would he call?

"He'll call."

"You don't know that." She didn't want to get her hopes up.

"I have a feeling."

"What is it with you and your 'feelings'?"

"I was right about Lucy, wasn't I?"

Charly sighed. "You were."

"Is he a believer?" She heard a slight hesitation in her mother's voice.

"I don't know, Mama. We didn't go there."

Mom reached for her hand and squeezed. "Then we need to pray about it."

"I already have been."

Her mother nodded and began to pray. "Lord, God, we ask for favor tonight. We ask that You touch Rance's heart if it hasn't been touched before, and that You would strengthen it if You have. All this for Your sake, and for Rance's sake, and not for our own."

Charly kissed her mother on the cheek. "Thank you, and good night. I have to be at church early tomorrow. Praise band has practice before Sunday School."

"I'll be ready when you are. Love you, baby girl."

"Love you, too, Mama."

She picked up her sandals from the foot of the bed and turned out the light in her mother's room, then made her way to her bedroom.

What did the Bible say about being "unequally yoked?" It was always a mystery to her, and it hadn't come up before. Maybe she had missed the mark by not finding out more about his spiritual life.

It might be a moot point. He might never call again. He might think she was the most boring girl he'd ever dated. As she stared at herself in the mirror, she shook her head. Maybe he's not the one.

WHEN HE GOT HOME, Rance picked up his phone. Was it too soon to call? Maybe a text. He'd had a great time with her. Maybe they could spend Sunday together. It was too soon. Maybe she hadn't been as impressed as he. She wasn't like any girl he'd dated before. In fact, he figured his friends would declare her not "his type," whatever that meant. He hadn't had time in the last three years to do much more than skim the surface of dates anyway. Many of those dates had been fix-ups, and none of them garnered a second thought, much less a second date. Charly Livingston was different.

His phone vibrated in his hand. Mom. He didn't want to talk to her at this point. She wanted him to make her feel better. To justify her abandoning one son and deceiving another. His deep sigh did little to alleviate the irritation he felt at this moment. He pushed the button.

"Hi, Mom." That was all.

There was a slight pause on the other end. "Rance, I need to talk to you."

"About?"

"Well, about your father."

Dead silence.

"Which one? The one that fathered me or the one I've called 'Dad' for twenty-eight years?"

An audible sniffle over the phone made him stop and close his eyes. The remark was uncalled for. She was his mother, after all, and he was raised better. "I'm sorry, Mom."

"No, sweetheart, I'm the one who's sorry. I was wrong to keep you in the dark. This is what happens when you let lie pile on top of lie."

"Nobody's perfect." He shook his head in disgust with himself. This was the best he could come up with?

"I know you're hurt. Ashton was so angry with me for telling you before he got home. There were a few things he wanted to go over with you before you left."

"What 'things' did he want to go over?"

"He wanted to make sure you understood his position. He didn't have to marry me. He didn't have to make you his son, but he did." She paused. "He wanted to have more children. I was the one who was afraid."

"Afraid of what?"

"I was afraid after a while I might fail all of my children. I couldn't risk it."

What could he say to this? Maybe, "Thanks Mom, for depriving me of not only a brother, but any other siblings I may have had?" Or perhaps, "So you decided to smother me with attention and cheat the man I thought my father out of his own children?" It was so messed up.

"It's late, and I've been working doubles this week. I'll come down in the morning if Dad will be home." Should he call Ashton Butler "Dad?"

His mother cleared her throat and sniffed. She was trying to pull herself together before facing her husband. Then the muffled sound of two voices. "That sounds good, Rance." She paused. "Everything I did was to protect you. I wanted you to know."

"Good night, Mom."

"Love you, Son."

He hung up without answering.

CHAPTER NINE

A smile bloomed on Charly's face when she saw Tom, Lucy, Hayes, and the twins enter the back of the sanctuary and sit in the pew behind Emma and Sophie. Still new at playing guitar for the praise team, she let her innate shyness dissipate as she let the joy of seeing her family sitting in their rightful place at Calvary Church. Sure, they ran late today, but what couple with brand-new twins wouldn't?

Concentrate. Lydia gave her a thumbs-up from her spot as vocalist on the platform. She glanced over at Sarah, back at the keyboard for the first time since Beau was born six weeks ago. It was so good to have her back. Sarah winked at her and turned to the music on the stand. After an opening of the traditional "Doxology," the band was leading worship.

Praise God from whom all blessings flow!
Praise Him all creatures here below!
Praise Him above all heavenly host!
Praise Father, Son, and Holy Ghost!
A-men!

So many blessings had come her way. Praise God, indeed, for these precious new babies. Her life wasn't perfect, but it was blessed. She had her mother, her brother and his family, a job she loved. What more could she expect?

A life of her own, perhaps? Don't go there. Not now. Concentrate on the music. It's what I'm here for at this moment. "For such a time as this."

Sometimes it was hard, being selfless. Wow. If you call yourself selfless, did you kind of undo the whole selfless part? She wondered if she was, or if it was easier for her to skim the surface and do what was expected of her. Fly under the radar. For quite some time, it had been her goal. She kept her head down, did what she was supposed to do, and nobody knew what was going on inside. If they did, they would be appalled.

After the worship set of songs, she pulled the guitar strap over her head, laid her pick on the music stand, and removed the earbud from her ear. Her preference would have been to rush down the aisle and sit with her mother, brother, and family, maybe hold one of the twins, but her desire to stay unobtrusive sent her to a seat beside Lydia in the "amen pew" behind the keyboard.

Now it was time for the weekly guilt-fest. The last few weeks Charly wondered if the pastor had talked to her mother. She was sure the sermons were meant for her because for a while now all the messages she heard hit her between the eyes.

And today was no different. *For you are saved by grace through faith, and this is not from yourselves; it is God's gift— not from works, so that no one can boast.* Ephesians 2. Ugh. It's not as if she didn't know her salvation was from grace. It felt like it wasn't enough. She worked.

GRACE. Emma latched on to the pastor's words. She knew grace was God's gift, and He had given it to her in abundance. It had nothing to do with anything she had done.

If she hadn't believed in God's grace, she wouldn't have survived her husband's death. Without warning, one day he didn't wake up. He was twenty-nine years old and had survived two tours in Afghanistan, only to be taken out by an undiagnosed heart problem. She took Sophie's hand and squeezed it, smiling when she saw the look of confusion on her daughter's face.

Had she neglected her daughter by not having a father-figure in her life? Sophie was a smart, well-adjusted girl who was more of an adult than she had been at fifteen. Had she left something vital out of her daughter's upbringing by swearing off men?

She kept busy. She had a business to run, a daughter to raise, church work, community work, and all the school events a varsity soccer player and band kid had to attend. It was a good life.

Not that she was bragging. She hadn't made it a good life, God had, and she knew it.

She had to admit that sometimes, in the dark of night or the mist of morning, she was lonely. She didn't expect to become a widow at twenty-seven. She didn't expect to raise a daughter alone, but God became her refuge, her constant strength in times of trouble. Funny how those verses came to her when she needed them. Sometimes it was with an emotional mom or bride, and sometimes it was for her own edification.

A tiny cry behind her made her smile and glance over her shoulder to see Lucy digging into her bag for a pacifier which was not welcomed by Miss MariAnne.

What was this feeling deep inside of her that she wanted to feel again? God? Do you have more parenting in me than Sophie?

She shook her head and would have laughed if it weren't the wrong time to do so. Surely not. She was too old for this.

When she looked over at her beautiful daughter, more similar to her dad every day, she was amazed. God was doing a work in both their lives, and she was so thankful. Daniel would be proud.

HIS MOTHER KISSED him on the cheek when he came through the back door. He let her but didn't return the kiss. The drive down from Georgetown gave Rance plenty of time to think, but it didn't serve to clear his head. He was still angry. He did realize one thing. He was disappointed.

Ashton Butler, the man he had called "Dad" all his life, sat at the breakfast table.

"Good morning, Son." Ashton pushed his breakfast plate aside and looked down at his coffee cup.

"Dad."

His mother brought over the coffee pot and a mug. "Let me get you some coffee."

"I'm good, Mom. I drank a big cup on the way down." He noticed his mother had a difficult time meeting his eyes.

He sat across from Ashton, next to his mother, at the round, oak table. It had been the kitchen table since before he could remember. It's where all the "family meetings" were held, where discipline was meted, where bills were paid, and where games were played. A multi-use piece of furniture.

"Mom said you had some things you needed to tell me." The ball was in their court. Let them try to explain why his entire life was a lie.

His mother put her hand on her husband's arm. Whether it was to give him strength or to gain it for herself, he didn't know.

"Rance, I'm sorry you've been dealt such a blow." Dad looked up at him, a mist of tears in his eyes. "Now you know, and I wanted to let you know I never considered you less than my own son. You were mine. As far as the world knows, you are my son. My parents questioned our marrying in a hurry and never said another word once I told them we had made our minds up. I'm sure they wondered when you were so early, but that's how they are. They keep quiet and go on."

"Did you ever wonder why I never felt close to them?" Rance gazed into his dad's face, feeling the hurt in his chest as if there was a knife sticking out of it.

"They're not demonstrative folks, as you know."

"Maybe if we'd had other children . . ." Mom pulled her hand away and twisted at a napkin. "I was so afraid."

"And what about Sam? Did you know he went to prison?"

Tears began to stream down her face. She whispered. "Yes."

"There's no reason to upset your mother, Rance."

"No reason? She tells me my life is a lie, you're not my father, and I have a brother I've never met, and you don't want me to upset her?" He stressed the last word. "I know all families have their quirks. I'm not naïve. Did you know that I learned what I know about my family from the Internet? I looked up my father's family, their business, and the news articles about Sam's indictment."

His mother looked up at him, the sorrow on her face palpable. "I can't undo the past, and I don't expect you to forgive me. I only told you now so you might be able to help him."

"Help who? Sam?"

"No, your father. Clifton Watson."

CHAPTER TEN

*R*ance looked down at the chart in his hand. He'd known it would happen since "the talk" with his mom and dad. Clifton Watson. His biological father. His father, and the father of the brother he never knew. After his Internet detective work, he wondered if he wanted to meet this family he had never known about.

Flipping through the information, he frowned. The person listed as next-of-kin was odd. No family, just his lawyer, William Schumaker, here in Georgetown. In a way, it made sense. The man's father was dead, his son was in prison, and he didn't know Rance existed. Had he never remarried?

Armed with a little information and a lot of uncertainty, he entered the hospital room. He wasn't ready for what he saw. Besides the usual machines, tubes, and wires present in a patient with kidney failure, the man's face stopped him in his tracks.

When Clifton Watson turned to see who had come in, a small smile lit his face. No recognition, just an easy smile and brilliant blue eyes. It was like looking into a mirror. The lines in his face indicated his sickness and age, but the smile? It explained the question of who he looked like when it was certain he didn't take after Ashton Butler, the man who was, to the world, his father.

"Mr. Watson, I'm Dr. Butler." He shook the hand that extended to him. "I'm in residency, working with Dr. Hobgood, and he wanted me to check in on you."

"Always good to meet a friendly face. Not that the nursing staff isn't great. They take good care of me."

"How are you feeling today?" He couldn't stop staring at the man.

"As well as can be expected, I suppose. You're the doctor, you tell me." Clifton chuckled. "I've been given a death sentence. Or maybe it's a life sentence. When you're as low on the list for kidney transplants as I am, you start thinking more and more about the life to come, when all this is over."

Rance tilted his head. This wasn't what he expected.

"Your numbers aren't where we want them to be. However, if a kidney became available, and it was a match, your chances would be good. Without it, dialysis is as good as it gets. What about your family? Any possibility of a donor there?"

A cloud came over the man's face but soon lifted. "Most of my family is gone, and those left are either not a match or are not willing to donate a kidney. Can't blame 'em. After all, I've lived my life, and they have theirs still to live. I'm sure some of them think I don't deserve it."

"I see." He didn't see. Where was the man his mother described? Where was the workaholic she said was so hard to please? The man driven to impress a father who ruled with an iron fist?

If he hadn't learned about Clifton Watson, he might have been looking at this man in the mirror in the coming years without any clue as to why it had happened. What had happened to change him?

"I won't keep you . . ."

"As you can see, I'm not going anywhere." The rumble of his bass voice with a tinge of sarcasm made Rance grin.

"Not for a few days anyway. Is there anything I can do for you?"

The older man narrowed his eyes and shook his head. "No, but if you have time to stop by, I wouldn't mind a visit. I have a son . . ." He looked down, breaking eye contact, swiping at his nose then waving his hand in dismissal. "I have a son, a little older than you. He's in prison." He winced as if it pained him to say it. "I didn't raise him right, but I pray that by the time he gets out, he'll be a better man than I was at that age."

"I'm sorry to hear that." Rance squinted, trying not to show any emotion."

Clifton shrugged. "That's life. God's in control if we let Him. It took me too long to let Him, I guess."

"I always figure we make our own way."

Clifton chuckled. "I used to think that way. I guess getting old and sick makes you rethink a lot of things." The faraway look in his eyes made Rance wonder.

"You know that old Elvis song, 'My Way?' Well, it's wrong. I spent a lot of time full of pride, thinking I could do everything my way, like my daddy did. It didn't work out, and I'm glad it didn't."

He left his father's hospital room as soon as he could, over-whelmed. This man didn't fit the description his mother gave him. What had she said? She'd "had enough."

Unacceptable. There had to be more to the story.

Doctor Hobgood strolled toward him. "I see you met Mr. Watson. What did you think?"

This man didn't want to know what he was thinking, because

it had nothing to do with his medical status and everything to do with recent information.

Rance cleared his throat and nodded. "His numbers were somewhat better today but not great. Dialysis is helping, but not fast enough."

The older man took the chart from him. "I agree. I've tried to get him higher on the transplant list. So far, nothing. Goes to show that status can't buy you everything."

"What can you tell me about him?"

"One of the founding families of Georgetown County, owned a cotton plantation, then the mill, then went to paper. I daresay the Civil War was a blip on their economic family tree."

"Have you known him long?"

"Most of my life. We went to school together here in George-town. I went into the military, so I was away for a while. While he was enjoying college life, I was serving in Vietnam. The GI bill paid for my degree when I got out. Always a great guy to be around. His old man was something else."

"Any idea what caused his problems?"

"Undiagnosed high blood pressure, alcohol, and cigarettes. Plain and simple. He tried too hard, for too long, to be like his daddy, and it almost killed him."

CHAPTER ELEVEN

Lucy and Tom were on their first date since the birth of the twins, and Charly thought they would never leave. They had celebrated the twins' due date the day before. She had been waiting a month for a chance to have the twins and Hayes to herself, and she didn't want to miss one minute of their time together. She was in the home where she grew up, pretending, for a little while, that it was her home and her babies. Who knew when it would happen for her?

She was cleaning up the leftover mac and cheese from Hayes's plate when she heard a little voice begin to cry out in distress. She looked at the clock. It was suppertime. Evan. She was hoping that she would only have to feed them one at a time, so getting one up without waking the other was foremost on her mind when her phone buzzed with a text.

Is this a good time?

A smile tipped her lips as she read Rance's text. As much as she wanted to talk to him, hungry babies wait for no man.

"Hayes?"

"Yes, ma'am?"

She had to smile at the preschool gentleman. "I'm going up

to feed one of the babies, and I wanted to let you know where I would be."

He sighed. It was the story of his life, these days, she was sure.

"Okay. Can I watch TV?"

She nodded then picked up the remote and helped him find a show. "Here you go. I'll be upstairs if you need me."

"Thanks, Aunt Charly."

"Welcome, sweetie."

She tapped a quick reply.

Babysitting, hungry infants, bored Hayes. Call me in an hour?

She pulled her bottom lip between her teeth. He might be busy in an hour. She sighed as she watched her phone even as she walked up the stairs to the master bedroom where two bassinets held their precious cargo. Another buzz.

Sure. If I'm asleep and it's later, I didn't forget. Soon.

She sent him a "thumbs up" emoji.

Residencies were hard. She knew that. A hospital resident's time was not his own, and Rance seemed to be one who was determined to get as much out of his experience as possible.

He called. Okay, texted, the modern equivalent. He communicated, and that was enough to put a smile on her face.

She tiptoed into the bedroom. It was Evan. Always the hungry little man. She picked him up, glad she had brought two bottles up with her, because he wasn't going to wait for anything, and about halfway through his bottle, his sister MariAnne started squirming.

"Your sister is not as loud as you, young man. What do you think about that?"

No answer, only a steady gaze into her eyes as he pulled on the bottle as hard as possible. Concentration.

"I have a feeling you'll be as big as your daddy at this rate." She chuckled as he drained the last drop from the bottle and looked up at her in utter contentment. "Pretty good stuff, huh?"

Before she could get him on her shoulder for a burp, he set forth a belch that would make a grown man smile.

She laughed and kissed his forehead. "Well, Mr. Evan, I guess you enjoyed that one, didn't you?" She laid him in the bassinet and turned on his mobile before picking up his sister.

"Hello, Miss MariAnne. I suppose you want your supper too?" The steady blue eyes followed her every move. As soon as she was picked up, she seemed to relax into her arms. No rush, just contentment. "You're getting used to waiting for brother, aren't you?" The infant latched onto the bottle and proceeded to slowly and methodically drain it.

Twins. What would it be like? She observed the seamless way Lucy and Tom worked together. How would it be to have a mate who was so in sync with you that you didn't have to verbalize what was needed?

Her brother was a blessed man. Lucy was a blessed woman, even if she did have to be married to her brother. Smiling down at the drowsy MariAnne, looking over at the kicking and cooing Evan, she wondered what the future held.

Into her peaceful mental meanderings came the sound of footsteps up the stairs. "Hey, Aunt Charly, can the babies watch TV with me?"

He leaned across her knees to kiss his sister and then went to hang over the side of the bassinet to get his brother's attention. Both babies knew him already and stilled when they saw him. Was she like that with Tom? Probably. She had always, even now, thought he hung the moon.

She grinned at Hayes. "What do you think they'd like to watch?"

He pondered a moment, chin in hand, back on her knees. "MariAnne would prob'ly like a princess movie, but I think Evan would like to watch *Cars*. What do you think?"

"You know, princesses like *Cars* too."

"Really?"

"Do you know who helped your daddy fix your granddad's old car?"

"Who?" He was curious.

"Your mama."

"Mama fixes cars?"

"She does." She tucked MariAnne into one elbow and scooped Evan up in the other. "Your mama can do anything."

"Anything Dad can do?"

"Almost. But she can't arrest bad guys."

"Oh. That's pretty 'portant, isn't it? I'll bet she could if she had a badge like Dad's."

"I'm sure she could. Now, let's see if we can get these two angels in their bouncy seats and get that movie going."

He scrunched up his face. "They're not angels, they're babies."

"'Til they start getting into your stuff, they'll be a little bit of both."

That made him laugh as he skipped down the stairs. He had no idea.

This is how a beautiful girl spends her Friday night. Babysitting twins and a four-year-old. Rance grinned as he looked at her text. He imagined she was enjoying every minute. What would that be like? Having no nieces and nephews—that he knew of anyway— he hadn't spent much time with small children. The obstetrics and pediatrics modules of his residency had been an eye-opener and made him realize that he liked kids.

Who knew?

He set the timer on his phone to go off in an hour. He wanted to talk to her. He hadn't seen her in a week and hadn't had time to call or text. His résumé wasn't going to build itself, so he had worked on it diligently in what little spare time he had.

What was next? He had thought he had his future set. Finish medical school, find a killer location for his first assignment, then settle down and get married, move to a beach house on the coast near Charleston. Work hard, play hard, and then . . .

What was it that Clifton Watson had said? That God was in control? Since when? Ashton Butler taught him that a man makes his own way. His natural father had followed this rule at one time as well.

It made sense.

He closed his eyes for what seemed like five minutes when he heard his phone's timer go off. It had been an hour.

He scrolled through his recent calls and touched Charly's name to call her.

After a couple of rings, he first heard what he figured was a movie in the background, a shuffle, and then a breathless "Hi!"

"Everything okay?" He laughed as she chuckled.

"We're having a great time. Hayes is convinced that Evan is loving the movie *Cars* and that we should watch a princess movie next for MariAnne. I hate to burst his bubble, but the only reason they're awake is that he keeps jumping in front of them."

"It didn't take long for them to catch on to the fact that they're loved by their brother, did it?" Rance was glad Charly couldn't see the sad smile on his face.

"Don't tell Tom, but he's an amazing brother. Jared, too, even though he's not my brother."

"They're pretty close, aren't they?"

"Um-hmm. They met in high school and have been best friends ever since. I tagged along with them every chance I had. What about you? I figure you have a group of buddies you 'hang' with?"

"Yeah, although we've scattered quite a bit since college."

"Internship is rough, isn't it?"

"Sometimes. Once in a while we get together and go water-skiing or parasailing. Stuff like that."

"Guys stay busy. We girls? We go shopping or get our nails done." Her laugh tinkled over his phone. "And I don't know if I could go parasailing or not. Heights and I do not get along. My head goes all wonky."

"Once you've experienced it, you love it. So, I guess we won't be going bungee-jumping any time soon? Or skydiving?"

"Uh, no. I can get on a plane, however as much as I love it as a time-saving device, I white-knuckle the whole ride."

"Noted. Speaking of going, I was wondering if you'd like to go out again. I had a great time last weekend." He heard a muffled laugh from Hayes and found himself smiling.

"I did too, and I'd like that." Did he imagine it, or could he hear a smile in her voice?

"The Dave Matthews Band is having a concert next weekend, in Charleston, and I happen to have tickets for the Saturday night concert. Interested?"

"Am I? Love them!"

"I was afraid they would be too old school for you."

"Remember, my brother is twelve—get that—twelve years older than me, so I grew up listening to his music, not mine." Her laugh was a tonic.

"Great. Then concert it is. Are you busy tomorrow?"

"Not anything firm. Lydia and I plan to go with Jared to look at a few rentals that Crawford and Benton have available."

"Sounds as if you're getting ready to spread your wings."

His chuckle made Charly smile. "Yes, I think it's time. Would you believe it was Mom's idea?"

"That's awesome. I had a feeling she was a pretty amazing mom from meeting her."

"She is. She's been through a lot and always comes out of it in style. I'll bet you have a great mom too."

He paused, which made her wonder.

"Of course. She's gone through a lot too."

An unexpected silence on the other end of the line made her wonder if he was still there. "Rance?"

"Sorry, the signal blanked out for a minute."

She didn't think it did, but she would go with it. "I thought the call had been dropped or something." Or something.

"Anyway, you want to meet for lunch tomorrow? Maybe go to the beach?"

"That sounds nice. We could go out to Pilot Oaks. They have a private beach, and they've built a little beach cabana down there with a bathroom and changing rooms."

"I've never been there. I've heard it's nice. Isn't it a bed and breakfast?"

"Kind of. Sarah's parents run it. They try to have it available for ministers and missionaries who need a time of retreat or a home on furlough. It's a great ministry and such a beautiful place. It's also a venue for weddings. Sarah and Jared had their reception there."

"Tell you what, how about I bring a picnic lunch, and text me when you think you'll be there, and I'll meet you?"

"I like the way you think." She chuckled into the phone, more excited for the picnic than the concert.

"It's a date then."

"I'll be waiting for you."

The conversation ended, and Charly put her phone on the table next to her chair.

"Was that your boyfriend?" Hayes, once again leaning over her knees, dangling his feet, stared into her eyes. Could he look any more like her brother Tom?

She felt the heat infuse her face. Who needs a mirror when a thermometer would tell you when you're blushing furiously?

"It was Rance, and he is my friend."

"Is he a boy?" This kid was serious.

"Yes, he's a boy."

"Then I guess that would make him your boyfriend."

What do you say to that kind of logic? At four, Hayes Livingston was a very astute individual when he stopped long enough to think things out. This time, he had.

AFTER HANGING UP WITH CHARLY, Rance was wide awake. No going to sleep now. He had a few choices. Call up a buddy and see what's happening around town, night-life-wise, go to the gym and work out, or work on his résumé. Relaxation was out of the question with that hanging over him, so résumé won out. And for that, he might as well go to the hospital and use the free Wi-Fi and network resources he couldn't get here at the apartment.

He looked around his surroundings. The hospital was more of a home to him now than the apartment. He hadn't spent any time here except to sleep and eat take-out. His mom had never been here. She always made an excuse when he mentioned her coming up to see him.

He guessed now he knew why. She was afraid of running into Clifton or J. H. Or Sam. At that, he got up, grabbed his laptop, and slammed out the door. He was angry, and he didn't have time for it.

When he got to the hospital, the large sweet tea from McDonald's had slaked both his thirst and his anger, and he felt better. As he exited the elevator on the fourth floor, something made him turn left instead of right. He found himself outside of Clifton Watson's room and after a pause, went in.

When the older man looked his way, a smile lit his face. "A little late for a visit, isn't it?" His gravelly voice made Rance smile and then dim when he wondered what he would think if he knew that he was his son. "What, no scrubs? You must be off-duty."

"I am. How are you, Mr. Watson?" He shook the man's hand and stood at the foot of the bed.

"Better than I deserve. Hobgood said that I went up a little higher on the list today." He paused and had a faraway look in his eyes. "I was glad but in a way hated to hear it. That means someone either died that was ahead of me or died to donate a kidney. A mixed blessing, for sure."

"I understand." He tilted his head. "Or maybe someone on the list received a living donation."

The half-smile on Clifton's face grew as he nodded. "I'll take that thought any day."

"I'd better get to work."

"I thought you were here because you couldn't stay away." He chuckled. "I know you're a busy man. What are you working on?"

"Résumé. I finish up here in about a month, and I'm already looking at placements after my residency."

"Got family close by?"

Rance looked down and shook his head, smiling. "I do, sir."

"Don't neglect them. It's not worth it. If there's anything I'd do different, it would be to treasure my family." He shook his head. "Two ex-wives and a son in prison, and I have to take responsibility for that."

"I'm sure there's more than one side to every story. Right now, I'm keeping my options open."

"No girlfriend?" Clifton narrowed his eyes at him.

Rance coughed in surprise. Was the guy psychic? "Not official."

"I had a feeling. Don't keep your options too open if you like her."

"Yes, sir. I'll keep that in mind."

"Now, see you do. Get on out of here. You've got better

things to do than entertain a sick old man." He waved him out the door, grinning.

"Have a good night, sir."

"Thanks, son."

Rance got out the door before he realized he called him "son."

CHAPTER TWELVE

Spring, when a young woman's fancy turns to thoughts of… weddings. But the planning and hard work comes long before that. Months before for most of her weddings.

Emma got out of the car at Tom and Lucy's house, smiling as she heard young Hayes in the back yard and a baby crying inside. Lots of life in this household.

Tom's sister, Charly, met her at the door, holding a sleeping MariAnne. "Hi, Emma, Lucy's changing Evan. Blowout." Charly wrinkled her nose as if the smell was still in the air.

"Ouch. It's been a while, but I remember those."

Hayes picked that moment to careen through the screen door and into the hallway. "Hi, Miss Emma. Did you come to see the babies?"

"The babies, and you too. How is the big-brother business going?"

"Good. They sleep and poop a lot."

"They do, don't they? Give them time, and they'll be good playmates for you."

"I hope so." He looked troubled for a moment, and then his face cleared. "Where's Sophie?"

"She's at a friend's house. She'll be upset I came to your house without her."

"Yeah. Sophie's pretty."

Emma exchanged a smile with Charly. "Do you think so?"

He nodded with enthusiasm. "When I get bigger, I want to go on a date with her. Aunt Charly went on a date."

Charly turned bright red and cleared her throat. "How did you know that, young man?"

"I hear stuff."

"Oh, you do, do you?"

"When people think I'm just playing, I'm really listenin'."

Emma tried to choke back a laugh. "I guess we'll have to be careful what we say around you, won't we?"

He seemed to think about that a minute. "I hope not. Tell Sophie hi for me, 'k?"

"I will, Hayes."

Lucy came in the room with Evan. "Fresh as a daisy. That particular blowout was far-reaching. I even had to change clothes."

The ladies laughed as she handed Evan to Emma. "I could tell you wanted to hold one, and I didn't dare take MariAnne away from Charly. "She winked at her sister-in-law. "Besides, I don't think there's any danger of mess. It's hard to believe one baby could hold that much ick." She turned to Charly. "What time are you meeting Jared?"

Charly looked at the clock. "In about forty-five minutes. You two go ahead and talk business, and I'll mind the babies."

"I don't think I want to let this one go." Emma cuddled little Evan closer, relishing the feel of him in her arms.

"That's fine. I'll be in the living room, and if you need me, holler." Charly sauntered into the next room, leaving Lucy and Emma in the kitchen to talk business.

"So, what's coming up?" Lucy got out her calendar as Emma pulled hers from her bag.

"We've got the Rowan wedding next weekend at Atalaya Castle, then the Bennington wedding the following weekend on the beach and grounds at Pilot Oaks."

"Aren't you glad Sarah had her reception there? It's turned into such a great venue."

"It has. Robert and Linda are great to work with too." She looked down at the drowsy baby boy and back up at Lucy. "How are you doing? I don't want to push you to get back to work before you're ready."

Lucy gave her friend and partner a tender smile. "I know. I'm doing okay. You know how it is with infants, there are good days and bad days, and with two, it makes it that much more volatile. If I can help you behind the scenes for a while, I'm glad to do that. Charly mentioned that she might be available to help on a part-time basis this summer."

Emma perked up. "Would she? That would be perfect. I could use the help at the venues."

"Charly?" Lucy shouted into the next room, making baby Evan startle and his face begin to crumple. "Oh, I forgot. I'm so used to shouting for Hayes or Tom in this big house." Lucy shrugged when he relaxed. "I guess he's getting used to it." Her quiet laugh made Emma laugh too.

Lucy was a tonic, as she found out upon meeting her, planning Sarah's wedding. Funny how an offhand comment about becoming her "paht'ner" came to fruition in such a blessed way.

"Yeah, Luce? I got MariAnne to sleep and in her bassinet."

Lucy looked at Emma. "See? She's great help."

Emma laughed. "Charly, would you consider working part-time for me this summer while Lucy's still on maternity leave? For pay, of course."

"Would I? Yes! My summer class will be Monday through Thursday, but I'll have Fridays and Saturdays free."

"Unless you have a hot date."

"Lucy . . ."

"Hey, the cat's out of the bag, per Hayes, remember?" Emma laughed at Charly's reddening cheeks.

"Yeah, well, we'll see. I would love to help you out. Date or no date." Charly winked and sashayed back into the living room, turning back to blow them both a kiss.

"I DON'T KNOW, Jared. I've never lived in an apartment before. Part of me thinks it would be cool to try it, and part of me wonders about living so close to other people. You know?"

"But, Charly, look at the light coming into this room. I could paint here all day." Lydia sighed.

Jared had taken the ladies to a few rental condos that were available for long-term rent, as opposed to vacation rentals. In the Pawley's Island area of the Grand Strand, vacation rentals were the bread-and-butter of Crawford and Benton Real Estate, but they still did residential sales and rentals.

"I understand." Jared pursed his lips in thought. "I do have one place that's not listed. Not yet anyway."

"Condo or house?"

"House, right on the beach. It's small but nice."

"Where is it?

He quirked an eyebrow at her. "It's Sarah's beach house."

"Are you serious?" Charly's eyes bugged in surprise. "You would rent that?"

"You are kidding me." Lydia put her hands on her hips and stared, deadpan.

Jared shrugged. "It's sitting empty. From time to time we let people stay there if there is an overflow at Pilot Oaks, but most of the time it's just collecting dust, and it's too nice to not be used. We wouldn't rent it to just anybody, after all. Y'all are family."

She flung her arms around Jared's neck and squeezed.

"Jared, you're the best brother in the world, and at this point I would even tell Tom that!"

"So . . . you're interested?"

"Depends on how much rent we're talking." Lydia eyed him shrewdly.

He gave them a number that was well below the going rate for the condos and houses they had looked at today.

"No, really, how much?" Charly glared at him.

"Your glare does nothing. I live with Sarah, remember? Charly, if you're living in the house, we'll feel better about it and won't have to check on it as much. And you won't be renting from the company; you'll be renting from us. I had it put in Sarah's name when we got married."

"Does it still have the blue leather couch in it?"

"'Fraid not. We took that to the new house on Pilot Oaks Road." He nodded his head and sighed. "I helped pick that couch out, you know."

"I've heard the stories, including how that was Tom and Lucy's first date."

He laughed, the red tinge on the tips of his ears adorable. "Good times, great couch."

Charly looked at Lydia with raised eyebrows. When she got the affirmative nod, she stuck her hand out. "Mr. Benton, you have a deal, and I'll throw in free babysitting. Shake on it, and don't you dare spit on your palm."

He shook both their hands and grinned. "You're no fun. I have the keys in the car if you want them now." He raised his eyebrows.

"You knew about this all along, didn't you?"

"Maybe. When Sarah heard you were looking for a place, this was the first place she thought of, so it was her idea. She liked the idea of you living there, and it was her last place to live as a single girl. She and Lucy had a great time staying together right before the wedding."

"I guess it worked for her, didn't it? Who knows, maybe it will be the last place I'll live as a single girl." She winked at Lydia and gave him a pointed look.

He frowned. "Anything I should know?"

She was sure the warmth of her face told him everything he needed to know.

CHARLY PULLED in the driveway of what she would always consider "Sarah's beach house," and parked beside Jared's SUV.

He dangled the keys on his finger, smiling at their excitement. "Who wants to do the honors?"

Charly and Lydia looked at one another, then nodded. "We turn the key together." Charly grinned at Jared. "I still can't believe it."

"Believe it. And enjoy it." He looked at his phone to check the time. "If you ladies are all right, I'll leave you to it. I've got another appointment in twenty minutes, and I'll just make it if I leave now. Any questions before I go?"

"Don't we need to sign a lease?"

"No lease between family. Come by the office sometime this week and I'll give you all the paperwork you'll need for changing the utilities. I want you to enjoy this house and consider it yours while you're here." He checked the time again. "Gotta go. Have fun."

"You know we will." Charly gave him another hug for good measure, and after unlocking the door with Lydia, she watched as he backed out of the drive.

Her own house. Well, kind of. Their own house. This could spoil a person. Some of her friends had rented during college, but this was different. It wasn't a decrepit apartment with particle-board furniture from the big box store.

But this? After Jared left, Charly and Lydia poked around the house alternately twirling and squealing all the way to the French doors that overlooked the patio and led to the beach. She felt overwhelmed, giddy, blessed.

"God, You knew this was going to happen all along, didn't You? Thank You. Forgive me for doubting You. You've put me close enough to all my people and my church, and I can still check on Mom and get to her in a hurry. But You have all that in mind, too, don't You?"

She poked around the kitchen, smiling as she remembered coming over when Sarah and Jared lived here after their wedding.

Out of the awed silence came Lydia's chuckle. "Do you remember how full this house was after the wedding shower?" It was full to the brim of wedding gifts, and the cabinets were overflowing as they made this their home during the renovation of their forever home on Pilot Oaks Road.

Charly nodded. "It was crazy. Wouldn't have been a problem at Jared's house, but it's a good thing the stuff was here when the hurricane hit."

"Definitely."

The rose bush by the front door had been pruned, and flowers lined the sidewalk. All they needed to do was bring their things in and make it into their home.

Lydia looked at her phone. "Yikes. I was supposed to be at the store fifteen minutes ago. I haven't told Mom and Dad yet." She looked up at Charly, wide-eyed. "I expected this to take longer than a half a day."

"Like, maybe, two half-days?" Charly giggled girlishly.

"Uh, yeah, at least." Lydia winked. "Gotta git. See you later?"

"Yeah. Rance and I are going to the beach later. Maybe we'll see you?"

"Maybe. Depends on the customers today. Last week we had a run at the last minute, and it was after seven before we closed.

I'll need to start packing, so I'll see you at church in the morning."

"Gotcha. Just think, next week, we'll be living here!"

"On the beach!" The girls hugged and laughed once more, taking a selfie of the two of them before they parted.

Charly was still wandering around when she felt her silenced phone buzz with a text. Her smile grew wide when she saw that it was Rance.

How's the apartment hunt? Still on for this afternoon?

He wouldn't believe how well the house hunt went. She sent him the address and the selfie of the two girls inside the house.

Success! Meet me at my new house!

Was she being forward? Silly. She was an adult. He was an adult. It wasn't like she was arranging a tryst.

Nice. Be there in a few.

She was glad she thought to bring her beach bag with her, so she could change here.

Now. Furniture. It was somewhat furnished for rental purposes and not her style. Maybe she would get Tom to bring her a few things from the attic of their home place, and chances were Lydia's folks had excess stuff too. Time for an archaeological expedition. Lydia would be up for that, she was sure.

She punched in her mom's number. She couldn't wait one more minute.

"Mom!"

"Charlotte? Is that you?"

"Well, besides Tom and Lucy, who else would call you 'Mom?' Yes, it's me. We found a place! Well, Jared found it, and it was Sarah's idea, so I guess you could say Sarah found it."

"Slow down, sweetheart! Where is it, and will I approve?"

"You'll love it. It's Sarah's beach house!"

"Sarah's house? Are you sure you girls can afford it?" Leave it to Mom to worry about money.

"Yes, Mom, I can afford it." She gave her the amount of the

rent. "I know, it sounds too low, and I'm sure part of it is because we're family, but, oh, Mom, it's amazing."

"I went over there after the wedding. Very easy to navigate, even for me." There was a pause. "There are a few pieces Tom put in the attic that would be perfect for that house."

Charly laughed. "I've been thinking the same thing. I remember an old kitchen cupboard that has been up there ever since I remember. Painted white? Remember?"

"Oh my, yes. That was my grandmother's. It has a flour bin and built-in sifter. Not much use for it these days, but it's a nice piece of furniture. Mama had it hauled up there when I was a girl. Only the best, most modern for her at the time."

She walked into the kitchen and dining area, looking at a blank wall. "We have the perfect place for it."

"It'll be nice to have those old things used again. I think there's a box of extra kitchen stuff up there too. Neither Lucy nor I could stand to get rid of it, and she had a house full of stuff from her house in Kentucky, so we packed it up for you, when you might need it."

"I'm so glad you did. Something about using the old stuff that you and Grandma used makes it more special."

Her mother's soft laugh warmed her. "We'll get you set up, young lady. I wish I could be more help."

"Don't you worry about that. I'm meeting Rance and going to the beach for a while, so don't look for me before dark. Need me to pick up anything on my way home?"

"We're 'bout out of butter, so better pick it up if you want any on your toast tomorrow."

Charly laughed. "Will do. Text me or call if you think of anything else. Love you, Mama!"

"Love you, too, sweetheart. Be careful."

"I will."

She pushed the button to end the call and headed out the door to get her beach bag, thinking the whole time. Note to self. Patio furniture and welcome mat.

RANCE DROVE up to the quaint beach house in time to see Charly closing her car door, carrying a bag. He got out of the convertible and slammed his door, smiling at her excited wave.

"It's pink!" He laughed as he stood in front of the house, taking it all in.

"And don't you forget it, mister." She came and stood beside him, admiring her new abode.

"Wow. I never knew anyone to find a house and take possession as fast as this."

"Then you never knew anyone that has an 'in' with a great realtor." She winked at him and nodded.

He noted her high color and grinned down at her. "Can I see the inside?"

"Of course. Jared had the keys with him when he brought me out here. I need to remember to get extra keys made before I go home tonight."

She was proud of her new place, he could tell.

"This is great. If I had a place this nice, I might spend more time there."

"Where do you live?"

"Oh, it's a little apartment in Georgetown not far from the hospital. Vintage 1980s." He laughed and wrinkled his nose. "Mirrors everywhere."

She winced. "Ouch. Most of this furniture is Crawford and Benton stuff, for rental purposes, so we'll bring our own furniture in. Mom's got a ton of stuff in the attic from when we traded houses with Tom and Lucy."

"Wait, you traded houses?" Interesting family.

"Yes. When Mom went blind, she needed to downsize and

wanted to sell the home place, but instead, Tom offered to trade houses with her. He wanted to raise his kids in the old house where we grew up, and it's a good thing, because his family started growing right off the bat." Her giggle made him smile.

"You are all close, aren't you?" What was that little pang that he felt in the region of his heart? Was it a little jealousy?

"We are. We've had to stick together. I don't know what I would do without my family. Lyd and I are ready to find out how to live on our own, and something tells me we won't have a hard time."

"You won't. At least your family is still nearby, and you won't be alone. This isn't much more than a mile from your mom's house."

"And about that far to Tom's. I know Jared's giving us an unbelievable deal, but when he offered this place, we couldn't pass it up."

He could see the thoughts tumbling upon each other in her head. She is woman, see her plan. He walked over to the French doors. "You are right on the beach. This is amazing."

"I know, right? It's all public beaches through here, but it's houses instead of condos, so it's never crowded like it is at the Huntington Beach entrance."

"If I owned this, I don't know if I could rent it out."

"Oh, Jared and Sarah live down the road from Pilot Oaks, so they have access to the beach any time they want. Speaking of access, I brought my stuff in to change. If you want to change here, we can "beach" from my own backyard if you'd like.

"Sounds great. I'll bring in the food and my bag." He grinned. "Congratulations on the place. It suits you." He turned and went out the front door, whistling.

CHAPTER THIRTEEN

Charly stopped at the yellow light heading out of Georgetown. The last day of school was a long time coming. Her mental list of things to pick up rattled through her mind, along with the to-do list that she had completed for closing day. Her room was inventoried, her desk cleared, and it was ready for next year's students.

Thankful didn't begin to cover what Charly felt. She was blessed, and she knew it. A great house, a great family, amazing best friend, and Rance. Where did he fit in? She wasn't sure yet, but the more time they spent together, the more she felt comfortable with him. He seemed to enjoy her company, too.

Moving in to the pink beach house took little more than an afternoon. Now all she and Lydia had to do was tweak and organize, and they would be done.

Done in time for summer classes to start and the wedding season to start. She sighed. She was so close to getting her master's degree she could taste it, but it would be so nice to have a summer off for a change. She went from graduating to starting her master's last summer and took classes during the school year as well. Three more classes and she'd be done. This time next year . . . wow. The quicker she finished, the more time she could give to her mom and living her life.

When she crossed the rivers into the Pawley's Island zip code, she smiled and waved at this and that acquaintance, her mind racing the whole time. It had been a busy week.

Maybe that's why she'd had this little knot of anxiety in the pit of her stomach. Everything was going well. Nevertheless, she felt a little empty inside. But why? She was getting things done according to plan, her family was well and healthy, and she was dating a great guy. What was the big deal?

She hadn't spent much time with her Bible lately. God understood. Didn't He? Her prayers were more off-the-cuff while driving than getting into the Scripture and then listening to what God had to say about it.

What was it Paul had said? In Romans? Oh yeah. It was something about the things I know are right, I don't do, but the things I don't want to do, wrong things, these things I do. So confusing. It wasn't as if she were doing anything wrong. She was doing all the right things. Wasn't she?

What day was it? Wednesday. She heaved a deep sigh. Church night. She had hoped to have an evening, especially this first evening of school being done, to continue settling in. In the summer months, Lydia worked at the shop until seven on Wednesday evenings. Rance was working the night shift, so she knew he wouldn't call. Mom would want to go to prayer meeting. No choir for the summer, so forty-five minutes of prayer and the usual "organ recital." That is, everyone sharing the latest in physical maladies for themselves or their loved ones or anyone else they may have met once.

She would go. It would disappoint her mom if she didn't. Her phone buzzed on the seat next to her. She glanced over to see "Rance" on the ID.

She pushed the Bluetooth button on her steering wheel to connect to her phone and answered. "Hey!"

"Hey, yourself. Are you driving?"

"Yes, speaking to you hands-free, so we won't get pulled over."

He chuckled. "I thought it sounded like speaker. I won't keep you. Looks as though I'm free tonight. Want to grab a bite? I could help you move furniture around if you need me."

She laughed and then sighed. "Sorry, I'm tied up with church tonight. Prayer meeting is at six, and I take Mom."

There was a moment of silence on the phone. "Hmmm. Okay. Mind if I tag along? We could get something to eat afterward?"

"Are you sure? I mean, it's not a regular service or anything."

"Hey, I'm at loose ends this evening. I got a great nap this afternoon, and I'm raring to do something. Anything is better than sitting around here or studying for the licensing exam."

"Don't say I didn't warn you."

"Wouldn't dream of it. How about I meet you at the church. Calvary?"

"Yes. I'll try to beat six and get there ahead of you."

"Is that unusual? Being early?" His teasing tone made her smile.

"Very funny. Sometimes, yes. It happens when I've had a busy day, week, and year. You get the idea?"

"I do. Last day of school?"

"Yes, and I'm so relieved I can't stand it. My summer classes don't start until next week, so I have a week to get settled in." She sighed again.

"You need a break, young lady."

"Thank you, I didn't realize." Her sarcastic quip came out before she had time to rein it in. "Sorry. I think your saying that is kind of a takes-one-to-know-one remark."

"Very true. We're a little alike in that respect."

"Hey, I'm at home. See you at six?"

"See you at six. Go in and put your feet up for a little bit."

"You, too, Dr. Butler."

She ended the call, listening to his laughter as he hung up.

As of now, the evening looked a lot brighter.

"I WONDERED why you wanted to get here early for a change." Her mother laughed when Charly told her that Rance was meeting them at the church.

She huffed. "I'm early sometimes."

"Not in recent days which makes me late as well." It was obvious her mother was trying to reprimand her daughter without embarrassing her. "Not that I'm complaining. Tom doesn't have room for me in their vehicle with all those car seats."

"That's true. I don't mind a bit coming to get you. It's not that far out of my way. I'll try to do better." She sighed as she turned in the drive of Calvary Church. "I've been really tired lately."

"How come? Something bothering you?"

There goes Mom's antenna again. "No, end of the year stuff, and classes starting next week, and moving. The usual." She laughed, hoping to throw her mother off the scent. "Did I tell you I'm going to be working for Lucy and Emma part-time, while Lucy's on maternity leave?"

"Are you sure you have time? You do know that you don't have to get your master's done all at once, don't you? You have three more years to finish it."

"I'll be fine. I know I have plenty of time. I want it done."

"I think you're pushing yourself too hard. You always have. Between making close to a 4.0 in college and watching over me like a hawk and now having a full-time job and a part-time one, you haven't left enough margins in your life."

"I learned it from the best, you know."

"I often wish I had slowed down a little bit while I could and enjoyed life more when I was younger. Now I have no choice."

Charly's heart dipped. The last thing she wanted was for her mother to worry about her. But if she didn't talk to her mother, who would she talk to? Except for Lydia, she had lost that close contact with friends that she had before everything changed and her mother went blind. When that happened, Tom was working, doing the same thing she was, which was spending all her time working or planning to work. She didn't want to be thirty and still single, and for some reason she felt as though she had to hurry and get it all done, just in case.

Just in case what?

She put the car in park and turned to face her mother. "I'll be fine, Mom. Don't worry about me. Hey, at least I'm dating. When Tom was my age, he still lived at home."

"That's true. So Rance is meeting us here?"

"Yes, and there he is now. See? We're not that early."

"I didn't want to have the preacher faint on us." Her mom's laugh tinkled across the parking lot, making Rance smile as he walked to them.

"Good evening, Mrs. Livingston, Charly."

Mary Ann extended her hand to him. "How are you, Dr. Butler? Welcome to Calvary Church."

"Thank you, ma'am." He turned to Charly. "Did you get to put your feet up?"

She rolled her eyes and put her hands on her hips. "What is this, worry-about-Charly day? And yes, I put my feet up while I scrolled through Facebook and checked my email. How's that for recreation?"

Her mom spoke up. "A little sad, if you ask me."

Rance laughed out loud. "You took the words right out of my mouth." He squeezed her mother's hand. "Somebody has to keep her in line."

"We'll make a pact to make sure she has fun this summer. How's that?"

Charly looked at the clock on her phone and shook her head in disgust. "Excuse me, I'm standing right here, and it's time to go in, or we'll be late as usual."

Rance twisted his lips in a mischievous grin. "Yes, ma'am." He held his hand out to them as they approached the door. "Ladies first."

THIS WAS DIFFERENT. Rance hadn't been nervous about his first visit to Calvary Church, but he wasn't expecting a group of twenty-odd people, all of whom turned to look at them as they walked in.

He saw Sarah at the piano, playing a soft hymn melody, and Jared stood and shook his hand as they passed him in the aisle.

They took their seat and were asked to stand and sing a hymn. At least it was a familiar one. Who hadn't heard "Amazing Grace" at least once in their lives? Elvis even sang it in his concerts.

> *Amazing Grace, how sweet the sound,*
> *That saved a wretch like me!*
> *I once was lost, but now am found,*
> *Was blind, but now I see.*

Not considering himself a singer, he accepted his side of the hymnal Charly offered but did not sing. He smiled at her and read along as she sang.

> *'Twas grace that taught my heart to fear,*
> *And grace my fears relieved;*
> *How precious did that grace appear*

The hour I first believed.

He had a vague recollection of hearing the song when attending church with his grandparents. A pang hit him when he realized they weren't his grandparents.

Through many dangers, toils and snares,
I have already come;
'Tis grace hath brought me safe thus far,
And grace will lead me home.

The Lord has promised good to me,
His word my hope secures;
He will my Shield and Portion be,
As long as life endures.

The verses continued. The last one. Was this true? Did God promise good to him? He expected good out of life, if he worked hard enough for it. This seemed to be his dad's philosophy. And what had Clifton Watson said? "God's in control, if we let Him."

When we've been there ten thousand years,
Bright shining as the sun,
We've no less days to sing God's praise
Than when we'd first begun.

No less days than when we'd first begun. Infinity. Eternity. It wasn't something he spent much time pondering. Science had never done a good job explaining it, and he figured it was off in the future, so why worry?

EMMA CLOSED her eyes as the next verse seemed to wash over her.

The Lord has promised good to me,
His word my hope secures;
He will my Shield and Portion be
As long as life endures.

The Lord was her shield and portion. He promised good. He promised hope. She opened her eyes and looked over at Sophie, sitting with her friends in the "amen corner" where the youth seemed to congregate. She caught her eye, and Sophie winked.

She sat there, alone. Was she lonely? Sometimes. Sometimes it would be nice to have a man around to reach high shelves, to crack a silly joke, or, if she were honest, to hold her.

Where was this coming from? She held an infant, and all of the sudden she wanted the last fifteen years back?

No, God's amazing grace had buoyed her from the beginning. When Daniel was gone, it had been herself and Sophie. Both sets of parents helped as much as they could, but they had trials of their own. She had leaned on God. It never occurred to her, until now, that God's "good" for her might include personal happiness and fulfillment as well. Maybe someone needs a help-meet they haven't found yet. Maybe she needs support she doesn't yet know about. And Sophie? What did she need?

"God, if You want me to dip my toes back into the dating pool, You're going to have to give me a clear sign. I'm not putting a time limit on it, but I'll be available for what You want, not what I want. Otherwise, I'm happy the way things are."

Are you?

Was that her own mind, or was it one of those God-whispers?

Charly was surprised when the pastor, Bro. Bill Macintosh, stood and had Ben, the song leader, hand out a half-sheet of paper.

"I know this is unusual for our Wednesday night prayer time, but rather than go through taking prayer requests, I've printed up the prayer list for you. If there are any additions, let me know after the service, and we can add them. I wanted to have a little more time tonight for our devotion."

No organ recital? She felt a giggle bubble up and glanced over at Rance to see him raising an eyebrow at her. She shook her head and whispered, "Later."

After several called out additions to the hospital and prayer list, Bro. Bill opened his Bible and placed it next to his hymnal. "Tonight I want to talk about grace. I asked Ben to sing 'Amazing Grace' to get us kicked off and wanted to take one hymn verse at a time, looking at what the hymn writer was talking about when he talks about this amazing grace we have through Jesus Christ, our Lord. I'll be expecting participation from the congregation, as well."

He looked over his glasses at the people in the pews and grinned, garnering a few chuckles.

She had heard this hymn all her life. She'd watched a movie about it. She had done sign language to it. What more could she learn about "Amazing Grace?"

Her sigh garnered a poke in the ribs from her mother, so she set her lips in place to sit through the message, planning instead to complete a mental to-do list. The first verse irritated her anyway. The last line, "was blind, but now I see" seemed to rub in her mother's blindness. If God was so gracious, why did He take her mother's sight? And was nobody else angry about that little fact?

She found herself stewing, wondering at the anger she was feeling. She glanced over at her mother. She was smiling and nodding affirmation. How could she sit and take this? Grace hadn't brought her mother "safe thus far." She was blind, she was a widow. And where was the "promised good?"

She felt Rance shift in his seat. Was he uncomfortable? Was this too much for a first-timer? She glanced over at him, struck by the intensity of his gaze on the pastor. A nudge of guilt wafted through her soul. She didn't know what was going on in his heart, and what hit her was that she hadn't asked.

An infant's hiccup caught her attention. Jared was bouncing baby Beau on his shoulder, and tears filled her eyes. Jared and Sarah looked as if they had the perfect life. Money was no object, they had a good marriage, and all their parents were still alive, but they had suffered their trials as well. Jared was critically injured in the hurricane the year they got married. The stillbirth of their first child a few years later was devastating. Beau was part of their healing. God's grace had brought them through. It was nothing they did. It was all God.

She closed her eyes. Thank You, God. And forgive me, God. Help me to be better. Help me to trust more. Help me to depend on You and not myself. It's not easy, and I'm still a little angry. Help me to not be angry. Please?

She looked up as the pastor was wrapping up.

Bro. Bill looked over at Ben. "Brother Ben, could we sing the last verse of 'Amazing Grace' without any music?" He waved at Sarah as she began to rise. "Keep your seat, Sarah. I want us to listen as we sing. When we've been there ten thousand years." He paused. "Ten thousand years. Sounds like a vast amount of time, doesn't it?"

Nods and amens from all around made Charly smile.

"And to think, after ten thousand years, we'll still have that many more years, and more, and more. God's grace is what gives us eternity to praise. Amen? Let's sing, considering this our prayer, and then you'll be dismissed."

The congregation rose to sing the last stanza. The voices were beautiful, the message more so.

CHAPTER FOURTEEN

"Do you want to grab something to eat? I'd love to treat you both." Rance held the door for Charly and Mary Ann as they exited the church, his hand resting on the small of Charly's back.

"You two kids go ahead. This old lady needs to get home and into her pj's." Mary Ann laughed.

Rance lifted his eyebrows and looked around. "I don't see any old ladies around here, do you?"

Charly laughed. "I do not."

"Well, thank you for the invitation, but, Charlotte, if you'll drop me off by home, I'll take a rain check."

"Then I insist on escorting you to the car." Rance took her hand and placed it on his arm. "And I plan on honoring your rain check."

Mary Ann inclined her head and bestowed a smile that looked for all the world like Charly's. Easy, loving, genuine. "Thank you kindly."

He looked over at Charly. "Want to meet at your house? Then we could decide what to do?"

She tilted her head. "Sounds good. I'll be there in ten minutes."

"Make it twenty and drive safely."

"If you want to go in, there's a key under the pot of geraniums on the porch." She laughed when he shook his head. "I know. Original, huh?"

"I'll be waiting for you."

"Thanks, Rance."

He caught her gaze again before he swung down into his car. She looked tired and a little emotional. Maybe a walk on the beach instead of a round of putt-putt golf? Maybe a little fried chicken? That would do it. Drive-thru chicken and a walk on the beach. It would be good for both of them.

And maybe he could find out what was going on in that pretty head of hers.

Before he put the car in reverse, his phone pinged with a text. It was Dr. Hobgood.

Call me. Important. Clifton Watson.

As he stared at the text, he felt his heart seize up on him. Had his biological father taken a turn for the worse? Would he die before he found out he had another son and his ex-wife had lied to him for twenty-eight years?

He waved at Charly as she exited the parking lot. As soon as she left, he called Dr. Hobgood. He answered on the second ring.

"Butler?"

"Yes, sir. What can I do for you? You said it was important, about Mr. Watson?"

"Yes." The doctor cleared his throat loudly. "When did you submit samples to be tested for a match with Clifton?"

"Yesterday, sir. Are they already back?" Usually the turnaround, on a rush job, was three days.

"They are, and you are a seventy-five percent match. Is it possible you're related to Clifton Watson?" He paused. "And does he know you've indicated an interest in becoming a living donor? It's not an easy surgery, son."

"I have reason to believe I am related to Mr. Watson. He doesn't know, and I'd like to be able to talk to him before you say anything, if possible."

"I trust you know what you're doing. Let's meet and talk about this in the morning. Say eight?"

"I'll be there, sir. And thank you for letting me know."

"I'll pray for you. Like I said, it's not an easy thing you're thinking about doing."

"I appreciate it."

They ended the call, and he sat there, staring at the church building.

The last time he talked to Clifton, his father, he told him God was in control. How could he possibly know? All those people in there tonight. What did they know of God's grace? They all seemed to understand it.

At this moment, his stomach told him he was hungry, and his gut was telling him he had a lot of thinking to do.

BY THE TIME Charly got home, the shadows were lengthening, but there was still plenty of daylight for whatever they decided to do. She felt reticent, as if she needed to sit still. Wait. Listen.

When she entered her front door, she had to smile. There, spread out on her breakfast bar, was a full KFC meal: chicken, potatoes and gravy, slaw, and biscuits.

"How did you know I needed biscuits tonight?"

He shrugged. "I had a feeling. Plus, I needed comfort food too." His eyes dimmed. "Hope it wasn't too presumptuous of me."

"Not at all. I would be glad to go somewhere, but I didn't want to be around people tonight."

"I'm sorry . . ."

"No, not you, I mean other people." She could feel the heat rising from her neck to her cheeks. Why did she have to be blessed with such a fair complexion that blushed at the drop of a hat? Real smooth, Charlotte Anne.

"Oh." His face relaxed in a smile.

She twisted her lips in an embarrassed grin. "I see you found everything."

"Including ice-cold sweet tea. It is the bomb." He held up his glass and looked at it with adoration. "Amazing."

She gave him a slight curtsy. "Thank you, kind sir." She pulled out her ultra-Southern drawl. "Ev'ry Southe'n girl has to learn how to make sweet tea before she leaves her mama, you know." She took a glass from him and nodded at him in her most genteel manner as he pushed her stool in for her.

"I was not aware, but it is a wonderful skill to have." He laughed. "Tell me, is sweet tea on the list for debutantes in this neck of the woods?"

"Well, it should be." She took a sip and sighed with pleasure. "Do you mind if I bless our meal?"

He looked surprised but not entirely. "Of course not."

She felt nervous. She had prayed in front of people all her life, but this felt different. It wasn't one of those public "should" prayers, but an intimate, moment with God along with someone who might not be a believer.

"God, thank You for this food and for Rance for providing it. Thank You for the time we spend together, and for his friendship. Thank You for the message we heard tonight, and for Your amazing grace. In Jesus' name I pray, Amen."

He turned toward her with a gentle smile. "That was nice."

There was the heat in her face again. "Thanks." She concentrated on putting a napkin in her lap and then pulled her hair over her shoulders.

"Tonight was interesting."

"I was afraid you would be bored. I'm glad Bro. Bill mixed it up a little bit tonight." She grinned and selected her piece of still-hot chicken. Why was she so nervous?

"No, not bored. Grace is not a topic that comes up in my everyday conversation." He chuckled.

"Well, now you can think about it when you jump out of an airplane or bungee off a cliff."

He laughed out loud. "I might." He sobered. "I may not be doing either of those for a while."

She glanced at him and stopped short at the frown on his face. "Anything you want to talk about?"

"I've had family stuff crop up. I won't bore you with the details."

"I respect your privacy, but if you need someone to talk to, I've been told I'm a pretty good listener."

"I'm sure you are. I'll know more after tomorrow, but thanks."

They ate in companionable silence, broken by a comment now and then.

"I can't eat another bite." Charly held her stomach.

"Maybe a little stroll along the waves?" Rance motioned toward the French doors with his head, raising his eyebrows.

Charly nodded. "I think that would do the trick."

THE STIFF OCEAN breeze blew the cobwebs from Rance's mind. So many things to think about. If he had doubt that Clifton was his biological father, his doubt was gone with a seventy-five percent match in blood and genetic testing. Fifty percent was acceptable for blood relations.

He had been so lost in his own thoughts since the phone call, he almost forgot the girl next to him, and she was hard to forget. He was beginning to realize it, the more time he spent with her.

Charly was quiet, sensitive to the fact he was pondering. Some girls would take his silence as a sign he wasn't interested. He had a feeling Charly wasn't like most girls he had dated.

He reached down and took her hand, and she rewarded him with a brilliant smile. A fleeting thought prompted him to kiss her, but he didn't. She had a very kissable mouth. Instead, he drew her hand up to his elbow and pulled her closer as they walked, her hand tucked into his arm.

From a distance, he could see bonfires on the beach in the Huntington Beach State Park section. He was glad to be away from the fray. At one time, he would have been in the middle of it.

"Penny for them?" He squeezed her hand and linked their fingers, stopping her for a moment. She looked wistful.

She grinned. "It'll cost you more than a penny, mister."

"Okay, piece of chicken for your thoughts?" He winked and then chuckled as she blushed.

"I was thinking about the service tonight."

"What about it?"

"Well, about you."

"What about me?" He tensed. Here we go. She's concerned for my soul. An inner sigh tried to get him to back away from her, but instead he steeled himself for the conversation.

"I don't really know you, do I?" She dropped her eyes. "My spiritual life, my church life, is such a big part of me and has been forever, it seems, and I don't know where you stand, or if you even believe in God." She looked away at the ocean for a minute. "I guess I've never been faced with this before now."

He looked away for a minute. When he looked back at her, he was at a loss. "Not something I've been faced with, either."

"You said the service was interesting. In what way?"

He thought a minute. "I guess I never thought about God as a person who thought we were important. I've heard the 'God is in control' thing but never thought about it applying to me." It didn't make much sense, to him, as he said it.

"I know what you mean. I'm confident in His grace, but sometimes I let myself get angry with God." She bowed her head, obviously embarrassed. When she looked up, there was a mist in her eyes. "And then I push Him away." She wrinkled her nose at him. "I don't recommend it."

"Does He care when we get angry?"

"Oh, I think He cares, and I think He understands. That's what I hold on to. If I thought I'd lose my salvation because I get angry, I would have given up by now. God doesn't hold a grudge. Unfortunately, sometimes I do." She shrugged. "I'm not very good at this."

"I think you're doing fine. My parents never went to church. I went a few times with my dad's parents, but it was so boring. It was a lot of standing up and sitting down and kneeling. I don't remember it being personal the way this was tonight."

CHAPTER FIFTEEN

*P*ersonal. It was an interesting way to think about God. Could it be He cares about individuals on a personal level?

Rance still had it on his mind as he drove to the hospital the next morning to meet Dr. Hobgood. He had decisions to make. Was he willing to sacrifice a few months of his life to donate a kidney to a man who, according to his mother, forced her to run away and leave both him and her son?

Sure, he had only met the man a couple of times, but he felt as though they had a connection. He liked the man. He didn't seem to be the monster to which his mother compared him. Or did his anger toward his mother make him look at Clifton through rose-colored glasses? Was he considering this to spite her? To get even?

He walked into the hospital annex and turned toward the elevators to go to the kidney specialist's office suite on the fourth floor. He was here for information, not to sign a contract. Surely there was another family member who could donate? What about this brother in prison?

He entered the empty waiting room and acknowledged the

receptionist who was gathering things to start her day. He was early, at the doctor's request.

"You must be Dr. Butler." Her eyebrows shot up when he smiled, not an unusual happening for him. He sighed.

"I am."

"Come on back. Patients won't be arriving until nine, so you've got him all to yourself."

"Thanks." He made his way through the long hallway of examining rooms to Dr. Hobgood's office at the very back. The doctor was going through a thick file on his desk and looked up when he heard Rance's soft knock on the doorframe.

"Rance, good to see you." He stood and shook his hand, gesturing for him to sit in the soft leather chair in front of his desk.

"Thanks for letting me come in early. I'm not ready to commit to anything, understand."

"Wise decision."

"Not making one?" Rance chuckled.

"Not making a rash one." Dr. Hobgood looked at the younger man over his reading glasses. "Have you spoken to Mr. Watson?"

"Not about this." Rance paused, putting his elbows on his knees, linking his hands together in front of him as he leaned forward. "I've come across some information in the last few weeks leading me to believe I haven't been in possession of all the facts of my heritage." He wasn't ready to say out loud, yet, that Clifton Watson was his father. Somehow saying it made it too personal, too real. He had to stay above the anger and hurt that went with this knowledge.

"And because of this information, you are not surprised you were such a close match."

Rance nodded. "Exactly. I know he has a son in prison. Was he approached about his father's condition?"

"He was. He offered as soon as he heard, but he wasn't a

good match. That, plus his long-time drug abuse has put his own health at risk."

The doctor shook his head. "I've known Clifton for a long time and knew his father. He wasn't always the man you see now. He was hard and tough on his son as his dad was on him, and they didn't get along most of the time. I understand his son, Sam, has had a change of heart while in prison, and I think it got Clifton's attention as well." He took a deep breath. "Sad situation."

"Where is the son?" An idea was taking hold. He had no idea if it was a good one or not, but it was an idea.

He'd never visited anyone in prison before. There's a first time for everything.

FOR THE FIRST time in a long time, Charly dreaded the beginning of a summer session of classes. Up to now she had been able to get most of them done online, and now she was down to the last few classes. This particular one required on-campus attendance, four days a week for four weeks. It would keep her busier than she preferred, and even more now that there was a certain blue-eyed young doctor vying for attention.

Driving north on Highway 17 toward Coastal Carolina University in Myrtle Beach, she shook her head in disbelief. How did someone like Rance find himself attracted to someone like her? Not that she was an ogre or anything, but, seriously. Rance Butler? He was someone special. She was so not special.

"God, I don't know what You've got in mind for Rance and me, but it's a little scary." The niggling fear and insecurity was always there, simmering beneath the surface. She could hide it for a little while, but sometimes it swamped her and she felt as though she couldn't breathe. Some people would call it a panic attack. She looked at it as one more way God didn't care about her as much as everyone thought.

She pulled into the parking lot closest to her building on the campus of her alma mater and pulled out the schedule. Since this class met so often and for so long, she could only take one class this session. This made it a little less daunting.

She felt herself relax. More time to work with Emma and more time for Rance. The thought of his brilliant smile and bright blue eyes made her insecurity a little lower. Being on campus didn't hurt either. There are comfort foods, and there are comfort places. This campus was one of her comfort places.

Bag in tow, she headed to her class, noting the slow progress of the students heading to the first day of class. Most of them had coffee in hand, including herself. She was thankful there was a coffee shop with a drive through on the way into town.

There were several familiar faces and a few new ones, all ready to delve into a graduate-level education class.

She turned to sit and found herself face-to-chest with one of her classmates who had apparently been eyeing the same seat.

"Oh, sorry, I didn't see you." She looked up to see a rather thin young man towering over her, smiling awkwardly.

"That's a new one. Usually people notice me for nothing but my height. And the weather up here is fine, by the way." He gestured for her to take the seat in his stead.

"How . . ."

He held his hand up. "How tall am I anyway? Six-feet, seven inches."

Charly laughed. "You've taken all the guess-work out of meeting new people, haven't you?"

"May as well. When you're me, you know where the conversation is going to go, and it's my height. By the way, my name is Jake. Jake Prince." He stuck out his hand.

She accepted his firm handshake with a smile. "Charly Livingston. Where do you teach?"

"Special ed at Waccamaw Middle. You?"

"Georgetown Middle! Why have I not seen you at any department meetings?"

Jake grinned. "I got the job last week. I was at an elementary school in Myrtle Beach this past year and wanted to move into middle or high school this year."

"Hard to get down to their level, huh?" She couldn't stifle the giggle threatening to burst forth.

He pointed to her and laughed. "Very funny, but somewhat true. I stayed bent over so much I was afraid I would end up stooped before my time." He rubbed the back of his neck and waggled his eyebrows comically. "Hey, would you be interested in carpooling? I'm renting a place at Surfside."

"Sure. I'm between Murrells Inlet and North Litchfield, so I go right through there."

"Great."

They exchanged cell numbers and looked up in surprise when the teacher spoke to them directly. "If you're both done arranging your date, we'd like to get started."

Charly felt the heat rise to her hairline and shifted quickly into the seat, Jake folding himself into the seat behind her.

She felt her phone buzz with a text, so she carefully and unobtrusively opened it to see a text from Jake.

Does this mean we're dating? Because it usually is much harder for me.

Controlling her laughter was proving harder than she ever thought possible. Maybe this wouldn't be such a bad summer after all.

CHAPTER SIXTEEN

Before the information that was an explosion to the world as he knew it, Rance would have used his day off to sleep, study, or maybe talk Charly into goofing off with him at the beach all day. She had class today, so instead, he was driving two and a half hours to Ridgeland Correctional Institute, about an hour or so south of Charleston.

He had a brother there. He shook his head at the thought.

He flipped through the radio stations, trying to find some old-time rock-n-roll. When he scanned through to a clear station, a few words caught him.

Amazing Grace, how sweet the sound . . .

It was, and it wasn't, the song from his visit to Calvary Church. A little different rhythm, and then there was a chorus added, talking about chains, and being set free.

Set free from what?

He hit the scan button again, looking for something he didn't have to think about. When all he could find was modern country, he switched the radio off. He had nothing against country music, but who could beat the classics? He pushed a button and a CD started playing Johnny Cash. It was one of those "best of" compilations with songs from various times in his career.

When the music started, he sighed in relief. Maybe it was "Folsom Prison Blues" or "Ring of Fire." Those were great songs, made you feel good. Or maybe "A Boy Named Sue." He remembered the first time he heard it. It cracked him up every time.

This sounded like a slow one but not too slow. He passed through Charleston and had a fleeting thought he needed to talk to his mother again. He wasn't ready.

When he heard Johnny's voice, he swerved in the road. In his low, gravelly voice that sounded strangely similar to Clifton Watson's, the words he had been trying to avoid hit him.

Amazing Grace, how sweet the sound . . .

RANCE SAT at a table in a room full of tables, waiting for his brother. His brother. All his life, he'd wanted nothing more than a brother or sister. Didn't matter which, but a big brother? That would have been the best.

Then to find out he did, indeed, have a brother, and said brother was sitting in a penitentiary two and a half hours away, only an hour away from his mother, was a slap in the face.

He lifted his head when he heard a buzzer and a loud clank then a shuffling across the floor. He stood and held out his hand. "Rance Butler."

"Nice to meet you, Rance. Sam Watson." They shook hands and sat, both staring at one another.

"I know we've never met, but you look familiar." Sam gave him a half-grin. "Don't suppose you've ever been in trouble with the law?"

Rance chuckled. "No, not beyond a few traffic violations. Nothing the state police would have been interested in."

Sam tilted his head and frowned in confusion. "Sounds as if you know more about me than I know about you."

"You could say that." Rance shifted nervously in his chair. "I've met your dad, Clifton Watson. He's a pretty sick man."

"I know. I wanted to be the one to give him a kidney, but we didn't match up. Funny. I'm more like him than anyone, and I wasn't a match."

Sam wasn't what he expected. He was calm, a little emotional when it came to his dad. How would he take the news of a twenty-eight-year-old bouncing baby brother?

"We did find a seventy-five percent match."

The man across the table sat up straighter. "Seventy-five? I've done a little research. That's better than average. Has it been set up yet? Is Dad able to have the surgery?"

Rance looked at him seriously. "It hasn't been set up yet. The donor is still deciding whether or not he should do it."

Sam pounded the table with his fist and shook his head. "How could he not? I mean, sure, it's major surgery, and the recovery time is pretty intense, but to save a life?" He paused, took a deep breath, and narrowed his eyes. "Sorry. That was the old, angry me talking, but then the old me wouldn't have thought much about saving Dad's life either."

"You aren't close?"

"We are now. Now that I'm in here and can't do anything to help him. I hope he lives long enough to see me out of here, able to make a fresh start."

"I understand." Rance looked down at his hands. How could he broach the real reason he was here? "How much longer?"

"Another two months." Sam looked straight into his eyes. "You look like pictures of Dad when he was younger. I was always told I resembled my mom, but I don't have many pictures of her."

"Do you remember much about her?"

Sam leaned back in his chair, his eyes narrowed as if taking a measure of the man across from him. Rance was positive he was wondering what made his family so interesting to him and was questioning whether or not to share intimate details about his childhood.

"What kind of doctor did you say you were?"

Rance grinned. "I'm finishing my internship at Georgetown General. I'm on rotation with Dr. Hobgood, your dad's urologist. Right now, I'm an MD."

"Thought so. I've talked to psychologists and psychiatrists, and they're much better at questioning."

"Yeah, well, I'm here on a personal mission, not a professional one."

"You're the match, aren't you?"

Their eyes locked, so similar, and yet the lines around Sam's eyes told of a life lived in difficulty and excess. Six years between them put Sam in his mid-thirties, most of his life without a mother, or at least without his own mother.

"I am."

"You asked about my mother. The last time I saw my mother was before school the day she left. I was in first grade. She packed my lunch, kissed me goodbye, and hugged me tight, then sent me on my way to the bus. She stood at the door and waved as the bus pulled away. When I got home after school, Dad was home early, and she was gone. He was drunk and sent me to my room. I'm pretty sure I cried all night, and by the next morning, Dad fixed my cereal and told me we'd talk about it later. I didn't want to be late for school."

"Did you?"

"Talk about it? No. Occasionally I would get up the nerve to ask about her, and he would only say she needed to leave and wasn't coming back. I asked my grandfather about her once, and he slapped me. He said he told her not to darken the door of the house and told me to never mention her again." Sam's eyes never wavered from Rance's.

He looked down then back up at his brother. "I guess you stopped asking after that?"

Sam nodded. "I found out later she had remarried, but that was all. She hid her tracks pretty well."

"Not that well. Somebody knew where she was."

"How do you know?"

"Because two weeks ago she told me I had a brother, and that his name was Sam Watson."

CHARLY WAS LAUGHING as she answered her cell phone.

"Rance!"

"You sound awfully chipper for having been in class all day."

"Sorry. Jake was telling me about one of his students."

"Ah, teacher talk."

"I can hear your eyes glazing over even on the phone."

Rance chuckled. "No, I'm sure many of my hospital tales are as bad."

"Are you off today?"

"I am. Thought about hitting the beach for a little while, if you're going to be home soon."

"I will be there in . . ." She paused and looked at the landmarks they were passing, ". . . ten to fifteen minutes."

"Awesome. Want me to pick up a pizza?"

"Perfect. I had peanut butter and crackers for lunch, and they are definitely gone."

Rance laughed. "I skipped lunch, so I'll be sure to get a large."

She glanced over at Jake who was pantomiming a love scene as he drove. She whispered, "Stop it!"

"Did you say something?"

"Oh, I was telling Jake something. He was about to miss our turn." She bugged her eyes at the driver, who laughed out loud.

"Right. All right then, I'm on my way back from Charleston, so I'll be about a half hour."

"Perfect. I'll make the tea."

"Absolutely." He sighed. "Thanks, Charly."

"For what?" She frowned into the phone. "Something wrong?"

"No, we'll talk later."

They ended the call, and Charly whacked Jake on the arm.

Jake grabbed his arm and raised his shoulder. "Ow, woman, you don't know your own strength."

"Pu-leeze. You've been hit harder by preschoolers."

"You are not wrong." He laughed. "So, Ra-ance is the hunky boyfriend, eh?"

"Seriously, two syllables?"

"It sounded more simpering to say it in that tone."

"I do not simper."

"No, but you do get all starry-eyed when you talk to him on the phone."

"Just you wait. It'll hit you one of these days."

He scrunched his face in a comical wince. "I hope not. Looks painful."

"Love is patient, love is kind—"

"Not jealous, boastful, proud, rude. I know the drill." He paused then turned to her for the punch-line. "Bible drill, that is." He winked at her.

She shook her head. "You're hopeless."

"Thought you'd never notice."

CHAPTER SEVENTEEN

Charly made a pitcher of tea and put plates on the counter as she unloaded the dishwasher. Jake was so funny. Since they started carpooling, he kept her laughing all the way to class and all the way home. He didn't make her feel breathless like Rance did, but he was sweet. She needed to find him a woman. Hmmm. She might know the perfect one.

About the time she pulled plates and glasses out of the cabinet, there was a gentle knock on her screen door.

She ran to the door and unhooked it, smiling.

"Hi, Rance, you were quicker than I expected!"

"Hey, you." He leaned over and kissed her gently over the box of hot pizza.

"What was that for?" She felt her face warm. It was sweet. Not a heart-shattering first kiss, but she'd take it. She felt like a puddle of goo anyway.

He continued gazing at her. "I've wanted to do that for a long time."

She gave him a gentle smile. "Have you now?"

"I have. I may do it again if it's all right with you." His half-grin threatened to undo her.

"I could be persuaded." She glanced down the box in his hand. "Hungry?"

"Starved." He raised his eyebrows when she glanced up at him. "For pizza."

"Me too. No class until next Monday, a project turned in today, and the next one not due until next Thursday."

"Great. Now tell me about this carpool-Jake-fella. Do I have anything to worry about?"

She gave him a quick kiss on the cheek. "Not a thing. He makes me laugh and saves me gas."

"Good. I thought about inviting him to go rock-climbing with me and maybe forgetting to tie him off—"

She held up her hand to stop him. "Not necessary. I think you would like him. He's hilarious. I'm thinking about introducing him to Lydia."

"Hmmm . . ." He arched a brow and nodded thoughtfully. "Mind if I change into my trunks in your bathroom?"

"Go ahead. Want to eat on the patio?"

"Sure. Less sand in the pizza."

"Exactly." A laugh bubbled up in her. "You sound better than you did on the phone."

"I am better, thanks." He winked at her and made his way to the bathroom with his bag.

"Can't wait to hear about it."

HE DIDN'T plan to kiss her today. There she was, opening the front door for him, for all the world like a wife welcoming a tired husband home from a hard day at work. It seemed the most natural thing in the world, and he simply went for it. Hey, a guy could dream.

Dressed in his navy and white trunks and a blue t-shirt, towel over his shoulder, and sunglasses on his face, he met her out on the patio, pizza and tea in place.

"Perfect."

"The pizza, the tea, or me?"

Was she flirting with him? Nice. "All of the above." He sat in the chair next to her and looked at her with a half-smile, relaxing for the first time today.

"How was your day?" She handed him a plate and opened the box of pizza, pulling a piece from the slices. The cheese strung so far he had to rescue her by sliding a finger along the cheese to break the contact with the larger pie. "Thank you."

"My day was what you would call interesting." He wasn't sure how to tell her about his day. Should he tell her? Would she understand the crazy situation he found himself in?

"Interesting, huh?"

"Yeah." How much should he share?

"Probably more interesting than mine."

"Depends on how you look at it." He raked his hand through his hair and grimaced. "There have been a few things to happen in the last few weeks."

"You mean besides the general-all-purpose grind of an internship?"

"Totally. Well, almost totally, outside of the internship."

"Okay." She looked puzzled as she took a bite of the hot pizza. "Ouch, ouch, ouch. Burn." She took a large swig of iced tea. "Why do I do this every time? Sorry. Continue if you'd like."

He looked at the slice in his hand and quickly set it back down on his plate. "I think I'll let mine cool a little."

She took another sip of the refreshing liquid and fanned her open mouth. "I'm a cautionary tale, aren't I?"

He laughed. "You definitely are when it comes to hot pizza."

"I think I'll let mine cool a bit too."

He leaned back again. "You haven't met my family yet. They're an interesting bunch."

"You've mentioned your parents and grandparents, and that you always wanted a sibling."

"Yeah, well, right before we went out on our first date, I went down to Charleston for a last minute visit. I hadn't been in a while, and in the three years I've been here, my parents have never been up to Georgetown to visit me. I always thought it was a little odd. When I was at Clemson, they came all the time, but here? Only an hour away? Never."

She gazed at him. "I can tell it hurts you."

"I didn't think much about it until Mom said something about me needing to call Dad more often, and then I mentioned he had never called me, and they'd never come down for a visit." He shook his head. Why was it hard to simply come out and say it? Because her family was normal, and he had thought, until two weeks ago, his was too.

He looked at her and then looked away.

"Charly, she told me I have a brother."

"What?" Her eyes widened in surprise.

"A brother." He looked at her. "That's not all. The man I've always thought my father, is not."

"Oh, Rance." She reached out to touch his hand as it rested on the table.

"Once she started telling me, there was no stopping her. She ran away from my father and my brother and made a deal with my grandfather to never see them again. She didn't know she was pregnant with me when she left, and she basically disappeared. Went back to her maiden name, met Dad, and they married, and he was the only one who knew I wasn't his."

"Why did she tell you now?"

"Apparently she found out, or someone told her, that my grandfather, my biological dad's father, has died recently."

"Was she afraid?"

"According to her." He shook his head. "I've met my father. He doesn't seem the harsh man she described, unless it was her father-in-law she was afraid of, instead of her husband. My father. Wow."

"People change."

"They do, and sometimes people are wrong."

"What about your brother?"

"I met him today."

"Okay, this is turning into a huge deal." She took a bite of her cooled pizza and then wiped her hands on a napkin. "My 'how was your day' has gone into overdrive."

"Hey, you asked."

She grinned. "And I want to know. You can't stop now."

"I went to the correctional facility where Sam is being held. My brother is Sam Watson, and my father is Clifton Watson. He's in the hospital at Georgetown waiting for a kidney transplant."

Charly sat there, her mouth hanging open, wide eyes blinking in confusion. "Wait. You said your brother's name is Sam Watson?"

"Yes." He watched as she got up from the table and began to walk around then turned back to him. "You know him?"

She stopped, her arms crossed at her chest. "I've never met him, but I know who he is."

"And?"

"He was caught embezzling relief funds after Hurricane Rosa and tried to implicate my brother. Tom and Lucy were the ones who caught him."

"You're kidding me."

She shook her head grimly. "He was also involved in a situation that almost killed Jared several years ago."

He wiped his hand over his eyes and slung his head back in a huge sigh. "Great."

"I mean, it's been five years. Surely your mother knew about it. It was all over the regional news, especially since Sam worked for the state police."

He looked into her eyes, holding her in place. "Charly, how do you think your mother will feel, and Tom and Lucy are going to feel when they find out the brother of the criminal they helped put away helped to deliver their babies, and is now dating their sister? And Jared and Sarah?" He closed his eyes and shook his head in disgust.

SUNSETS AREN'T the main focus of the beaches of the East Coast, but tonight, sitting on a towel on the sand, Charly leaned her head onto Rance's muscular shoulder and watched the shadows lengthen as the tide started going out. He had told her everything except how he felt about it all. Maybe he was still processing the information.

They sat, fingers linked together loosely, saying nothing except occasionally when a thought would come to them.

After one such period of silence, Charly raised her eyes to his. "Why would they be upset about our dating? You had nothing to do with any of it."

He gave her a half-smile. "I know, but people have a way of surprising you with what they will and will not tolerate in relationships. Bad seed and all."

"We just started dating. It's not like we're married." She huffed a little, looking away to avoid his gaze.

"True. And who knows what will happen once this internship is over? I may not be here much longer."

She turned and looked at him, stricken. His leaving had never come up. She knew interns didn't stay where they were working, usually. She had thought maybe . . .

"You never considered that, did you?"

She shook her head and drew in a deep breath. "No, not

really. I've been working hard to be spontaneous." She gave him a rueful smile.

"Me too." He pulled his fingers from hers and stood, holding out his hand to her. "Walk a little?"

She nodded and reached up to him, hanging on to his hand as they walked.

The beach had emptied at suppertime, and being a weekday, they had it to themselves. It was like being on a desert island, if you didn't think about people in those houses along the shore. Even at that, the dunes between the houses and the beach insulated them from the world. Saltwater lapped at their feet as the tide went out, leaving a hard surface to walk on, the occasional shell or jellyfish left behind.

"What are you going to do?" Was it her place to ask?

"I have no idea. I'm a seventy-five percent match for a kidney for Clifton Watson."

"Have you told your mother?"

"No, I left pretty soon after Dad got home that night. When I went back later, I hadn't been tested yet."

She looked at him sideways.

"I know. I should have heard them out the first time. I was angry. Seriously angry." He blew his breath out his nose and pressed his lips in a firm line. "And I'm still angry. They lied to me."

"Anger is a normal reaction. I've been there a few times myself."

"I find that hard to believe."

"I've been angry at God, even."

He was quiet, pondering. "I wish I knew how much Clifton knows and what his father, my grandfather, had to do with it." He shook his head in disbelief. "I thought I had a normal family."

She sputtered in laughter. "No such thing."

"Yours seems pretty normal."

"All families have their quirks. I've been told it's all in how you react to circumstances, not the circumstances themselves."

"How does your family react to circumstances?"

She thought a minute as they strolled, the sun going down further. "We all face things differently, even in one family. With Tom, it's control. With Mom, shutting herself off. Sarah's told me that for her, it was withholding trust. I told you one way I react, and it's with anger. I guess I'm a little like Tom and Mom, where I shut myself off and pretend it didn't happen while I'm seething on the inside. Not healthy, I know."

He looked up and away from her and laughed. "I'm sorry, but you, angry? You're the most calm, quiet, in-control person I think I've ever met."

Using her best Bugs Bunny impersonation, she said, "You don't know me vewy well, do you?" She grinned. "Ask Lydia. She sees the real me more than my family."

He stopped walking and pulled her to face him. "When I'm with you, I'm not angry."

"I'm not either."

She watched as he reached out to tuck a stray strand of hair behind her ear and to stroke her cheek with his knuckles. When he put his hand on her waist and pulled her closer, she didn't resist, her doubts and fears vanishing in the depths of his blue eyes. A fleeting thought came into her mind, "what if he leaves?" vying for attention, but it was obliterated as soon as his lips touched hers.

CHAPTER EIGHTEEN

uying a panel van had been one of the best purchases Emma and Lucy had made for Quince Wedding Designs. You could have the big stuff—tents, tables, chairs, etc.—delivered, but all the little stuff took up a lot of space too. When her aging minivan bit the dust, the decision had been made to transfer responsibility for transporting goods to the business instead of her personal checking account.

Tooling down Highway 17 toward her supplier in Mount Pleasant, north of Charleston, she had the radio on KLOV, singing along to Chris Tomlin and his version of "Amazing Grace." She felt herself grin when she realized everywhere she went, that song seemed to be cropping up.

She thought about the song. She thought about God's amazing grace and about how she had held the world at bay, caring for her little corner of it, seldom thinking about how she could be part of change for someone else. It never really occurred to her. Maybe God had been protecting her while Sophie was little and while her heart was still so tender from her loss.

She pulled into Hodge Rental Equipment. This was where

the big stuff came from, and she preferred to see it before she rented it. Especially for a wedding at Pilot Oaks. She was looking for a specific chair and knew she could find it here. The plan was to take one with her to get approval from the bride and groom.

She walked into the showroom and smiled at the gentleman at the service desk. "How are you today, Ken?"

"I'm good, Emmaline, how are you? Come to see a man about a chair?"

She laughed. "I most certainly did. I'll bet you're just the man who can help me, aren't you?"

He came out from behind the desk. "I am. You mentioned the acrylic chairs. We have three different styles."

"At three different price-points, I'll bet."

"Yes, ma'am. Although they all look good to me." He led her to the platform where the different styles of chairs were displayed. "I can let you take one of each with you, if you'd like, or pick what you want, and we'll put it on your account."

She looked them over. All three would work, but the rental on the most expensive one was so far above the others, she eliminated it on the spot.

"That sounds good, Ken. How about I leave the most expensive one and take the other two with me? No need to bust the budget completely."

"Be glad to. Anything else I can help you with?"

"No, I'm heading a little farther into town for candle holders and such. Wish y'all had those."

The man grinned. "Too much frou-frou for us. We stick with the big stuff. Did you still want those tents on the twenty-eighth?"

"Yes. D'you mind if I look at my order for the date and make sure I have everything down I'll need? I'll have to call you with the order for the chairs after I get the okay."

"Works for me. Come on up to the desk, and I'll get it printed up for you."

As they walked up, a man strode up to the desk, obviously in a hurry. He nodded at Emma, his eyes widening in appreciation as she gave him a slight smile.

"How are things with the state police these days, Rafe?" Ken greeted the new customer as he printed out Emma's order.

"Pretty good, Ken. Been pretty busy. I decided to take a few days and work on my dad's yard. I brought in his Stihl mower for repairs."

He looked familiar, but it never surprised her when someone who looked familiar had been an attendee at a wedding she had planned. Over the course of ten years, she had worked a lot of weddings.

"Be with you in a minute, Rafe."

"I'm in no hurry." He leaned on the counter, looking across the store, seeming to will his breathing to slow.

"Okay, Emma, you look over your order, and I'll go get those chairs for you from the display, then I can get a few more out of the warehouse."

"I appreciate it, Ken. Bring them up here and I can carry them out."

She looked over the list of items, checking them off one by one. She looked up to see him coming back toward her, two chairs in tow. "Ken, I'm adding another small canopy. It's liable to be hot during the reception, and the musicians would appreciate it, I'm sure."

"No problem. Mark it on that list, and I'll add it in the computer."

"I did." She nodded at him and then looked down at the chairs. "Well, I'd best be on my way. Thanks so much, and I'll call you on Monday about which chair to put on the bill."

"Sounds good. Sure you don't want me to carry those out?"

"I'll carry them for you." The man at the counter spoke unexpectedly.

"Oh. Well, all right, if you don't mind." She held her hand out. "Emmaline Quince, Quince Wedding Designs."

"Rafe Jernigan, detective with the South Carolina State Police." He paused as recognition dawned on his face. "Was your husband Daniel Quince?"

She raised her eyebrows and looked at him brightly. This didn't happen often, these days. "Yes, did you know him?"

"We served together."

"Afghanistan?" She spoke quietly. Daniel was a good husband, and a good father. He wasn't the same when he returned from there.

He nodded and looked down. "It was tough over there. Daniel was a good friend, kept me out of some pretty bad scrapes."

She smiled sadly. "I'm glad to hear it. It wasn't the same after he came back."

"Not for any of us. He was one of the good ones. Some of us weren't so blessed. I remembered his wife was a redhead, though. He kept your picture right here." He patted his shirt pocket and glanced at her, head still dipped a little. "Let's get this stuff loaded."

"Thank you, Detective Jernigan."

"Call me Rafe."

He carried them out and smiled when he noted the signage on the side of the van.

"Anything for a fellow Georgetown County citizen."

"You're from Georgetown?"

"Originally from Murrells Inlet, left there when I went into the service, then my parents moved here after my sister died."

"I'm sorry."

"Old news. Died after a car wreck when she was eighteen.

Daniel and I were football rivals in high school." He grinned. "I took him down more than a few times."

It had been a long time since she laughed with a man, and about her husband, no less. "He's not here to defend his honor. I wish I'd known him back then. We met in college."

"He always had this smile on his face, you know? And a lot of black hair." He shook his head and pointed to his scruffy red head. "I got stuck with this. No wonder he got all the pretty girls."

She opened the back of the van for him to set the chairs inside it. "I'd be the last person to criticize a redhead. Thank you so much for your help. Now I need to make a few more stops before heading home."

"You're welcome, Emmaline Quince. It was nice to meet you." He grinned at her, hands in his pockets.

"Thank you, Mr. Jernigan, so glad to meet you too."

"Rafe. I've carried your chairs."

She tilted her head a bit. "Rafe then."

RAFE WATCHED as the panel van left the parking lot heading toward Charleston proper. Daniel Quince's widow. He'd heard about Daniel's unexpected death while he was on leave after Annabelle passed but couldn't bring himself to go to the funeral. He was in a bad place then. It was bad enough he'd signed on for another tour after Daniel decided to go stateside and resign his commission, but combining the loss of his support system, the tragedy of Annabelle's death, and the anger that came with it was a recipe for disaster in his personal life.

He left the rental company that was also a repair shop for Stihl brand equipment and headed down the road to his parents' house. He flipped on the radio, and there it was, again. "Amazing Grace."

"Lord, if there's something You're trying to tell me, go ahead. I'd like to listen to a different song if it's okay with You."

He chuckled. Six years ago he had been at the end of his rope. His latest girlfriend had dumped him because if he wasn't working, he was drunk. He'd always heard about the downward spiral that you went through to hit bottom and hadn't believed it. Now he did. When he got suspended for hitting a suspect he was interrogating, they sent him to mandatory rehab. It was that or sit in a jail cell.

He was fortunate. No, he was blessed. He was able to get into a faith-based rehabilitation center across the state in Spartanburg. He met God there.

He hadn't thought about Georgetown in a while. He spent a lot of angry years trying to push his hometown area out of his mind, and it became habit. Until the day he met Sam Watson and realized the anger he'd held on to over Annabelle's death was misplaced.

"God, if you hadn't found me before then, I'd have killed him."

This was how he prayed. As he went. He wouldn't call himself much of a Christian, but he was a child of God, and that was what mattered. He learned the hard way. The fact that Jesus loved him so much He died on the cross for him was all that mattered.

God was good. He hadn't seen Sam in a while. While he was in Charleston, he thought he might head down there one day.

RANCE'S first thought the next morning was of Charly and the afternoon they spent on the beach. In the forefront of this thought was the feeling of her lips on his. He had kissed his fair share of princesses, but Charly was different. It felt different.

Next thoughts were less distracting and less enticing.

With his licensing exam completed and with excellence, Rance had more time to concentrate on his future and on whether or not to become a living donor for a man who didn't know he was his son. He was tired of dealing with this issue himself.

He was still following Clifton Watson's progress, and he was not doing well. His numbers had stabilized at one time but now were swinging out of kilter, creating a need for dialysis more often, so he was back in the hospital.

He strolled down the hallway toward his room and stopped right outside when he heard a familiar voice. It was his mother. He stepped inside the door to see her wipe tears from her eyes. "Mom?"

"Rance. I thought I might run into you here."

Clifton Watson was lying in his hospital bed, pale, as if in shock. "Rance. Dr. Butler. You're my . . ."

Rance flattened his lips in a firm line, trying to tamp down his anger while looking from his mother to the man who was his father. "Apparently, I'm your son."

"How long . . ."

"I've known for about three weeks. You?"

"About three minutes." Clifton looked up at his ex-wife. "Anna. How could you . . ."

"I was scared, Clifton. Your father . . ."

"You left your son. It affected him, you know. He needed you. I needed you."

Rance watched as the scene played out in front of him. The man wasn't lashing out, simply stating facts. The bare hurt in his eyes and the tears on his face denoted sadness and regret, not anger.

He pulled a chair over for his mother to sit in and pulled in another for himself. "Tell us why you did it. Why did you leave?" Looking over at Clifton's monitors, he was concerned. "Are you okay?"

Clifton closed his eyes for a moment. "Dazed and confused, but I'm fine. Anna, you could have come to me."

"At that point, I didn't know you. You were turning into your father, and he hated me. He was souring you on me and did everything he could to undermine me with both you and Sam."

"I was working hard, but we were starting a new line of business. It was for our future. I know I wasn't easy to live with . . ."

"Easy? You were never home. When you were, you complained all the time, yelled at Sam and me."

"I would have talked to Pop. You know that."

"No, you wouldn't. So I did. I talked to him. I don't know if it was the hormones talking or what. I told him how I felt, and I couldn't take it anymore. He told me I should leave. I was holding you back. I said, fine, I would take Sam with me, and he forbade it. He said if I didn't leave Sam, his only grandson, he would ruin me, have me committed. He would do whatever it took to protect his empire."

"He said that?"

"He didn't say empire, but he did say the other. I almost took him anyway, but I didn't have the courage."

"You know Pop died a few months ago." Clifton never took his eyes off of Mom. It was as if he were looking at a ghost.

"I saw it in the paper." She looked haggard.

"Did you know you were pregnant with Rance when you left?"

She met his eyes and shook her head. "No, I didn't. By the time I did, your father had wangled the divorce, and I had signed a waiver of parental rights. Did you know what you were signing?"

Clifton brushed a hand over his face. "Probably not. Pop offered to take care of the divorce so I wouldn't have to deal with it and Sam at the same time, and I let him. I was so stupid. What kind of a man does that?"

Rance's mother looked down at her hands. "What kind of a

woman lets it happen?" She looked up at Rance and at her ex-husband. "I ended up in the hospital when I moved to Charleston, with a nervous breakdown. That's when I found out I was expecting Rance."

"You could have come to me." Clifton's face, once pale, was red with frustration.

Rance glanced at Clifton's heart monitor before he took his mother's hand. "Why didn't you tell me all of this the other week?"

She put her other hand on his cheek. "My baby boy. I was so ashamed. Things have not been perfect for Ashton and me, but we've had a good life. When I learned Clifton was sick, I knew I had to tell you."

"How did you know?" Clifton looked at her curiously.

"I still have friends around here." She lifted the left corner of her mouth in a sad smile. "Clay Hobgood's wife, Diane, let me know. She's the only person I've kept in touch with in the area."

"Dr. Hobgood?" Rance's eyebrows went up.

"I've known Clay for a long time." Clifton lifted his lips in a half-smile. "I should be angry at him for sharing patient information, but I'm not. He's a good man."

"Believe it or not, I have kept up with Sam. I'm so sorry for the trouble he's been in. I feel as though it's my fault."

"I raised him the only way I knew how, like Pop raised me. Too hard. He wasn't ready to take responsibility for his actions in high school or college. I should have known he wasn't ready for police work."

CHAPTER NINETEEN

Charly laughed when Lydia finally emerged from her bedroom on Saturday morning, black and purple hair sticking up all over the place, and the eyeliner expertly applied the day before showed up in various places under her eyes.

Lydia gave her a warning look. "What?"

"You are so not a morning person." Charly poured her roomie a large cup of coffee and scooted it across the breakfast bar."

After a long swig of the sweetened liquid, Lydia spoke. "News flash."

"What's your schedule today?"

Lydia stretched and then leaned an elbow on the bar. "Nothing. I told Mom I needed a day off. I know Saturday's not ideal, and I usually can juggle about as much as can be thrown at me, but today I'm too pooped to party."

"You've been burning the candle at both ends, as my mama would say." Charly put her cup in the dishwasher and closed the door. "More margin."

"Yeah, and my mom says I can sleep when I'm dead. Go figure. Think your mom would adopt me?"

"In a heartbeat, but you know you'd miss your parents."

"I would, and I know I need to get out more. Non-work-related, that is. What about you?"

"I'm helping Emmaline with a wedding this afternoon, so I'll meet her at Atalaya around ten this morning to set up."

"Speaking of margins . . ."

"I know, but with Lucy out of commission, I thought I'd pitch in. For me, it's temporary." She stopped and looked at Lydia pointedly. "Speaking of which, I know a guy . . ."

Lydia glared at Charly. "You're kidding me. You, fixing me up on a blind date?"

"Turnabout's fair play. Not a blind date at all. He is a sighted individual."

"Ha ha, Ms. Special Ed Teacher." She took another drink and put down her cup. "Who is this person who can't get his own date?"

"I'm sure he could. His name is Jake, and I have class with him. He's my carpool ride."

"You mean Jake-giraffe-like-Jake? What is he, six foot four?"

Charly coughed. "Um, actually, he's six foot seven. What does that have to do with anything?"

Lydia sighed. "Probably nothing. Apparently working the barista shift at the hospital hasn't snagged me a young doctor, unlike some people." She gave her friend a dirty look. "But I'm not bitter."

"Of course you aren't." Charly gave her a cheesy grin. "Maybe we could double?"

"No movie dates. You can't get to know a person at a movie."

"Right."

"You realize he is a full foot and a half taller than me?" Her sigh could have taken down a wall. "Set it up. I'm not getting anywhere like this."

"You haven't looked in the mirror yet, have you?"

"Actually, yes I have, and I wanted to see your reaction. So there."

"You are incorrigible."

"I know, and that's why you love me." Cheesy grin returned.

WHEN RANCE OPENED his email the next morning, the first thing he noticed was a message from one of the recruiters who had his résumé. He hadn't put specific places on his list of desired locations, but he decided to limit it to the South if at all possible.

This one sounded interesting. Nashville, Tennessee. Nashville had a lot going for it. Lots of restaurants, music, night life. Anything you'd want was there, and it would be far enough away from his parents, all of them, to feel like he had a life of his own.

He hit the "reply" button and started typing an upbeat response, welcoming an opportunity to talk with them. Then he stopped. Charly. Charlotte Anne Livingston. What about her?

Was he in love with her? Too soon to tell. She had no hold on him. At this point, no one did. Before, he would have taken his mother's feelings into consideration when planning where to live and work, but these days? The anger still flared up when he thought about all the years she could have told him about his father and brother.

All those years wasted because she was afraid of a mean old man.

Occasionally a bit from the song, "Amazing Grace," came to him, and he shoved it aside. He wasn't ready to extend grace, and until he was, he didn't want to seek it for himself.

Charly believed in that grace. How could he live up to such a lofty ideal? That was just it. He couldn't.

Maybe it would be better to break it off before they got in too deep. When he kissed her the other night, it was unexpected. Oh, he had played out all kinds of scenarios in which he ended up kissing her. He hadn't expected it to be as sweet as it was.

But sweet didn't get you a plum position at Vanderbilt Hospital.

THE DAVE MATTHEWS concert at the North Charleston Coliseum lived up to the hype. A sold-out crowd of thirteen thousand people couldn't be wrong.

Rance said all the right things and laughed at all the right places, but Charly could tell something was bothering him, and she had a good idea of what it could be.

When she suggested a walk in Waterfront Park, Rance didn't question going into the historic district.

"I would offer you a piece of fried chicken for your thoughts, but I don't have any on me." She squeezed his hand as they faced the harbor.

He turned and smiled at her. He looked tired, as though he'd endured several sleepless nights. "It might cost you your company over a cup of coffee before we head home."

"I can guarantee I'd be willing to pay that price." She winked at him. "What's going on?"

He shook his head soberly, gazing out at the water. "Way too much. You worked a wedding today, didn't you? How'd it go? How's your class going? Prince Charming still giving you rides to school?"

"Way to deflect the conversation, Rance. The wedding went off without a hitch, class is going well, and yes, Jake Prince is still keeping me entertained all the way to Myrtle Beach and back." She gave him a sideways glance. "I'm thinking about fixing him up with Lydia."

He nodded thoughtfully. "You sure you don't want to keep him on the string, just in case?" He gave her a half-smile.

"What's wrong?" She was serious. He wasn't himself, and she didn't quite know how to deal with it.

He tugged her hand toward the lighted Pineapple Fountain in the heart of the park. It was warm out, but she felt a chill run through her at his silence.

"I'm going to Nashville next week."

"Okay, that sounds nice. Any particular reason or shouldn't I ask?"

He shrugged his shoulders. "I got an invitation from Vanderbilt Hospital to talk to them about a job."

"In Nashville."

"In Nashville." He turned, looking down at their hands clasped between them. "It may be a good opportunity for me."

"I'm sure." She swallowed, confused. "I mean, Vanderbilt."

He looked up at her, squinting in a pained expression. "It might also be a way to get away from my family."

"And me." Her gaze faltered. She did not want to cry. After all this was a summer romance. He was finishing up his education, she was in the middle of hers, and he had places to go. She was here. In South Carolina.

"That's the kicker."

"I get it." She was going to be a grown up about this. He looked at her closely. "I really do."

"Charly . . ." He shoved his hand through his hair and started pacing. "No, Charly, you don't. I'm not who you think I am. I'm not even who I think I am or was."

She had no hold on him. She was this close to giving her heart to him, but there was always a little seed of doubt. Probably a little God-pause. He wasn't a believer, and he wasn't sure about his life right now. For that matter, neither was she.

HE COULD TELL she didn't get it. The only sane thing in his life right now was Charly Livingston. He felt like himself when he was with her. Even when he was confused and angry, she had a way about her.

She needed a man with a solid foundation. At this point, he had no foundation. Her religion was important to her, to her family. His family? They lied, they cheated, and they stole. At least that's what he was learning, lately.

"You deserve better than me, Charly."

Her eyes widened until he thought they would pop out of their sockets. She put her hands on her hips and looked at him with intensity. "Rance Elliot Butler, you're crazy."

He took a deep breath. She was mad now. He could deal with anger better than stoic heartbreak.

"Charly."

"Rance." She was calming down.

"I've got things to work out. Maybe this week, while I'm gone, we both need to do some thinking." He took her hands again, pulling her closer this time into the circle of his arms. "I'm not saying I never want to see you again."

"Are you sure?" She started fiddling with his loosened tie.

He laughed. "I'm not sure about anything right now." He tugged. "Look at me." When she did, he shook his head and sighed. "You make me a little crazy, did you know that?"

"Crazy in a good way, or crazy in a bad way?" The smile she tried to hide began to break through.

"To tell you the truth, I'm not completely sure."

CHAPTER TWENTY

"That you?" Lydia's voice called out when she heard the door close.

"It's me." Charly's sigh could have started a tidal wave, and that's all it took to bring Lydia out of her room.

"What's wrong? Did he break up with you? Did you break up with him?" Her eyes got wider the longer she stared at her best friend.

"None of the above, but close. Does that make sense?" Tears threatened to fall, and she was afraid nothing she could do or think was going to stop them.

"Oh, honey, what happened?" Lydia turned a light on in the kitchen and started heating water in the tea kettle.

"I'm not sure."

"What do you mean?"

"I mean, I'm not sure. Rance has stuff going on with his family. I mean major stuff. He told me he's going to Nashville next week to talk to a hospital. He may be moving to Nashville, Lyd." Her wide eyes, filled with tears, met Lydia's in heartbreak.

"Okay, he's meeting with people in Nashville. Doesn't mean he'll get the job."

"Oh, they'll want him. Who wouldn't?"

"Listen to yourself. I know he's Prince William and Chris Pine all rolled into one for you, but there are lots of good doctors out there, and I'm sure they're talking to more than one person. Rance is great, but I wouldn't count him out yet."

"He told me I deserved better than him."

"Hmmm. He is struggling deeply with something, isn't he?"

Charly nodded. "He said we needed to take this week to do some thinking."

"What about praying?"

"I know I will be, but I'm not sure about him." Charly twisted her lips in a frustrated grimace. "That's another thing."

"God."

"I think he believes there is a God, but he's having a hard time with the concept of God caring about individuals, especially with what's going on right now."

"I won't ask what that is, because it's none of my business, but is there any way all this can point him to God? Because if that doesn't happen, I don't see a future for you two."

Lydia was power in a small package.

Charly laughed through her sniffles. "You sound like Lucy. Tell me how you really feel."

"Always. That's what best friends do, and Lucy is my role model, you know." Lydia winked at her.

"I know. Honestly, this is not something I ever expected to happen."

Lydia nodded sagely. "Because up to now you've never dated someone who isn't a Christian."

Her statement hit hard. All those times, as a teen, when she considered dating someone, this was the number one criteria. Was he a Christian? Now, she was letting her guard down, and she wondered if this was a type of punishment. Was she settling for less than God's best for her life?

Charly stared at Lydia. "Then I guess I'd better start praying, hadn't I?"

"And I'll pray too. And while we're at it, let's pray me up a guy, okay?"

"Gotcha."

"YOU'RE AWFULLY QUIET TODAY. I've told you three jokes and you have barely grinned." Jake was doing his best to entertain her this Monday morning, but she wasn't feeling it.

"Sorry."

"Rough weekend? Ra-ance in trouble?"

She gave him her best stink-eye. "Rance is in Nashville, meeting with a recruiter." There, she'd said it. She hadn't even told her mom, and now Lydia and Jake both knew.

"Whoa."

She looked over at him and noticed his raised eyebrows. "Yeah. That's what I thought."

"When did he tell you?"

"Saturday, after the concert." Ugh. She felt the pressure in her chest that always brought on the tears. Not now, not right before class. Stop it. Stop it right now.

"Are you okay?" He looked over at her, compassion in his eyes. "You can talk to me if you need to."

"Thanks, Jake. You're a good friend." A great friend. Why couldn't she fall for someone like him?

"Do you mind if I pray for you?"

"Mind? Why would I mind? Please, I need all the prayers I can get. I don't know what's going to happen. Maybe God doesn't want us together." She paused, her pulse beginning to ramp up. "Or maybe I shouldn't care so much what He thinks. If He loves me, the way He says he does in the Bible, then doesn't He want me to be happy?"

She was beginning to get angry. Defensive, even.

"Hang on."

"I mean, why would He let me fall for a guy like Rance if He didn't want us to be together?"

"Uh, free will? Just because something is out there doesn't mean we have to go for it."

"Yeah, free will." She huffed. "It would be easier if God would tell us what to do. Step-by-step instructions."

"He did. It's called the Bible. Mind if I pray right now, while we're driving?"

"As long as you keep your eyes on the road." She felt her face begin to heat in embarrassment.

"Noted. I make it a habit to not close my eyes and bow my head in prayer while driving." He grinned at her and winked.

"Thank you." She pursed her lips. "Sorry to be a whiner."

"God, you know Charly has a problem. It's not only a boyfriend problem, but a problem knowing what Your will is for her life. She loves You, Lord, but she's a little irritated with You for some reason, and I pray You will reveal the reason to her and soften Rance's heart toward You. Send someone to Rance to be a witness to him even now, while he's in Nashville. And help Charly not to be mad at me so we can have fun again. While You're at it, send me a girl who cares as much about You as I do. In Jesus' name, Amen."

"Amen." Charly reached over to touch his fingers on the steering wheel. "Thanks, Jake. I needed that."

"I did too. I figure if you're going to say you'll pray for someone, may as well do it on the spot."

Charly blew her nose and gave him a half-smile. "By the way, I have this friend, Lydia."

He looked at her, and she saw some fear in his expression. "I'm happy for you? Let me guess. She's six feet tall and has a beautiful complexion."

Mopping up her tears, Charly finally felt a laugh coming out of her mouth. "Not even close."

AFTER GETTING SETTLED into his room at the Sheraton Grand in downtown Nashville, Rance waited in the lobby for Phil Rickman, the recruiter for Vanderbilt Hospital. They were going out to dinner where Phil would prep him for the interview tomorrow. About ten minutes early for their appointment, he looked around the lobby. Charleston had it in spades when it came to nice hotels, but this one was over the top. His room had a view of the entire downtown area, and any amenity he could think of was at his disposal.

Dressed in jeans and a sports jacket, he crossed his ankle over his knee and steepled his hands as he looked around, thinking. His first thought was how comfortable this leather club chair was and wondered if he could get one like this.

He should be thinking about his prospects, about what it would be like to live in this city. It wasn't as old as Charleston, but the vibrancy was enticing. Charly would like it here, he was sure.

And there he was. Charly. He'd said they both needed to think about things this week, so he was thinking. Mostly about how he had left it last Saturday. He had thought about showing up at church the next morning to see what it was like, but he didn't want to give her hope where there might not be any. And could he see himself in this kind of a life?

Instead, he had spent Sunday morning doing laundry and packing for the trip. He hoped Charly was having better luck avoiding the elephant in the room than he was.

God. What was He all about anyway? Clifton, his father, had said He was in control. If He was in control, why had He let his mother make decisions that affected so many people? Hurt so many people?

He shook his head. This particular rabbit trail led to frustration, and he didn't have time for it. Phil was walking across the lobby toward him, so he stood with a smile.

"Phil, good to see you." Rance shook the older man's hand. He had seen his picture online but wasn't expecting the real-life image of a cowboy standing in front of him.

The tall, weathered man in cowboy boots stuck his hand out and shook heartily. "Good to put a face with a name, Rance. Good flight?"

"Great. A two-hour flight beats a fourteen-hour drive any day."

Phil laughed. "I hear ya. Hungry? I'm hankerin' for some Tennessee barbecue, how about you?"

"Sounds great. I understand you guys do it right up here."

"You understand correctly, young man. You been to Nashville much?"

"No, somehow I've missed it except for the airport."

"We're a hub for the South, seems like. Martin's is down the street about a half-block. Can't beat it. Up for a walk?"

"Sounds good."

They made their way down the street. Being a Monday, the crowd was lighter than he was sure it had been on the weekend. They passed honky-tonks, shops, venues, and hotels and met every kind of person you can imagine in a busy downtown during summer tourist season.

"I called ahead, and they told me no problem getting a table. If they're full in the front, they have outdoor seating in the back."

They arrived at the restaurant and saw a few people outside waiting to get in. "I'll check on the reservation and see what's what." Phil went in, and Rance stayed out on the sidewalk, looking around, enjoying the warm breeze and the tantalizing smell of hickory-smoked barbecue.

"Come on in. They've got a place for us."

The hostess, clad in jeans and a company t-shirt, showed them to their table and took their drink order. When Phil ordered a Coke, Rance echoed the order, not sure how ordering a beer would look at this juncture.

"What do you think of Nashville, son?" Phil was a gregarious man, met people as easy as a knife through butter.

"Nice town, what I've seen of it."

"If you want to be in medicine, music, or church work, Nashville's the place to be." Phil put his menu down and looked up when the waitress approached.

"Hi, I'm Randi. What can I get you gentlemen?" She had a pad and pen ready and spouted the special so fast Rance almost had to ask for a repeat.

Instead, he gave her his brightest smile and said, "What do you recommend?"

The flush on the waitress's face told him he still had it. Not bad.

"If you've never been to Martin's, I'd either recommend the pulled pork sandwich with slaw or the ribs with wet sauce."

Phil nodded assent. "Can't go wrong either way. I'll have the ribs. Full rack, young lady."

"Good deal. Baked potato or fries?"

"Baked potato and slaw."

"Got it. And for you?"

"I'll go with the pulled pork and homemade potato chips. No slaw on my sandwich. Could I get it on the side?"

"Not from around here, huh?" She laughed. "That's all right. You'll convert eventually. Everybody does." Randi took their menus. "I'll get this put right in. Need any more to drink?"

"No, thank you. Maybe later."

"Alrighty then."

"Nice girl."

Phil snorted. "Gunnin' for a nice tip, but Randi's all right. She's worked here since high school. Got a kid to raise, so I usually give her a pretty good tip."

"TELL ME ABOUT DR. RANCE BUTLER."

Phil was getting down to brass tacks. They had chatted through the meal, and when they were both done, he pushed his plate to the side and leaned forward, waiting for Rance's answer.

"I grew up in Charleston, only child, did well in school, and finished my third year of residency in Georgetown."

"Stayed pretty close to home. How was that? I only ask because most of the time when someone does their internship in their own backyard, it means they want to stay close to home, and yet, here you are in Nashville, about as far as you can go and still be in the South. Not that I blame you for limiting yourself to the South." A smile tugged at Phil's mouth, then disappeared.

"Maybe it's time I spread my wings a little more."

"Tell me about your family."

"Well, as I said—"

"Tell me what's not on the résumé."

Rance paused, looking the man in the eye. He wasn't comfortable answering truthfully, but then he wasn't comfortable with the truth at this point.

"My parents still live in Charleston. I haven't lived there since I left high school except during breaks. I've been on my own since medical school at Greenville."

He shook his head. "Good enough. Remember, in your interview, they can't legally ask you personal questions about your family. Sometimes they'll try to weasel info out of you that's not their business to begin with. Got it?" He winked.

Rance gave him a half smile and a sigh of relief. "Got it."

"Got a girl back home?"

"I . . . don't think you can ask me about that." Rance looked at him, unsure.

Phil laughed out loud. "Aw, interview's over. I'm askin' out of curiosity now."

"Then I'll have to answer like this. Maybe."

Phil stopped laughing and nodded, never taking his eyes off him. "Sounds like a transition time for you in more ways than one."

Rance snorted. "You have no idea."

"AND WHY IS IT, once again, that I would want to go out with Jake the giraffe?"

An afternoon on the beach beckoned, and so did girl time. The large beach towel laid out on the sand just down from their little pink beach house was the perfect place to set up a date between two of her favorite people, and Charly was determined to get someone's romantic life on track if hers wasn't.

"Lyd, he's great. He's quirky, like you, and if you keep saying it, you're going to mess up and call him that to his face."

Lydia twisted her lips and dug her fingers into the sand. Charly knew she was trying to avoid the subject.

"I'm sure he's been called worse."

"Probably, but it's not nice."

"And one thing I am, mostly, is nice."

"I'd say mostly you're quirky, but we'll go with that." Charly laughed as Lydia flicked sand onto her freshly oiled legs. "Hey!"

"Double with you and Rance?"

"Maybe." Charly paused and started doodling in the sand. "I'll have to talk to him when he gets back."

"He doesn't have a cell phone?" Lydia's raised eyebrow made her wrinkle her nose.

"Yes, but I don't want to bother him."

Lydia's lips flattened in a line. "He hasn't called since he's been gone, has he?"

"Nor texted." She looked up at Lydia. "He said we needed a week, and I guess he's sticking to it."

"Hmm. And you have to be as tough as he is, right?"

"Well? What would you do?"

"The same thing." She gestured with both hands lifted to the sky. "Ugh. Men, right?"

"Can't live with 'em . . ."

"Aunt Charly! Lyddie!" A flurry of activity ran to them in the form of one Hayes Livingston, his mother trudging behind with all the trappings of a mom and preschooler on the beach.

"Whoa there, bud! You're getting sand all over us!" Charly laughed as she hugged her nephew and spat sand out at the same time. After the hug, he ran with his bucket and pail straight to the edge of the water, where the sand was damp, and started digging.

"Sorry, ladies, with the twins, we haven't had much beach time this summer, and when Tom suggested he take care of the twins and me bring the tiny tornado to the beach, I jumped on it. Next summer will be totally different with toddlers, so I'd better enjoy it while I can."

"Never apologize for beach time. We all need it, right, Lyd?" Charly grinned at her sister-in-law. "I can't believe you fit into your old swimsuit."

"I can't either, except running after Hayes and caring for twins is very slimming." She laughed and looked down at the visible stretch marks on her side. "It's not perfect, but I'm glad I could get into it." She rubbed the blemishes and grimaced. "I need to look for a one-piece."

"Lucy, we were discussing men and how they are frustrating." Lydia looked pointedly at Charly, who rolled her eyes behind her sunglasses and sighed.

"Oh, you mean the old 'Can't live with 'em, can't live without 'em?' Been there, done that."

"See, told you she was the one to talk to." Lydia poked Charly in the side.

"What's going on in your version of 'The Doctors' or 'The Young and the Restless' these days?" Lucy giggled at her own joke and wiggled her eyebrows as she made her nest on the beach towel next to theirs. She lay flat on her stomach with a happy sigh, her head on a small beach pillow. "Oh my goodness, the sun and breeze feel good."

"Rance is in Nashville."

"Okay, Nashville is nice. Visit? Vacation?"

"Job interview."

Lucy lifted herself up on her elbows and grimaced. "Ouch."

"Yeah."

"So . . . did he tell you he was going?"

Charly nodded. "Last Saturday, after our date. He said we needed to think about things. Which is his way of saying he needs to think about things. Maybe he's right."

Lucy was quiet, pondering as she turned to look at Charly. "Maybe he is. Maybe he wants to see how serious this thing is between you."

Charly lifted her hands in frustration. "We just started dating. How serious could it be?"

"Humph. Remember me telling you about me and Tom? I thought I had found my one and only, only to have him ignore me for nearly a year."

"He was going through stuff, though."

Lydia spoke up. "You said Rance was having family issues. Might those be part of his problem?"

"Maybe." Charly sat up and cradled her knees, resting her chin on them as she watched Hayes fill the bucket then empty it in a pile. She grinned. "He also said I made him a little crazy."

"All right then, we have progress." Lucy put on her

sunglasses and leaned back on her elbows. "When they admit that, you almost have them in the bag."

"Tell me I don't have to wait a year until he comes around?"

"Hard to say. Now me, I didn't stand around pining after Tom. First, I was hurt, then I got mad, then I started dating again."

"Really?"

"Football coach."

"Wow."

Lucy looked over at her, deadpan. "He liked steak. Rare. Lots of it."

Charly and Lydia laughed. "A real manly-man, huh?"

"I guess. When I found out Tom was definitely manly and was also good at cleaning and organizing, I knew I had hit the jackpot. With Ben, I would have been chained to the stove for the rest of my life."

Charly nodded. "Tom does make good biscuits."

"Oh my, yes. Better than me, and I know his secret."

"Lard." Lucy and Charly both said the word in tandem, and all three girls laughed.

Lucy looked out at her son and the waves and smiled. "I don't know what I was thinking to almost let him get away. I guess God had it all along. It certainly wasn't anything I did."

Charly picked at the edge of the beach towel. "This is part of the problem."

"What is?"

"God. Rance isn't, well, I don't think he's a Christian." She paused. "I think he believes, to a certain extent . . ."

"He either believes or he doesn't. It's not something you can work your way up to doing."

"I know. It's the first time I've ever let myself be interested in a non-believer."

"Been there too. I dated a guy in college who didn't believe in God or any higher power. I thought I was in love with him.

We had so much in common outside of faith. He didn't believe in anything, but he said he respected my beliefs. It took me a while to realize that while he might respect me, how could he respect God if he didn't believe in Him?"

"What happened?"

"I told him about Jesus, and how important He is to me." She shrugged her shoulders. "We dated a while longer, but it wasn't the same. I think he was actually jealous of Jesus."

"Did he ever come to Christ?" Charly was amazed at this revelation. She was so glad to have Lucy, who still had so much about her she didn't know, for a sister.

"He did later. I saw him not long before I moved down here, at a meeting at the university. He was involved in a program working with troubled teens, making a presentation to teachers. He came up to me during the break and hugged me, told me when he met the girl who became his wife, she led him to the Lord, but I had planted the seed."

"That's great." For that guy. But what about Rance? Would she plant the seed only to have someone else reap the harvest?

Lucy leaned over and put her hand on Charly's. "I know, not very encouraging, but you never know how the Lord is going to work. He could be with someone right this minute who knows Jesus."

Charly nodded. "That's what Jake and I prayed yesterday."

"Okay, you didn't say Jake the giraffe was a praying guy." Lydia sat up straight, her entire body on alert, bright smile on her face. "Now, tell me more about Mr. Prince, and feel free to share with him my contact information."

CHAPTER TWENTY-ONE

It had been a whirlwind, and this was the first chance Rance had to think about anything except putting his best foot forward. The longer he stayed in Nashville, the more he enjoyed it. He could imagine living here. In the morning he toured the hospital, and after lunch he had free time to explore. He rented a car and drove around different areas of the hilly city and discovered hidden gems along the way.

The downtown night-life was great, and there were no limits to the recreational activities available. Close to the Smoky Mountains, he would have plenty of opportunities for extreme sports, as well as biking, climbing, and more.

Walking around downtown after a solitary dinner, his mind finally beginning to settle down, Charly came to the forefront. Maybe he would call her. What was she doing tonight? Oh, it was Wednesday. She was at church probably.

This was why he was spending the evening alone instead of with Phil, prepping for tomorrow's interview with the board. He had offered to come, and miss church, but Rance told him he thought it would be fine. He was enjoying a little down time.

People who went to church weren't always the people you expected. A high-profile professional headhunter? Why not?

In this country music town, gospel music was heard right along with wife stealin', heartbreak, and "friends in low places" to the point it all ran together. Until one particular song came up that all the country music stars and wannabes seemed to think they had to sing. Didn't matter if it was in church, in a honky-tonk, or on the street. It was the song that caught him. Every time.

Amazing grace, how sweet the sound,
That saved a wretch like me.
I once was lost, but now am found,
'Twas blind, but now I see.

Why did this mess with his head? He was no wretch. He didn't need "saving," but why now? Was it because of his mom? His parentage?

He loved his mom and his dad, but he was angry. So angry. As long as he stayed away from it, away from thinking about it, life went on, and he was fine.

Somehow Charly was lumped in with all of this. When he asked her out, he had thought of her as a pleasant escape from all of the turmoil, but she wasn't. She made him think, and thinking was the last thing he wanted to do.

The bar he was walking by had music loud enough to not only drown out the song he had heard earlier, but also his thoughts. That's what he was going for, right? Something to take the edge off. Something to drown out those thoughts that didn't serve any useful purpose except to bring him down.

He went in and made himself comfortable.

HE KNEW BETTER. His head pounded. His attempt to stop the train of thought leading to Charly and his family issues simply enhanced them the longer he poured the amber liquid down his throat.

He sat at the bar, flirted with the female bartender, and was rewarded with a few free drinks "because he was cute." Whatever it took.

On his winding way back to the hotel, he felt his phone vibrate. It was Phil calling.

"Phil. How are you, man?"

"Rance, what are you up to?"

"Just a little downtime, heading back to the hotel."

There was a pause. "You been drinking?"

"A little. Not much."

"I'll meet you at the hotel."

"No need. I'll head straight to bed, and you won't have to worry about me anymore."

"No, I'll be there in ten minutes. Drink some coffee."

"Probably good. Kinda got a headache."

"Yeah, I'm trying to keep you from having a worse headache in the morning."

"Thanks, Phil. See ya in a few."

Phil ended the call, and Rance looked through his texts to make sure he hadn't missed any. When he got to Charly's name, he paused, willing the blurriness to leave his sight.

Charly. "I miss you, Charlotte Anne Livingston. You probably wouldn't like me right now."

"Rance?"

Great. He'd opened the call list instead of the text list, and accidentally called her. He cleared his throat and shook his head to clear it. It didn't work. His head pounded much harder, but the buzz made him not care as much.

"Charly? I didn't mean to call."

"Oh." There was silence on the other end.

"How are you?"

"I'm . . . okay, are you?" She sounded worried.

"I'm fine. Heading in for the night, interview tomorrow. I'll be okay."

"Rance, have you been drinking?" Her voice was so quiet he strained to hear.

"Maybe a little, but not too much. I'm fine."

Silence.

"Charly."

"I'm here, Rance."

"I'm sorry, Charly." He said it and then started laughing. "Get it?"

"I get it." He heard a loud sigh. Was she crying?

"Gotta go. Phil's coming over to get me ready for tomorrow."

"Take care of yourself, Rance. I miss you."

For some reason, those words helped to clear his head, and the enormity of what he had done crashed down on him. "Charly?"

"Yes?"

"I'm sorry. I said you deserved better than me."

WHEN CHARLY HEARD the phone beep, ending the call, she simply sat there, staring at it, willing the tears to stop falling. She couldn't.

She was glad Lydia was still working at the shop. She didn't want to see anyone right now.

"Why, God? Why did You let me meet him? I never wanted to date someone who wasn't Your child, but I thought maybe, just maybe, You could use me to draw him to You."

The hurt and fear she felt when she realized Rance had called her by mistake because he was drunk had morphed into anger. Anger at God and anger at herself.

"I've worked hard for You. I've tried to do everything You wanted me to do, and when I try to claim Your promises? Where are You?"

I'm right here, where I've always been.

She had friends who had gone through hurts like this but never her. She stayed above it all. She told herself she was somehow closer to God because she was Charlotte Anne Livingston. Everybody expected her to be a good girl, so of course, she was.

Didn't she deserve some kind of reward? A special dispensation for having gone through the loss of her father, her mom's blindness, and now, this?

She didn't ask for much. Peace, quiet, a family of her own and maybe a little excitement in her life. The good kind, not this kind.

Then she thought about Rance. What was he going through right now? He felt betrayed on so many levels. A family that wasn't his own. A brother in prison for stealing and drugs. What if Rance had an addictive personality too? What if he not only drank but did drugs, and she hadn't found out yet?

She wanted to help, but this? This was too much. No. She couldn't deal with this. It was over between them, and when he came back, if he came back, she would tell him.

WHEN PHIL KNOCKED, Rance was waiting. He opened the door, his face revealing the penitence and sorrow he felt.

"Hi, Phil. Thanks for coming."

"What happened?" Phil's face was red. He was angry and a little out of breath.

"I thought I could handle it." Rance sat on the end of his bed, his hands in his hair as he leaned his elbows on his knees. "I'm not like this."

"I didn't think so. None of the background checks indicated any kind of alcohol or substance abuse."

"Don't worry, it won't happen again. Having fun is one thing but being out of control is another."

"What do you mean?"

He looked at the older man soberly. "I called Charly."

"Girlfriend?"

Rance nodded. "At least she was."

"I see." Phil handed him a large cup of coffee from the coffee shop down the street. "Drink it."

"I think I've pretty well sobered up, but I'll drink it anyway." He took off the lid and blew on the hot liquid, then took a swig, grimacing at the heat. "I messed up, Phil."

"Hopefully not so much you can't fix it. The girlfriend is not our problem right now. We need to get to the bottom of why you went on a bender."

"I wouldn't call it a bender exactly."

"What would you call it?"

Rance paused. His experience with alcohol had been limited. "I guess, for me, it was a bender."

"Thanks for admitting it."

"It's not as if I've never had anything to drink, but I never had much. My mom was scared to death of alcohol, and my dad never drank because he saw how it affected people in his job as a parole officer."

"What about college?"

"In high school and college I drank enough to get by and not get ribbed, and in med school I was too busy and tired to fool with it, so it wasn't an issue."

"Too much time on your hands today?"

"Too much time to think, more likely."

Phil pulled a chair over and sat across from him. He took a deep breath and looked at him closely. "I guess I'm not your typical head-hunter. When I take on a kid such as yourself for a job, I want you to be someone I can vouch for. Someone the company hiring can count on. I've had a few young folks who admitted to a little issue here and there, and I'm not here to judge. I think you can do better."

"Why?" Rance furrowed his brows and looked at the older man.

"Why?" Phil looked at him plainly. "Because I see something in you."

"Right." He still frowned and shook his head in confusion.

"I see potential. Whether or not you get this job, I feel led to help you find something. Not sure what it is yet, but there's something missing in your life."

Rance looked down. Phil was right. There was something missing. He'd always known it. His family? His brother? Purpose? One special girl for all time? What was it?

"I think you're searching for something and not finding it."

Rance jerked his head up. "Why do you say that?"

"Because sometimes I look at you, and there's a lost boy looking back. You've got it all, but something's missing, and I think it's right there." Phil pointed to the area of his heart. "Until you figure that out, there will always be a piece of you that is lost."

RANCE GRABBED his suitcase and closed the door quietly behind him. His flight was in two hours. Plenty of time to get checked in and wait. Waiting, thinking. This seemed to be his life these days.

The Thursday morning interview with the board of directors of the hospital went as well as expected, considering Rance had more on his mind than simply getting a job. Like getting a job at a major hospital was simple.

He loved medicine. He had known medicine was his pick from the time he could think about a career. Everything about it fascinated him. The idea of helping people came first, and then the idea of status didn't hurt.

Phil was in the lobby waiting for him.

"Ready to roll?"

"As ready as I'll ever be."

This was his shot. Nashville was in his top five cities he would consider for his first practice. He hoped he hadn't messed it up completely.

His phone buzzed with a voice mail in his pocket. He'd missed Dr. Hobgood's call.

"Let me get this, Phil, it may be important."

"Sure. I'll be in the car out front."

"Be right there."

Rance, Clay Hobgood here. Wanted to let you know that Clifton Watson has taken a turn for the worse. Give me a call when you get back to town.

He stared at the phone then at the car waiting outside the revolving doors. It would have to wait. He needed more time.

He loaded his suitcase in the back seat and got in beside Phil.

"Everything okay?"

"Not really. There's a situation I have to make a decision about, and faster than I wanted to."

"Not the girlfriend, I take it?"

Rance gave him a half-smile. "No, I may have made that decision the other night. The ball's in her court, now."

He nodded. "Rance, are you a praying man?"

Where did that come from? Had he given any indication he would be open to anything relating to prayer or to God, even?

"No, sir, I'm not."

"That's a shame. When I can't tell which way is up, I go to

God. I'm not sure where I'd be without Him. Probably divorced, sick, and passed out somewhere."

Rance looked straight ahead. "I don't think I'm so far gone, Phil."

Phil didn't say anything for a few minutes. He was maneuvering downtown traffic, getting to the on-ramp to I-40 toward the airport. "When I was your age, I wasn't either, but a few missteps threw me for a loop, and I crashed. Believe me, when you've never failed at anything, and it all comes down around you, it's a big fall."

"Sorry you had to go through that." Was this guy a mindreader? Was he on an episode of *Highway to Heaven*?

"Ha! I'm not."

Rance looked at the side of Phil's face as he drove, not understanding the smile residing there after what he had told him.

"If I hadn't hit bottom, I wouldn't be here."

"What if you'd kept going down?"

"Wasn't anywhere further down to go. I was ready to make a deal with the devil, so to speak, but God wouldn't let me."

"How's that?"

"Every time I tried to go a certain direction, I was blocked. I'd try to go 'round, still blocked. Finally, I gave up. I went in a bar to hear a new 'up and coming' band. I just wanted to get drunk or, more likely, stay drunk. Funny thing was, it wasn't a bar anymore. It was a mission. All they had was coffee and sweet iced tea. By the time I left, I was sober as a judge and wanted to sign this group with a record label. The group ended the set with—"

"Let me guess. 'Amazing Grace?'"

They were at a stop light, and Phil looked over at Rance and laughed.

CHAPTER TWENTY-TWO

"I've had it. I don't have to deal with this, and I'm not going to." Charly had ended her rant to Lydia, finally spilling everything.

"He actually drunk-dialed you? Wow. I've had that happen before."

"Really? When? Where was I?" Charly looked at Lydia as if she'd grown two heads.

She shrugged. "It was while we were at CCU. A guy in my art classes was in my study group for a general education class, and I had no idea he had a crush on me. He had my number for study group, and one night he tied one on with a few buddies and had to prove to them he had a girlfriend."

"You never told me."

"Because it didn't matter. I wasn't his girlfriend and he knew it, but I helped him save face with his friends."

"That's terrible. What did you say to him when you saw him?"

Lydia laughed. "Oh, I told him he'd better not ever do it again, and furthermore he'd better not ever get in such a shape again because I would be watching him, and Jesus was too. He's now married, has two kids, and is attending seminary in Winston-Salem."

It felt good to laugh. She hadn't spoken to anyone about the phone call, and she needed to share it with someone.

"He told me he was sorry, and I deserved better than him." Those stupid tears were back. "Oh, Lydia, what am I going to do?"

Lydia shrugged. "Pray. It's all you can do right now."

"I have been, but it seems as if I should be able to do something, you know?"

"Quit your pouting. Pray, and then listen. Remember the verse, 'be still and know that I am God?' The main part is the 'be still' part. Let Him work on it, and you leave it to Him."

ANOTHER TRIP to Mount Pleasant wasn't on Emma's list for the week, but wedding plan changes wait for no one. She was adding to her list and wanted to look at some new tablecloths she'd seen on their website.

She sighed as she drove into the parking lot right behind a pickup truck and trailer.

Rafe Jernigan. What were the odds of them meeting at the same place twice, in neither of their places of residence?

He was smiling when she got out of the van.

"Hello again, Emmaline."

"Rafe, fancy meeting you here." She laughed and felt herself blush.

"Came to pick up my dad's mower."

"Tablecloths for me, and I'm bringing an extra chair back."

"Let me get it for you."

"Thanks. Your vacation almost over?"

"Yeah, I'll be heading back to Columbia in a few days. It's

been nice to spend the time with the folks, though. They're not getting any younger."

"Neither are we." She chuckled.

"Hey, now, speak for yourself." He lifted an eyebrow. "We're not a day over twenty-nine, are we?" He winked.

"I wish. Just turned the big four-O." She shook her head. "Time gets away."

He carried the chair to the door, stopping before entering the establishment. "A mere child." He paused and smiled at her. "I know we haven't known one another long . . ."

"Seems like a long time." She smiled gently, pushing a stray auburn curl behind her ear. He was going to ask her out. She could feel it.

He raised an eyebrow. He was quite good-looking in a mature, red-head sort of way. Nothing like Daniel. His green eyes sparkled with energy. Where had this energy taken him, in the past?

"It does, doesn't it?"

She nodded, mesmerized by his gaze, until he looked away, breaking eye contact.

"Emmaline, would you consider having dinner with me? This weekend?"

The wedding at Atalaya was this weekend, Pilot Oaks the next. Her face fell.

"I'll be working."

"Working? Oh, you have a wedding."

She nodded and shrugged. "It's my bread and butter."

He gazed into her face. "Would you like a wedding date?"

"Really?" Her face must have betrayed her surprise, because he laughed.

"Yes, really. I'd like to get to know you, Emmaline."

Her lips curved up in a grin. "I think I'd like to get to know you, too, Rafe."

WHEN RANCE LANDED IN CHARLESTON, he considered a couple of options. Go straight back to Georgetown and try to fix things with Charly or go by his mom's house and try to learn more about his beginnings.

He decided to do neither. At least not now. When the choice came to go north to Georgetown or Charleston, or go south to Ridgeland, where Sam Watson was being held, he knew what the choice had to be. He went south.

As he drove through the checkpoints of the correctional institute, he noted the high fences with barbed wire on the top and the men with rifles in the turrets surrounding the property. His brother was here, and beyond the fact that he had never thought he had a brother, the idea he was in prison hurt.

He waited in the visitation room once again, watching as prisoners were escorted in and out. He looked at the visitors. There were wives, girlfriends, and parents. Some were children. Some, like him, might be siblings.

When Sam came out, he was carrying something, and when he saw Rance sitting there, he was surprised. "Hey! I thought it was Tom visiting me today."

"Tom?"

"Tom Livingston. He comes every other week pretty much, and we do a Bible study together."

"I've met Tom. He's a great guy."

"I'll admit I wasn't his biggest fan when he helped put me in here, but God has a way of changing our outlook doesn't He?"

Rance stared at his brother. He didn't know him. All he knew was what he had found online, about his arrest and subsequent conviction, and now his incarceration.

"Can you tell me about our father? About you? I've missed out on an entire part of my life, and I'm trying to fill in the blanks."

Sam looked at him sadly and then spoke. "First, tell me about Mom."

He should have led with that. Here he was feeling gypped for not knowing about his family, and Sam had been deserted by his mother, the one person you should be able to count on.

"I'm sorry. I've been pretty selfish, haven't I?"

"No, I understand." Sam held his hand up to stop Rance when he would have spoken. "I do. You've had a freight train run over you with information you never knew existed."

"Well, you've had a semi-trailer-truck, then." Rance growled out the words and then grinned.

Sam smirked. Was that a mist of tears? "You sounded like Dad just then."

"Nice."

"What's she like?"

"Mom? You know I've never had to describe her before. She's always been there for me, as far as I knew. She worries a lot, but I tried her patience, I'm sure. I 'live life to the fullest,' she likes to say, which means I was up for any daredevil stunt anybody suggested."

"Sounds like we would have had fun together."

"I imagine we would have." Rance nodded sadly. "I guess that's what makes me angry. We never had any say in all this."

"God's got a plan. He's in control."

"Clifton—er, our dad said the same thing."

"It's a fact."

"How do you know?" Rance still wasn't convinced. Those people at Calvary Church. They didn't seem particularly special. They welcomed him, were nice to him. Wasn't being nice part and parcel of being a good person?

"Because of where I was and where I am now."

"Explain. I mean, look around. Before, you were free. Now, you're in jail."

Sam laughed out loud. "Man, I was so not free when I got

here. I was mad at the world. I was mad at Dad, I had been mad at Mom so long it became part of who I was. I tried to frame Tom Livingston for stealing money so I could buy drugs. How low do you have to be to do such a thing? I was crazy when I got here."

"What about Jared Benton? What did he have to do with any of this?" It still wasn't making sense to him.

"Wow." Sam raked his hands over his face. "That's a tough one. I started drinking and doing drugs in high school. I started dating this girl I knew had a college boyfriend, but she was lonely, and pretty hot, so I didn't think about it as being wrong. One thing led to another, and one night I came in and she told me she was pregnant. She was afraid to tell her parents. I felt trapped, angry, and I hit her." He looked up at his brother. "I'm not proud of it. I got mad at Jared because he wasn't here. I didn't even know him, and I hated him. If he'd been here, it wouldn't have happened. Or maybe it would have. I don't know." He shrugged, shaking his head.

"What happened?"

Sam let out a deep breath. "Jared took care of her. He was driving her to Charleston to stay with friends when he had a wreck on a rain-slick road. She didn't make it, and he ended up with a concussion. Her parents blamed Jared for the wreck and for her pregnancy, which wasn't on him. He took the blame for over ten years, not knowing who was responsible. I knew, but I never said anything, never took responsibility for my own actions."

"Why did you go into law enforcement?'

"I didn't start out to be a cop. I majored in computer science in college and picked up a minor in law enforcement. When I graduated, I didn't want to work for my dad and grandfather, and there was a job opening with the SCSP. I got it then found out I was good at it. I was still doing drugs, thought I had it under control, and I was successful in my job, until I wasn't."

"What happened?"

"It's more what didn't happen. I left home, got out on my own, and decided I could become a different person. I did to some extent. It all came creeping back when I came back to Georgetown."

RANCE WAS STUNNED at his brother's story. He never expected to visit a man in prison and come out feeling as if he had been the one to be helped.

As he walked out into the sunshine, he stopped to look up. "Are You there, God?" He was a little startled when he heard a voice answer.

"He is."

The laugh he heard afterward drew Rance's eyes to the man coming up to him on the sidewalk.

"Hey, Dr. Butler, how's my favorite resident and baby-deliverer?" Tom held out his hand, and Rance shook it.

"Great. Call me Rance."

"All right, Rance it is. You can call me Sheriff." When Rance glanced up at him with uncertainty, Tom laughed. "Kidding. Call me Tom. I understand you've been seeing my sister?"

"I have. She's a special lady."

"She is. What brings you out here?"

Rance paused. It was getting too complicated for him to deal with on his own. According to his brother, Tom was a guy you could trust. Being Charly's brother made him hesitate, but maybe it was one of those "God-things" Sam talked about.

"I'm visiting my brother."

Tom raised his eyebrows in surprise. "Brother? I thought you were an only child?"

Rance grinned. "Charly told me you did a background check."

Tom reddened slightly. "Sorry, but—"

Rance held up his hand. "I get it. She's your baby sister. I would have done the same thing." Rance looked over, noticing a bench near the entrance, most likely for released prisoners to catch their ride. "Got a few minutes?"

Tom looked at his watch and then down at Rance. "I've got all the time you need."

Rance leaned on his knees as he sat on the bench, looking out over the parking lot. "I found out a few weeks ago I'm not who I always thought I was."

"Come again?"

"Don't worry, nothing illegal. The man I thought was my father is, in fact, my adoptive father, and my mother recently told me about my real father and the brother I never knew. Sam Watson." He looked at Tom, waiting for a flicker of something.

"Sam Watson is your brother? Half-brother?" Tom's face was impassive. He was good at interrogation, kept his cards close to the vest when he wasn't in a delivery room with his wife delivering twins.

"Brother. Mom was pregnant with me when she left, and my real father never knew until recently."

"Tough situation."

"I never had anything to do with God before. My parents never talked about it. My grandparents, well, adopted grandparents, took me to their church occasionally, but it never clicked with me." He looked up at Tom. "Since I started seeing Charly, God keeps coming up. Now even Sam is telling me about God."

Tom grinned. "Someday we'll have to tell you the whole story about Sam. It's pretty interesting."

"Sam's told me a little of it, mainly how you and Jared Benton pointed him to God."

Tom looked out over the parking lot. "It's interesting how people are put together for specific purposes, at specific times."

"Can't God simply take care of stuff? If He's all-powerful

and all-knowing, and loves us so much, why does he leave things for us to mess up?" He was beginning to feel more frustration than curiosity.

"This may not mean much to you right now, but the Bible is littered with people who made bad choices over and over again only to be forgiven and given a place of importance. Prostitutes, swindlers, liars, thieves . . . God loved them all. They made the decision to do sinful things, and then they made the decision to turn away from sin and follow Him."

"Sounds too easy."

Tom laughed out loud. "I know. I've been back and forth myself, trying to make it harder than it is. It's a free gift. You know what you have to do to get a free gift?"

"What?" Rance was totally baffled.

"Receive it."

CHAPTER TWENTY-THREE

The Baker/Rowan wedding, held at Atalaya Castle at Huntington Beach State Park, was going to be perfect. Such an interesting venue. What looked like a Moorish castle on the desert opened up to a green oasis complete with palm trees, wrought-iron accents, and what was once an art studio for a sculptor.

Charly had helped with more than one wedding at this venue since Lucy went into business with Emma. Before Hurricane Rosa, Sarah and Jared Benton had planned to have their wedding here. They changed to the church when damage to the property closed the venue for a season.

Clipboard in place, Emma was coming toward her, auburn hair shining in the bright sunlight, her summer dress the perfect color of blue to help her blend in but still look beautiful.

"Charly, could you go and check those tablecloths over on the far end? I was watching as they put them on, and the hems are not level. See how bad it is, and if you need to, help them take everything off and fix it. Got it?"

"Emma, are you all right?" Usually cool as a cucumber, Emma was flushed and a little out of sorts.

"I'm fine." She paused and looked at her young friend. She had to tell somebody. "I have a date."

"For the wedding? Emma, how long since—"

"Since I had a date? Let's see now . . . over ten years."

"Seriously? You haven't had a date since I was old enough to think about dating?" Charly giggled and hugged Emma tightly. "You'll be great. Anybody I know?"

"Probably not. I met him in Charleston. He was a friend of Daniel's, and they served together in Afghanistan."

Charly's mouth hung open. "Wow. What are the odds?"

"Seriously. He asked me out for this weekend, and I had this, so he asked if I'd like a date for the wedding. What could I say?"

"Is he cute?" Charly winked at her. "And what time will he be here so I can watch for him."

"He's cute, has red hair, and will be here for the reception. Then I can begin to relax."

"What's his name?"

"Rafe. Rafe Jernigan."

Charly frowned. "His name sounds so familiar. I know I've heard it somewhere."

"He said he grew up here, but after the service, his family had moved to Charleston."

"Interesting. Okay, I'll look for a cute guy with red hair. Big guy?"

"Kinda. Tall, looks like he used to be a soldier." Emma laughed, sounding more relaxed than she had earlier.

"What does Sophie think about it?"

"She's been after me to start dating for a while. I think she's come to the realization she may have missed out by not having a father-figure in her life."

Charly nodded. "It's tough. I had mine until I was a teenager, but it was hard. I can't imagine never having known my dad."

"I'm going down to the beach and see how things are looking

for the ceremony site." She wrinkled her nose in irritation. "It's hard to put it together without a crowd gathering."

"I'll keep things going here."

"Tell Sophie to make sure there's plenty of ice. If we need more, have one of the guys go for more. I'd rather have too much than not enough."

"Will do." Charly turned to walk back to the tables that needed checking. She stopped and looked back. "Does Lucy know?"

"Not yet." Emma twisted her lips, trying to hide her grin.

"Ha! I know something before Lucy! Finally!"

Emma shook her head and waved her on. "Go. Work. Now."

"Yes, ma'am." Charly saluted then skipped to the tables in the back to make them perfect.

Ceremony done, Emma looked over the reception area. She was good at her job, and the gentle smile on her face showed confidence in her abilities.

Rafe stood off to the side, avoiding the receiving line, watching Emma and wondering what would have happened if he'd met her before Daniel. She probably wouldn't have given him the time of day. He had been pretty rough back then.

"You must be Emma's friend, Rafe. I'm Charly Livingston." She held a tray of finger foods and smiled.

"Related to Tom?"

"Yes, he's my brother." She grinned. "You know him?"

"You could say that. We've met a few times. Nice to meet you."

"Thanks, same here. I'll let Emma know you're here. She'll be done in a few minutes. The receiving line is finishing up, and then they'll announce the wedding party, and then I'll give her a break and keep things rolling. She's got a place for you over at the back table."

"Sounds good. I'll wait for her here, if it's okay."

She nodded. "Fine with me."

As soon as the receiving line was done, he noticed who the bride was. Cynthia Baker. Annabelle's best friend and the girl he had avoided like the plague when she was a hormonal teenager with a crush on him. He chuckled and shook his head, then turned quickly when he felt a hand at his elbow.

"Hi Rafe."

Emma. She looked amazing. "Hey, yourself." He looked at the bride and groom and had to laugh. "If I'd known it was Cynthia Baker's wedding, I might have ditched."

She tilted her head curiously. "History?"

"Ancient. She was my sister's best friend and had a raging crush on me when she was a teenager."

"Well, I think she got over it." Emma laughed, noting the passionate kiss the groom gave his bride as the master of ceremonies announced them.

"Dodged a bullet there." He made a show of wiping sweat from his brow, enjoying seeing her smile and making her laugh.

"I'm glad you came."

"Me too. What kind of schedule do you have to keep here?"

"I'll be on call during the reception, make sure everything is going all right, then when the bride and groom leave, the clean-up crew takes over."

"Any time for a walk on the beach?"

She looked around and saw Charly. She pointed to the gate leading out to the sand, and Charly nodded with a smile. "As long as somebody knows where I am, I'm a free woman for about thirty minutes."

"Good, but then you look too pretty to go walking on the beach."

"Thank you, kind sir, but I recently supervised nuptials on

the beach, so I came prepared." She opened her bag to show flip-flops matching her dress.

"I like a woman who is prepared."

"Thirteen years of being a single mom has taught me a few things."

"I'm sure it has." He cleared his throat and held out his arm. "You look like you've done well for yourself."

She tucked her hand in the crook of his arm and walked out the gate with him. "It was tough, at first. Sophie was so little, and I had started wedding planning for fun. After Daniel died, I went full-time. God was certainly good during those times and still is."

"I hear you. I didn't have much time for God back then."

"I'm sorry."

He grinned at her. "Me too."

"What changed your mind?"

He looked at her intently as they stood on the beach. "It's been a while, but that doesn't sound like a first-date question."

She raised an eyebrow. "Hey, I'm forty. I figure why act like a twenty-something? I figure it's a good idea to separate the wheat from the chaff early."

He nodded and twisted his lips in a half-smile. This was no ordinary woman.

HAD SHE MESSED UP ALREADY? Emma strolled along the beach with a silent Rafe, wondering. Her experience with first dates was sketchy, but there was something about him. There was a sadness she sensed had nothing to do with the loss of his sister but had everything to do with the fact that he had spent many years pushing God aside.

He stopped for a moment, away from other people, and turned toward her. "You really want to know?"

"I do." She didn't reach for his hand, but she was tempted. His unruly red hair blew in the breeze and was more unruly when he raked his hands through them. She wanted so badly to touch the curls, to smooth them over to one side, but instead linked her fingers together and tilted her head. "It's not a deal breaker, so don't feel as if you have to share if you don't want to."

He nodded. "I get it. If I had a daughter, I'd be careful who I spent time with too."

"Thank you."

"I guess I started down the wrong path before I joined the Army. The usual stuff, drinking, drug use, and a little dating extra-curricular activity. When my sister, Annabelle, was in the wreck, I had found out she was pregnant, and it floored me. It made me mad. I guess anger, combined with a little PTSD from two tours in Afghanistan, made the violence worse and made the dependence worse. I was one unhappy camper."

"I can't even imagine."

He reached for her hand, and she let him take it. "I decided God, if He existed, was for other people but not for me. How could He take my kid sister? And how could He sit back and watch while she was fooling around, acting stupid? But then I wasn't exactly a good role model."

"Survivor's guilt?"

"Yes, on several levels. I'd lost a few of my buddies and couldn't figure out why they had to die, and I lived. I knew I was being unreasonable, and that's what unreasonable people do, they don't think straight. I unleashed my anger on the young man in the wreck with her and blamed everything on God and Jared Benton."

She blanched. "Jared Benton?"

He shook his head sadly. "Wasn't his fault, none of it."

"Wow."

"Yeah, and you know what? Jared forgave me even before I found out he wasn't responsible."

"He's a good man." She squeezed his hand, giving him a sad smile when he squeezed back.

"One of the best. I spent a lot of time angry with him, angry with God, and wasted a lot of time thinking about nobody but myself."

"What made the difference?"

"One night a few years ago in Charleston I came across Jared and Sarah. I was drunk, and I was mad at the world. It wasn't pretty, Emma. I found out a year later he wasn't to blame for Annabelle's death or the trouble she was in, and I came to him and apologized. He didn't like me scaring Sarah, but he told me the most important thing was that God loved me enough to sacrifice His Son to die for me. All I had to do was accept it was true and that it was for me. Nothing else mattered. Not my anger, not his or my guilt over surviving. Nothing. God's love was the important thing."

She grinned at him, a mist of tears in her eyes. "The Gospel in a nutshell."

"The Good News. That's when I started getting sober."

THE WEDDING RECEPTION was drawing to a close. Cake had been cut, toasts made, and the bouquet was about to be tossed. Emma walked over to Charly and Sophie after settling Rafe in a chair with a plate of food. It was almost over.

"So, ladies, are you going up for the bouquet toss?"

Charly laughed. "Not unless you do."

Emma let out one loud "Ha!" making everyone turn and look. She felt herself turning red. "I'll leave bouquet catching to you young folks."

Sophie poked her mother in the ribs. "Hey, how's the date going?"

Her mother smiled. "Very well. Thanks for asking."

"Good. He's a ginger. I like it."

Emma winked at her daughter. "I do too."

The three ladies laughed together as the master of ceremonies asked for their attention. The bride beckoned for the three of them to join the fray as the other single ladies assembled. Emma waved them off and pushed the other two forward.

She grinned over at Rafe and noticed at the entrance a young man that would certainly be of interest to Charly. Emma wanted to get her attention, but about the time Rance Butler got to her side, Charly was entirely too busy . . . catching the bouquet.

CHARLY LAUGHED as she easily caught the bouquet. Sophie was tickled pink, and Charly could feel her face turning pink. Very pink. Especially when she looked over and saw who was standing next to Emma.

What was Rance doing here? She thought he was coming home yesterday, but she hadn't heard from him. But then, she hadn't checked her phone since she started working this afternoon.

She walked over to him, and Emma excused herself to confer with the bride and groom about their exit.

"Hey." She stood there, looking down at the beautiful blend of real peonies, roses, and other flowers. Cynthia had spared no expense for even the "throwaway" bouquet. She loved peonies. Maybe she'd have them at her wedding.

"Hey, yourself." Rance took her free hand and pulled her closer. "I missed you."

She gave him a partial smile. "Did you?"

He looked down then away from her. "Charly . . ."

"Rance, I don't know if I can do this." She waited until he looked at her then tilted her head and looked him in the eye.

"I know we're different, but maybe being different is a good thing." He held on to her gaze and squeezed her hand. "Charly, I'm sorry."

She nodded and looked away, suddenly not wanting to meet his eyes. "It's okay." She pulled her hand away and rubbed her arm. She felt chilled.

"No, it's not." He looked around at all the people milling around in the aftermath of the reception and put his hands in his pockets. "We need to talk, and this isn't the place."

She dipped her head. "I need to help Emma get things wrapped up."

"Can I come over later?" His eyes pleaded with her to accept his apology. "Charly?"

She chewed on her bottom lip and looked down at the flowers in her hand. The decision to cut ties with him had been easy when he wasn't standing in front of her, but now she was so torn. She might be falling in love with him, and she didn't know what to do about it. "I'm not sure that's a good idea."

"Please?"

When she looked up, she was startled at the pain on his face, in his eyes. She couldn't refuse. "Lydia will be there, I should be home by eight-thirty or so."

"Okay. I'll be waiting."

CHAPTER TWENTY-FOUR

It had been a fun night, right up to the point when she saw Rance.

Working with Emma and Sophie, teasing Emma about first date jitters, surprise at Sophie's adult-like graciousness when meeting Rafe Jernigan. That he had known her father seemed to raise her first impression of him dramatically.

And then Rance came, and she was confused. "Lord, what am I supposed to do?"

The thought had occurred to her there might be no point in asking God for advice in this one. She was on her own, like she had been so many times before. What if God didn't care one way or another?

Or He did care, and she didn't.

What was the cliché poking her brain? "God didn't move, you did."

It was true. Everything she knew about God told her He was the same yesterday, today, and tomorrow. Was she?

No. Not even a little bit. Human nature means a lot of things go into how we are from day to day. Good days and bad days. Days when you feel good all day because the sun was shining, and days when it rains, your hair frizzes, and you have a sinus headache that won't go away.

Days when God feels near, like when a set of healthy twins are born four weeks early, and days when God feels far away because you've lost your father and your mother is going blind. Those were the angry days.

"I didn't deserve this, God. Mom didn't deserve this. What did we ever do to have You pull the rug out from under us that way?" She felt tears of hurt and anger begin to gather and brushed them away in irritation. She finally hit her steering wheel and shouted there in the privacy of her car. "Do You even love us?"

She let the tears fall until she arrived at the street to her house. She tried to mop up and drive at the same time, blowing her nose at the stop signs. "I want to believe again, God. I really do. I want to feel You inside me the way I used to. I want to rest in You, like You said to do. Your yoke is easy? It's felt hard. Really hard."

Then the song came to her again. This time there was no radio, no church service, just her and God.

Through many dangers, toils and snares
I have already come
'Tis grace hath brought me safe thus far,
And grace will lead me home.

Dangers: sickness, bereavement, sorrow. Toils: those times that are hard, like losing your dad, or taking care of a blind mom, or worrying about things you have no control over. Snares. The tough one. A snare is a trap. Sin is a trap. Self is a trap.

The Lord has promised good to me,
His word my hope secures;
He will my Shield and Portion be

As long as life endures.

"God, when did I get so caught up in myself and things only You can take care of, that I forgot You are in charge?"

HOW TANGLED up was his life supposed to be anyway? He had a perfectly normal life, successful internship, a great career looming ahead of him, a great girl, and then?

Boom.

A lie, pain, loss, gain, and heartache. Then he thought about all the people who had come into his life in the last few weeks and months.

He found out he had a brother. He met Charly. He learned about God. And the kicker? It all started because of two precious infants delivered by a doctor wearing muddy garden shoes who prayed.

Rance sat on the front porch waiting for Charly. Lydia had come in earlier, and after a brief, awkward conversation in which she invited him in to wait, he decided to wait for her out here in the darkness. He belonged there anyway. If what Tom said was true, God loved him. But until he made things right with Charly, he wouldn't rest easy.

God was too big for him to handle right now. Even if the gift was free, he didn't feel worthy of taking it, no matter how easy Tom or his brother said it was. Life couldn't be that simple.

He stood up, hands stuffed into his pockets, as he walked around, pacing up and down the sidewalk.

Life was meant to be hard. It wasn't some big "Kum-ba-ya" where you loved everybody, and everybody loved you, with a great big wonderful God standing over you, taking care of things before they hurt you. Uh-uh.

When he met Charly, life was going pretty well. Since they

met, it was like his life was falling apart, one piece at a time. Even with things going well on the job front, his personal life was in shambles.

He should focus on his work, to the exclusion of everything else. But then, apparently exclusively focusing on work was what his real dad did and look where it got him.

He raked his hand through his hair, wondering how many times he could do this without starting to lose his hair, which made him chuckle without humor. That would be about right. Not only lose his family and his girl, but his hair as well.

He stood straight when he saw headlights headed to the drive, Charly behind the wheel.

Was it over? He wasn't sure, at this point, whether he had it in him to continue the relationship. Was it a relationship? Was she that important to him?

As she got out of the car, he saw the tears in her eyes and the pain on her face. Yes, she was, but was he important to her?

"Why, Lord, does he have to be such a gentleman?" When Charly switched off the car, she momentarily squeezed her eyes shut, feeling the tears start up again when Rance walked over to open her car door for her. She squelched them. Now wasn't the time. Maybe later when it was over.

She gave him a timid smile as she grabbed her purse and bouquet and stood up next to him. "Hey."

"Hey, yourself. You okay?"

The tension on his face and in his voice was palpable. His brilliant blue eyes, visible in the dusky twilight, grabbed her and held on.

"I'm okay. I'm a little tired." She grinned and held up the bouquet. "Big day."

His lips lifted in a grin. "Looks like it." He looked down at his toes and then back up at her. "Want to take a walk?"

She nodded. "Let me take this stuff inside and put on something else."

"I'll wait on the patio."

Charly watched as he walked around the side of the house to the patio facing the beach. The spring in his step that was usually there, wasn't.

She went in the front door and straight to the kitchen to put the flowers in water. Whether catching the bouquet meant anything or not, she wasn't one to waste beautiful, fragile peonies in high summer.

"Hey, girl, where's Rance?" Lydia wandered into the kitchen from her bedroom. "And you caught the bouquet?" She started to squeal then saw the look on Charly's face. "Uh-oh."

Charly waved her off. "He's on the patio. Yes, I caught the bouquet, not that it means anything."

"It might. Stranger things have happened."

"Yeah, well, after tonight it might be more far-fetched than ever."

"Have you prayed?"

"Are you kidding me? I've prayed more this summer since I met Rance than I have in years."

"Hmmm. Sounds like you had some catching up to do."

"You think?" Charly's voice dripped with sarcasm, then she stopped. "I'm sorry. I've been irritated with God too long, and I'm realizing He wasn't the one that left, I was."

Lydia sat on the stool, chin in hand. "What do you think He's telling you to do?"

She lifted her hands in frustration. "That's the thing. I don't have any idea. I'm to the point I don't know what's God and what's me." She shook her head. "I need to change. We're going for a walk. Maybe a good ocean breeze will clear our heads."

"Or not. Be careful, friend. The wind and waves can sway you."

"It can also calm you. When I look at the ocean, it's like I'm finding out all over again how insignificant I am in the grand scheme of things."

"Except when it comes to God. You are precious in His sight. Don't forget."

Charly leaned over and hugged her friend as she walked by. "Thanks. I needed that."

RANCE TOOK off his jacket and laid it across a chair, then loosened his tie and collar. He sat, staring out at the water as the shadows crept up and darkness began to overtake the shore. The ocean was vast, and deep, but the darkness threatened to be deeper as he sat there, feeling icy fingers clutching at his heart.

"Still want to walk?" Charly had come up behind him without him noticing.

"Yeah. I didn't hear you for the surf."

"You were deep in thought."

He took her hand and led her off the patio and into the sand. "It's been a rough week."

"In what way?"

He noticed when she tucked her head to avoid looking directly at him.

When they got to the edge of the water, he stopped, and she had to look at him. "Charly, I don't know if I can do this."

"Do what?" She looked confused, troubled, and in a strange way, knowing.

"It's all too much."

She looked out at the water, catching a stray lock of hair whipping across her face. "I'm not sure what 'all' includes, but I think I agree."

"You do?"

"Rance, I think—"

"Charly, I'm sorry. When I realized what I had done when I called you, I was sick. I never wanted you to see that side of me."

She turned toward him with a sad smile. "I know. And I forgive you." She shrugged. "Nobody's perfect."

He had said those exact words to his mother, and the fact that Charly could forgive him, but he hadn't forgiven his mother hurt. "Charly, maybe we need to cool whatever this is between us." He closed his eyes to shut out the hurt in her eyes.

She put her hand on his arm, and he opened them. "I know." Tears stood poised to drop from her lashes, and it was making him crazy.

"You know?"

She nodded. "I need time. You need time. You're starting a new job who-knows-where, and I'm here. Your family is here, but you've got to figure that out too."

He put his hands on her cheeks and looked deep into her hazel eyes. "I'm afraid to lose you."

"Why?" She gazed at him, tears still simmering, a sad little smile on her face. He could kiss her right now, and they could go back to where they were. But could they? Could he?

"Because you're the best thing in my life right now."

"Which is why we need to be sure."

He shook his head and pulled her to him in a hug, so she couldn't see the emotions on his face. "The voice of reason. I've never had anyone like you in my life before."

Her voice was muffled as she hid her face in his shoulder. "If I'm the voice of reason, then bless your heart."

CHAPTER TWENTY-FIVE

Rance sat next to his father's bedside, staring at the man who had been kept from him his entire life. He figured this was what he would look like at this age. The same hairline, the same smile, jaw line. He shook his head. It was uncanny. Their voices were even similar. Fortunately he hadn't given in to the temptation to smoke at a young age, so his growl was less gravelly than Clifton's.

As he watched him sleep, he raised his lips in a half-smile. He wanted to know this man. He wanted to know what made him tick. Did nature or nurture make him want to try new things, live on the edge?

His eyes fluttered open. "Hey."

"Hey, yourself." He leaned forward in his chair, putting his face on a level with his father's.

"I hear they found a match."

"They did." Rance couldn't pull his eyes away from his father's, so like his own when he looked in the mirror.

"Don't do it." The smile on Clifton's face turned into a grave line of concern.

"Don't do what?"

"Don't go through with the surgery. I've had my chance, now it's your turn."

Rance looked down at his hands clasped in front of him. He shook his head. "I've got to."

"No, you don't." Clifton raised the hospital bed so he could sit up straighter. "Son, you don't have to prove anything to me. None of this is your fault."

"You've been kept from me all my life. I want to get to know my father and my brother." He gazed into his father's eyes. "If I don't do this, you'll die."

"It's dangerous."

"So is driving down the road or jumping out of an airplane, but I've done that too."

Clifton closed his eyes. Fatigue dogged him, Rance knew. He also knew if he didn't have the surgery soon, he would be too weak to survive the surgery, much less the recovery and the acceptance of the grafted kidney.

When he opened his eyes, he stared at the ceiling. "I jumped out of an airplane once." He smiled widely. "Biggest rush I ever had."

Rance reached for his dad's hand. "I'd like to jump out of an airplane with you someday."

Clifton looked over at him with a sigh. "I'd love to."

"You, me, Sam. He's getting out in about six weeks."

"He called a couple of days ago, said you'd talked." Clifton's brows drew together.

"What's wrong?"

"I know he's gotten his life back together in prison. I hope he can maintain it when he's out."

"Me too." Would Sam's faith carry him when he had all the freedom in the world? Or would he slip back into his old ways when it was available?

"God is good. All the time."

Rance didn't quite know what to say. "That's what I hear."

"That's what I know." His father gave him a straight look. "And I want you to know it too."

EMMA WATCHED CHARLY INTERACTING with their current bride, Kristi Brown, as she and her mother walked the property at Pilot Oaks. With Lucy tied up with twins, Charly's help for the summer had been a life saver.

Who knows? Someday maybe Emma would need help during a maternity leave. She stopped short. Where had that come from? She was forty years old, the mother of a teenager, and a businesswoman. She was also a woman who was looking forward to whatever God had next for her.

She smiled and caught up to the trio as they approached the swing overlooking the marsh.

"This is my favorite spot."

Kristi smiled. "I can see why. It's beautiful. Do you think we could have a few pictures taken here?"

Emma nodded. "We'll plan on it. I'll make a note to decorate it a little bit when we're decorating for the wedding." She wrote it down and noticed Charly did the same. Between the two of them, they would get this done.

The bride hugged herself and sighed. "It's going to be beautiful, and I'm convinced the weather is going to cooperate."

"We'll start praying for good weather now." Emma loved to see the glow a new bride carried with her. Even the "bridezilla" types, deep-down, had a glow of happiness and excitement. She missed that in her life. Could that be why she decided to continue with weddings after Daniel died? She wanted to experience happiness through other people.

And God had blessed her. She was successful in her field and did weddings from Myrtle Beach to Charleston. Someday, Sophie might join her in her business.

Her phone buzzed with a text. They were wrapping up this session, so she would check it later. She should see who it was.

It was Rafe. She closed the window and smiled as she put her phone in her pocket. "Ladies, do you have any other questions?

Mrs. Brown looked at her daughter then back at Emma. "I think you've covered everything. Of course we'll think of questions after we leave." She chuckled nervously.

"If you do, call me. That's my job, and it's what you're paying me to do: plan, arrange, and keep you posted. My goal is to help you enjoy one of the most special days of your life."

"Thank you so much. You've been a God-send." Kristi was smiling through a mist of tears.

Emma hugged her. "You couldn't have said anything to make me happier."

"How do I look?" Lydia twirled in front of the full-length mirror in the tiny hallway of the beach house, her purple sun dress and platform booties stylish and flattering on her petite form.

"Perfect. And your dress matches your hair." Charly giggled and then twisted her lips, trying not to laugh. "You do realize Jake is coming over to study, with me, for our final exam?"

"You never know, if I'm highly visible, he might get up the nerve to ask me out." She flitted around the living room and kitchen. "I'll be around, making cookies, mixing up sweet tea, cleaning the oven. You know, good-wife-material stuff."

Charly raised her eyebrows. "I don't think you have to go as far as cleaning the oven. It's self-cleaning."

"True. Maybe I could demonstrate using the self-cleaning feature."

She shook her head furiously. "Please, no. The oven gets up

to 900 degrees on self-clean, and stinks to high heaven. It would run us all out of the house."

Lydia's face fell. "Oh. Okay, I'll be quiet but ever present."

"Don't be a distraction. We need this class."

She splayed her well-manicured fingers on her chest and batted her eyes. "Who? Little ol' me? A distraction?"

"Yes, you." She looked out the sidelight of the door to see Jake's car pull up. "He's here, so you behave."

"Yes, ma'am. I'll do my best. Don't mind the galley wench." Lydia winked and backed into the kitchen.

Charly was shaking her head when she opened the door. In surprise, she blurted, "Flowers?"

Jake turned three shades of red. "Uh, they're for Lydia."

"Oh? Is there something I should know?" She looked at the flowers, then at Jake, and with her hands on her hips, simply snorted.

"What?"

"You've been texting, haven't you?"

His face relaxed in a smile. "Yeah. I like her, Charly."

"She's in the kitchen. Make yourself at home." She held her hand out, guiding him in the right direction as she closed the front door. At least somebody in her life was having fun.

RAFE WAS TORN. He didn't want to be pushy, but he wanted to see Emmaline Quince again. It had been a few weeks since their date, and he had almost called her several times.

"I'm getting too old for this." Sometimes talking to himself was the only thing that kept him sane. That and talking to God. "I'm acting like a teenager."

He snorted and sent the text. Hey

He didn't get a response immediately, but he saw where she had read it. She was either busy, or she never wanted to lay eyes on him again. After the things he had told her, he wouldn't blame her for the latter. She deserved so much better than him.

After about twenty minutes, his phone vibrated with a text.

Sorry. I was in a meeting. Hey yourself.

He grinned.

Busy tomorrow night? It's a Tuesday, so thought you might be free.

There was a pause. Great, she's rethinking answering the text.

Sorry, had to answer a text from Sophie. I'm free. Want to come over for dinner?

How about I take you and Sophie out?

Are you sure? I can cook.

I'm sure you're a great cook. ;) My treat. You girls like seafood?

We're from SC. It's required. LOL

Great. Pick you up at 6:30.

We'll be ready.

See you then.

OK. Have a good day.

You too.

He nodded and smiled. That wasn't so hard, now, was it? "God, I'm goin' on a date."

"Mom, you look great." Sophie leaned on the facing of her mother's bedroom door. "How many outfits have you tried on anyway?"

"Only six." Emma looked at herself in the mirror. White slacks, a gauzy blue top, and blue sandals that matched perfectly. Was it too much? She started to change the shirt. What time was it?

"Mom?"

"Is it too dressy? I don't want to be out of place."

"It's pants, top, and sandals. I think you'll be okay."

"Easy for you to say."

"Why? Because I'm wearing the same outfit I wore to school today?"

"Yes, and you look cute in anything."

"I guess I'm like you, Mom. Granny always said you'd look good in a feed sack."

"Granny was biased."

"No, she wasn't. She was proud of you, and I am too."

Emma sat on the bed and slumped. "Oh, Sophie, am I doing the right thing?"

"It's a date, Mom, and I'm going, too, remember? I met Rafe at the wedding, and he seemed nice."

Emma smiled and plucked at her bedspread. "He is nice." She looked at her beautiful daughter. "And he knew your daddy. Sometimes I wonder if it's as much a connection with him as it is Rafe himself."

Sophie put her hands on her hips and shook her head at the clothes spread on the bed. "Maybe a little bit of both." She shrugged. "I'll admit, I'm looking forward to asking him about my dad. Do you think that'll make things weird?"

"No, I don't. Rafe seems like the kind of guy who doesn't like to keep secrets anymore." She looked at her bedside clock. It was time. "He'll be here any minute. Are you sure I look okay?"

Sophie hugged her mom. "You look gorgeous, and I'm proud to have you for a mom."

Emma kissed her daughter's cheek. "Thank you, baby." The doorbell sounded, making them both jump.

"Showtime." Sophie stated the fact as Emma hurried to the door.

RAFE SMILED as the door opened. How did a guy like him get so lucky as to get a lady like Emmaline Quince to go out with him? She was beautiful.

"Come in, come in." Emma seemed a little nervous. Probably because this would be the first time they would be going out with Sophie and without a lot of other people around.

He stood in the entryway of her bungalow. "Nice place."

"Thanks. I've lived here for about fifteen years. Sophie's never known another house."

"I like these older homes. There's something about them."

"I agree. You can't buy character the way they built it a hundred years ago."

He nodded, taking in the woodwork and oak floors.

Sophie came into the entry. "Hi."

"Hey, Sophie. I'm glad you can join us tonight."

"Me too. Thanks for inviting me. You didn't have to." She grinned. "Nothing like being the chaperon on a date with your mom."

Rafe laughed. This kid had a good sense of humor. Like her dad. He hadn't thought about Daniel Quince in years, and now here he was, going out with his wife and daughter.

"You girls ready? I've got us reservations at Captain Dan's."

"Captain Dan's?"

"Yep. Did you know they're closing? The brothers who own it are retiring, selling out."

Emma shook her head. "I'm sorry to hear it. It's a popular spot."

"And the hushpuppies are to die for." Sophie grabbed her purse and handed her mom's to her. "I'm ready to get started, since it looks like my time with them is limited."

"Then go, we shall."

Sophie giggled. "You sounded like Yoda."

"Star Wars fan?"

"Uh, who isn't? Besides Mom, that is." Sophie cut a glance at her mother.

Rafe stopped in the middle of the sidewalk. "Are you kidding?" He looked from Sophie, with a wink, then to her mother, and back again. "That might be a deal breaker."

Emma locked the front door and followed them down the sidewalk. "Don't worry. Between Dan and then Sophie, I've been indoctrinated enough to carry on an intelligent conversation about both Star Wars and Star Trek."

"That's a relief. Thought I'd have to cancel the whole thing. Let me guess. You like chick flicks."

Rafe opened the car door for both Emma and Sophie. When he got in on the driver's side, she was thinking.

"I like the occasional chick flick, but you know what I really like?"

"Romantic comedy? Musicals?"

She grinned and arched her brow. "Movies with lots of explosions."

"You're kidding me."

She shook her head. "Give me a good *Mission Impossible* scenario any day over *Beaches* or *Titanic*. She shrugged. "Dan thought he hit the jackpot with me."

Rafe's smile widened. "I can see why."

CHAPTER TWENTY-SIX

R ance stopped short when he came around the corner, almost colliding with a double stroller. When he saw Lucy, he had to smile. He hadn't seen Charly in weeks, and he missed her family as well as the beautiful girl.

Lucy was corralling Hayes and pushing the twins and looking everywhere except where she was going. "Oh, Rance, I'm so sorry. I almost ran you over."

"You've got your hands full, haven't you?"

"Yes. Up to now I've had Charly or Tom to come with me for doctor's appointments, but Charly's finishing up her class, and Tom had something come up at work, as usual." She ended in a huge sigh. "I can do this. If I can give birth to 'em, I can haul 'em around. Right, Hayes?"

"Right, Mama. I'll help."

"I'll bet you're a good helper with these guys."

"Yeah. I bring diapers and pacifiers and make them smile. It's hard, but I can handle it."

"I'm sure." He laughed as Hayes demonstrated his ability to entertain his siblings and anyone else within sight or earshot.

"We've missed seeing you, Rance. How are things going with the internship?"

He could tell she wanted to inquire about his feelings about a certain blonde sister-in-law of hers. He couldn't go there. Not now.

"Good. I'm done. Now I'm finishing up paperwork and going for interviews."

"I understand you had one in Nashville?" Her eyebrows raised in question.

"Yes, and I've had one here, too, and in Charleston. I'm still considering them all." She looked concerned, and for good reason. He hadn't told Charly he was definitely going to be the live donor for his father's kidney transplant.

"I'm having surgery in a couple of weeks, so circumstances have put things off for now."

"Surgery? Is something wrong?" She leaned down and poked the pacifier back in baby Evan's mouth as he started squirming.

How do you tell somebody you're doing something like this? Is it bragging? He didn't want to be praised, but he would like Charly to know. "I don't know how much you know about my family, but my biological father is in need of a kidney transplant, and I am a match." He shrugged, trying to minimize his part.

She tilted her head and smiled at him, a little crease of worry between her brows. "Rance, do you mind if I pray for you?"

"Not at all. My father has been praying too. I would appreciate it." He looked down at his toes and then at her face. And I would appreciate it if you told Charly."

She put her hand on his arm and squeezed. "I will."

"Are you Aunt Charly's boyfriend?" Hayes had stayed quiet through their exchange, but his curiosity had gotten the better of him.

Rance knelt in front of the small boy and smiled. "I'm not sure right now, but as soon as I figure it out, I'll let you know. Deal?"

Hayes stuck his hand out for a shake. "Deal. My Dad says that's how men make deals."

"Your dad is right."

BLOOD TESTS and other medical tests done, Rance was approved for the match, and surgery was scheduled for three weeks from now.

When he walked into his father's room after getting clearance, he was surprised to find his mom and dad there. He was still trying to figure out what to call Clifton and calling Ashton "Dad" felt strange now that he knew he wasn't his father..

"There's the man of the hour." Clifton's bright smile helped to hide the weakness and fatigue Rance saw in his eyes.

"No, I'm only a body part." He hugged his mom when she rose and hugged his dad, as well. "What are you guys doing here?"

"I thought it was time we had a family meeting, Rance." Ashton smiled sadly at the boy he had called "son" for so many years.

"All right, what about?"

His mother smiled sadly. "I know you've been hurt that I didn't tell you about your father. I thought if I didn't think about it, it would stay hidden, and you would live your life blissfully unaware of anything in the past that didn't have anything to do with you."

"Mom—"

She stopped him with a raised hand. "I know. It had everything to do with you. At the time I thought it was the right thing, but I know now it wasn't."

Rance looked at Ashton Butler. "Did you know?"

He looked up and nodded sadly. "I did, from the beginning." He looked over at his wife. "I was so in love with your mother that I thought it wouldn't matter. You would be mine according to the law and everyone we knew. I let her talk me into keeping the secret and staying away from Georgetown County." He got up and paced the floor. "And now I see the likeness between you, I can see why she never wanted to come here lest she be found out."

"Son, I asked them to come." Clifton spoke, getting Rance's attention. "I wanted us to be together before the surgery, in case, well, you know."

His mother spoke up. "Clifton has been more than gracious to me, sweetheart. He's forgiven me, and I hope, in time, you can too."

Grace. Was this why he'd been hearing that song? Was this what Sam was talking about, and Tom?

He looked at his mother, then his dad, and his biological father. Bitterness rose up in him, and looking at the three of them, he could have lashed out in pain. He didn't. "I hope I can too."

Clifton cleared his throat. "Don't let it fester in you."

"How can I not?"

"Come over here, Rance." Clifton held out his hand to his son, who walked over to him reluctantly, and took his hand. "Your mom and me, we didn't start out right. I was ambitious and would have done anything to get a kind word out of my father. I knew it wasn't right, and when your mom left, I put all my bitterness and hurt on Sam. Now he's paying the price. You were spared until now."

Mom came to his side. "I'm going to visit Sam, if he'll let me. I talked to him on the phone last week, briefly."

Rance looked down at his mother then at the man in the hospital bed. They both looked sad, and he felt it too. Ashton Butler sat alone, acutely aware of his part in the deception.

"Sam gets out in a few weeks. I want to be there to pick him up. That will be the week before surgery." Rance stood straighter. He didn't know what else he could say.

Clifton rubbed his hand over his face. "I wish I could be there with you."

"I know. I'll bring him straight here."

"Rance?" His mother wanted to be included, he could tell.

He took a deep breath and looked her in the eye. "See how your visit goes, and we'll plan from there."

His dad came to stand beside him. "Son, will you forgive us?"

"I'm working on it. Right now, I'm not sure."

THE IDEA of another wedding soured her stomach. Charly hadn't spoken to Rance in weeks, and she was avoiding her family. She used school work as an excuse to skip Wednesday night prayer meeting. Sundays had been hard enough, but she had responsibilities. She wouldn't shirk those. Her class was over except for turning in a paper, so she couldn't use it as an excuse anymore.

The morning wedding would be beautiful. The private beach at Pilot Oaks was perfect, and the heat wouldn't be unbearable until time for the reception, and everyone would be safely up the hill and under the spreading live oaks in the garden of Pilot Oaks. The brunch reception suited the venue perfectly.

Charly sighed, wishing she were in her bed with the covers over her head. "Eddie, could you move the far-left table over about two feet? Perfect."

"What about the head table, there by the summer house?"

"Looks good." She smiled at Eddie Harper, her assistant and head roustabout for the weekend.

The rehearsal had gone well, and she was supervising the placement of tables for the reception the following morning, using last-minute changes in the layout as subterfuge to get out of attending the rehearsal dinner at a local restaurant.

She made a round of the outside space, visualizing the table-cloths and decorations on each table, the area under the awning for the band, and the cafe lights, unnecessary for a daytime wedding but beautiful strung between the trees. There were three candle chandeliers above the head table, their clinking crystals making a light show in the lowering sunshine of evening.

Inside, where hors d'oeuvres would be served, was already set up in stations for the guests to mingle while pictures were being taken. Platters were in place to hold the delicacies. There would be mini chicken and waffles, salsa egg cups, and tiny potato latkes with sour cream. Her mouth watered a little bit at the thought. The silver coffee servers were in place, as well as a juice bar both inside and outside.

The owners of Pilot Oaks, Robert and Linda Crawford, Sarah Benton's parents, were in the kitchen supervising the storage of the dishes and foodstuffs to be used early the next day. When she opened the door, the first thing she saw was a laughing Robert holding his grandson, Beau.

"Looks like the party is in here tonight." Charly sat down at the long kitchen table next to Robert and immediately began to coo at the precious baby in his arms.

"Anywhere this fella is, there's gonna be a party." Linda smiled, shaking her head as she watched her husband and his grandson. "He's been a long time coming."

"Did they get everything brought in?" Charly pulled her gaze from the beautiful Beau and looked at the neatly stacked dishes, cups and boxes of silverware.

"It's all here. I'm glad we decided to go with the commercial refrigerator and freezer. They've been great."

When Beau began to fret, Robert handed his precious bundle to Linda. "I agree. There's no way we could provide the services we offer without it." He tilted his head at Charly. "Are you sure you're okay with us leaving right after the wedding? We can stick around if you need us."

"No, you need to get started if you're going to make it to Kentucky by midnight. Are Sarah and Jared leaving earlier?"

"Definitely. They're packing up the car now and may actually leave out this evening and stop part-way there."

"And you're okay leaving the keys to this amazing place with Emma and me?"

Linda chuckled. "Charly, you're one of ours now, and we want this place to be a blessing for the Stantons and the Benningfields. I don't know them well, but Kristi's mother has been by here a few times with Emma, looking things over. I know how she feels, being a mama."

"I know you do. I also know you're anxious to show off this young man to your family and friends back in Kentucky."

Robert laughed out loud. "You have no idea. Abby and Trudy have face-timed Sarah so much, wanting a glimpse of Beau, that she'll be glad to be in the same room with them and let them try their hand at baby entertaining."

Linda poked him. "Now Robert, you're as excited to have all three grandbabies together as I am."

"Are Susan and Mike still considering moving out here?" Charly couldn't imagine living so far away from her brother.

"Eventually. Since Mike's parents live in Tennessee, it would be about as close for them to live here as there. I'm hoping we can convince them. I miss having both my girls."

Charly smiled. "I know you do." She looked around one last time. "Well, it looks like my work here is done. Is it okay if I go out to the swing? I showed it to Kristi, and she loved it. I thought about putting ribbons and flowers on the ropes so they can use it for pictures."

Robert grinned. "You make yourself at home, young lady."

"I will and thank you."

"You rest well, and we'll see you in the morning." Linda pulled her in for a hug while she was holding the baby.

"I'd better tell this fella bye." She kissed his plump, smooth cheek. "Bye, Beau. You be good for Mama and Daddy, you hear?"

THE SWING WAS A SPECIAL PLACE. She had been introduced to it as a kid, when she tagged along with Jared and Tom to swim on the beach down the path. It had been maintained over the years, so the wooden, porch-style swing was painted, and the ropes holding it in the huge live oak looked new.

Such a great place for pictures, both for the bride and groom and for guests.

She sat down for a minute, looking out over the marsh. It reached out farther than she could see from here. Peace. This place may have once been a bustling rice plantation, like the one where she grew up, but now it exuded peace, and she needed it.

Honestly, she thought if she were to plan her own wedding, she would like to have it here, on this rise, overlooking the marsh instead of on the beach. Beach weddings were all the rage because the sand was clean, and the sea oats and dunes were picturesque. But the marsh was special. It was alive.

Sometimes she wanted to feel more alive. Sometimes, like now, she felt the coldness around her heart and longed for it to melt. Being alive was more than breathing or feeling. It was knowing, experiencing.

It was having faith in something beyond yourself.

"I used to have faith in You. Is it still there, buried so deep I have to dig for it?" She grinned, listening to herself talk. It was like having a conversation with someone else. Actually, she was having a conversation. "God, where are You?"

She pulled her feet up on to the swing and sat, chin on her

knees as she hugged them, looking out at the gently waving grasses. A lone egret flew up and away, disrupting for a moment the peace of the place. The sound of frogs and cicadas were the background music for her thoughts. Her mind was too full for words at this point.

God was here. He was for her. He loved her and hadn't deserted her.

A tear crept out of the corner of her eye. "So why does it hurt so much?"

Maybe because she hadn't given her hurt to Him. She tried to take care of it on her own, in her own strength.

"I know better, don't I?" When her father passed, she had been strong for her mother. Everyone had been amazed. When her mother went blind, she stayed strong, wanting to keep things as normal as possible. But now?

Now she had hit a wall as tall and as solid as the walled gardens of the Charleston historic district.

CHAPTER TWENTY-SEVEN

Charly wiped her tears away when she felt her phone vibrate in her pocket.

It was Lucy. Are you still at Pilot Oaks?

Yes, about to finish up.

Could you come by the house before you go home?

Sure. Be there in about 20.

Great. CYA.

Charly smiled. As loquacious as Lucy could be in person, via text she was pretty no-nonsense. Of course, since the arrival of the twins she had no time for pleasure-texting.

She rose from the swing and stretched, looking around in the lengthening shadows of the tree from which the swing was attached. Yes, it was still her favorite place, any time of the day. "Thank you, God."

I love you.

She looked around and realized the voice she heard wasn't an audible voice, but the still, small voice you can only hear when you are still. "I love you too."

Her heart was full. She didn't want to lose this moment, but her brain was telling her she needed to get to Tom and Lucy's to see what was going on. She put her hand on the area of her heart, where it hurt, deep inside. "Help me, Lord."

I Am.

"Then why do I feel broken inside?"

My grace is sufficient for you, for My strength is made perfect in weakness. [2 Cor. 12:9]

It was one of those memory verses she had learned as a child. As an adult, she knew this was what God said to Paul, when he complained about the "thorn in the flesh" that kept him dependent on God. In fact, Paul praised God for giving him this burden because it kept him humble and in touch with God.

Humility was never one of the virtues Charly appreciated, although she liked to appear humble. She was the "good girl." The girl you could always count on to be there, to say all the right things, and to help the needy. It was her way of life. Her family legacy.

What was her individual legacy from God? Had she considered that?

She shook her head in confusion. Why did one have to become weak to be strong? The very idea was counter-intuitive from the human perspective. From the perspective of a believer, it made sense.

For you are saved by grace through faith, and this is not from yourselves; it is God's gift—not from works, so that no one can boast. [Eph. 2:8-9]

God's gift. She had been given life, simply because God loved her. That was huge. And He not only loved her, but everyone else every bit as much. And that included Rance.

As Charly drove up, she saw Tom putting his mower away. "You just about let dark catch you."

"Days are getting a little shorter, but the grass sure isn't. To what do we owe the pleasure?" Tom put his arm around her shoulders and walked with her into the house.

"You, bro, are sweaty." She cringed in his embrace.

He grinned. "Yeah, I know."

She poked him in the ribs with her elbow.

"Ow!" Tom laughed as she wriggled from his hug.

She ran up the back steps to the door where Lucy was standing.

"Tom, are you harassing your sister?" She stayed behind the screen. "Hurry up so the mosquitoes can't get in."

They hustled through the doorway and let the door slam behind them. "It's a big brother's prerogative to harass his little sister. It's called payback."

"What did I ever do to you?"

Tom crossed his arms and stroked his chin, thinking. "Hmmm, let's see now, there was the rip on my Power Rangers poster."

"It was barely there. The tape was loose."

"Humph. I noticed it right away."

"You've got to be kidding me." Charly shook her head in disgust.

Lucy had walked out of the kitchen to check on a crying infant. She came back in, hands on her hips. "Thomas Sumter Livingston, are you still whining about your middle-school *Star Wars* poster?"

"It was Power Rangers, and I hadn't even gotten to my *Star Wars* action figure collection she constantly rearranged."

Charly laughed and then felt the tears coming. A surge of love for her family overtook her as she threw herself into Tom's arms. She needed a hug only a big brother could give.

"Hey, I'm not still mad, I was teasing." He hugged her, and Charly knew he was shrugging and looking over her shoulder at Lucy.

She pulled away and grabbed a paper towel to mop herself up, then started laughing. "I needed that."

"What?" Tom still looked confused.

"A text from my sister-in-law, and lighthearted teasing and a hug from my brother. Thank you." She blew her nose noisily and threw away the paper towel.

"Glad we could help." Lucy hugged her. "Now, are you okay? You seem a little out of sorts."

"Ya think?" Charly shook her head and smiled. "I've been better." She waved her hand. "I'll be fine."

"It's Rance, isn't it?"

Charly looked down at her toes then up at Lucy. "I'm not sure anymore."

Lucy looked at Tom and tilted her head.

"What?" Charly frowned and then shook her head. "I forgot you wanted me to come by. What's going on?"

"Well, I saw Rance this morning."

She felt her face warm and looked away. "Did you now?"

"Actually, I almost ran over him with my entourage." Lucy grinned. "He was coming around the same corner I was with the double stroller and Hayes, and we almost collided."

"Maybe you should have taken him out." Tom quirked an eyebrow at his sister and gave her a mock glare.

Charly simply looked up and shook her head. "Seriously. We broke up, but it doesn't mean I want you to 'off' him." She turned back to Lucy. "Did you talk to him?"

"I did, and he asked about you. He seemed a little preoccupied."

"I'm sure he is. Between his family situation and job-hunting, he's had a lot on his mind."

"And you."

"And me what?"

"He's had you on his mind as well." Lucy walked over to the coffee maker and held up the pot. "Want to sit a bit?"

Charly sighed. She knew it sounded juvenile, but it was that kind of day. "I could use a good, stiff cup of coffee."

"It's been sitting here most of the day, so I can vouch for its stiffness."

Charly settled into a kitchen chair and took the mug from Lucy. "Sugar?"

"Here you go." Lucy scooted the sugar bowl to her. She sat at the table across from her, Tom on the end between them.

"What did he have to say?"

"Well, after I told him we'd missed seeing him—"

"Lucy!"

"Well, I have. He's great with Hayes."

Charly covered her face with her hands. "The break-up was mutual, you know."

"I know, but I have a right to my opinion, but that's neither here nor there. I asked how the job hunt was going, and he told me he'd had interviews at Charleston and here in Georgetown in addition to the one in Nashville."

"Here? In Georgetown?" She shook her head. "Why here? I mean, for an internship it's fine, but it's small compared to the other places he had mentioned." Lucy shrugged. "We didn't get into that. What I wanted to tell you is that he's having surgery, and he wanted me to let you know."

"He's going through with it, isn't he?"

"The kidney donation? Yes. I asked if I could pray for him, and he said he would appreciate it, and then asked me to let you know."

Charly swallowed. He wanted her to know. "When is the surgery?"

"He didn't say specifically, only that it would be in a couple of weeks. He said the job situation was going to be put on hold until after recovery from surgery." Lucy twisted her lips in a gamin grin. "Hayes got in on the conversation then. He asked Rance if he was your boyfriend."

"He didn't."

"He did. Hey, if you want information, take a four-year-old along. They cut through the red tape in a hurry."

"I have to ask, what did he say?"

"He said he wasn't sure, but when he figured it out, he would let Hayes know. They shook on it."

"Oh well, then, since they shook on it . . ." Charly shook her head and smiled. "I'm torn."

Lucy nodded. "I know." She looked at her husband and put her hand over his larger one on the table. "It took me a while to get over thinking I could control everything around me, including this guy here. I finally had to give up the idea of 'us' and start over. We had to get acquainted all over again."

CHAPTER TWENTY-EIGHT

Morning weddings were wonderful. The Benningfield wedding festivities at Atalaya Castle inside Huntington Beach State Park were over by mid-afternoon, and everyone hurried the clean up so they could have more free time. Charly drove the short distance to the beach house around four-thirty.

She would love to sit on the beach for a while. She and Lydia could go to the beach then order pizza and watch a movie tonight. That would be fun. It had been a perfect day, lower humidity than usual, although further inland, without the stiff ocean breeze, it got hotter and hotter. Summer in South Carolina.

She unlocked the door to wonderful smells coming from the kitchen.

"Lydia, what is that amazing smell?"

"It is my famous lasagna."

"Since when do you have famous lasagna?" Charly laughed. Lydia wasn't known for her cooking. Art, yes, culinary arts, no.

"Since I got the recipe from Sarah Benton, who takes pity on girls who are late bloomers like her in the cooking category."

Lydia opened the oven to check the progress. "It'll be done in about twenty minutes, and then it'll have to rest for at least ten."

The spicy smell tickled her nose, in a good way. "Is this for us, or are you hosting a dinner party?"

"I'm hosting a dinner party, and you're invited."

"Who's coming?"

"Well, Jake, of course."

"Of course."

"And Matthew."

"Who's Matthew?" Something about the way Lydia wouldn't meet her eyes made her suspect this wasn't simply a dinner party.

"He's a friend of Jake's. He teaches in Myrtle Beach."

"And who else is coming?" She arched an eyebrow at her roommate.

"Nobody else." Lydia smiled brightly.

Charly melted into a barstool. "Lydia, is this a fix-up?"

"It's a dinner amongst friends, and who has enough friends?"

"I do."

"No, you don't. You've moped around here long enough. It's time to get out there and face the world again. You've done nothing but go to school and work all summer."

"I was going to go relax on the beach and thought maybe we could have a girls' night in." She knew she was whining. She was tired, both physically and emotionally.

Lydia waved her hand dismissively. "We've had too many girls' nights in, if you ask me. We'll have dinner and play a few games. No pressure."

"No, not for you."

"You'll be fine. Now go get changed and help me with the garlic bread and salad. They'll be here in about forty-five minutes."

"Fine. I'll be here, but I won't have fun." She got up from the stool and put her hands on her hips.

"Not with that attitude you won't." Lydia rolled her eyes as Charly flounced down the hallway to her room.

CHARLY FUMED as she changed clothes, throwing her dress and heels in the corner as if punishing them for being there. She couldn't believe Lydia would fix her up. It was too soon. And she wasn't sure if it was over with Rance. After talking to Lucy and Tom, she wondered.

She pulled on jeans and a brightly-colored top that could be construed as being cute, if she were of a mood to look "cute."

Oh, well. Like Lydia said, you can't have too many friends, and he is Jake's friend, so how bad could it be?

She slid on her sandals and fluffed her hair, putting on extra lipstick before leaving her room. Taking a deep breath, she looked at herself in the mirror one more time and nodded. She'd get through this, and she would be as pleasant and charming as humanly possible.

The sound of the oven door opening told her she had better get in there before Lydia dragged her to the kitchen. She made the turn into the kitchen and stopped when she looked at the dish her roomie had pulled out of the oven. It was a little lopsided but looked edible.

"You know, for somebody whose main contribution to food preparation up to now has been chocolate chip cookies and scrambled eggs, this looks pretty good."

"Thanks. I think." Lydia gave her a dirty look and then smiled when she saw she had freshened her makeup.

"Have you met this guy?" Charly pulled the salad fixings out of the crisper drawer of the refrigerator and put them on the counter.

Lydia took a salad bowl out of the cabinet and placed it on

the counter in front of Charly. "No, but Jake says he's nice. He goes to his church, and they've been friends for a long time."

"Hmmm. We'll see. I make no promises. If things go south, should we have a safe word?"

Lydia simply stared at her.

Charly turned her face toward the counter, her back to her friend.

"I mean, just in case. What if I can't stand him?"

"Surely you can break bread and socialize with a fellow human being for a few hours. It doesn't mean you're agreeing to marry the guy."

Charly twisted her mouth, trying not to laugh. "I mean, I love Jake, but I can't imagine dating him. I would get tired of laughing."

"Maybe he doesn't share Jake's love of puns and alliteration. Although I can think of worse things."

Salad done, Charly turned and leaned on the counter. "Lyd, I'm teasing you, in case you didn't know."

"As irritated as you were earlier, I figured you'd be pouty all evening."

"Have I been that bad?"

"At times."

"I'm sorry. I promise I'll be good tonight."

"Thank you, Lord." Lydia raised her hands Heavenward, and then arched an eyebrow. "And will you promise that if you like him and he asks you out, you'll at least consider it?"

"I'll consider it." She paused, wondering if she should tell Lydia what Lucy had told her the day before. She looked at the clock. Still another twenty minutes before the guys would be there. "I didn't tell you what I found out yesterday."

"About?"

"Rance."

Lydia sighed. "He would rear his ugly head, wouldn't he? Not that he's ugly, because he's absolutely—"

"Yes, he is, and that has nothing to do with it. Lucy saw him, and he asked her to tell me he's having surgery."

Lydia sobered. "The kidney donation?"

Charly nodded, tearing up a little. "I feel like I should get in contact with him, but I'm not sure."

"Is it a feeling or a nudge?" Lydia looked her straight in the eye.

"I'm not sure. The fact he made a point to tell Lucy makes me wonder. Maybe I'm supposed to get in touch with him."

"Then call him."

"What if I mess things up? We decided to cool things down, think things through, and he has my number."

"And it sounds like he's had a lot going on in the last few weeks. Keep that in mind."

Charly held up her hand. "I know. It's not all about me."

"It's not about any of us. We're simply along for the ride."

The doorbell made them both jump.

Lydia's eyes grew round and she jumped up and down. "They're here!"

Charly held up her pinky, and Lydia hooked hers around it. "Best behavior. Promise."

Lydia hugged her and started for the door. "Relax and have fun."

"Yes, ma'am."

CHARLY COULDN'T HELP but have a good time. It was irritating how much she had laughed since Jake and Matthew had arrived. She almost forgot she was supposed to be on best behavior.

During the game of Trivial Pursuit, she sat back at one point, watching the others. She was skilled in very limited areas of the game, but this guy? He was skilled in all of them. Lydia had insisted on couple versus couple, and Matthew was clearly winning the game for the two of them.

"I'm curious as to where you got all your information on mixed drinks, my friend." Lydia glared at her over the board.

"I read, and I watch television. For some reason, random useless information sticks, and the science and nature stuff doesn't." Charly chuckled.

"Well, thank you for winning us another piece of the pie. It might be what wins the game for us." Matthew, striking with his dark brown hair and brown eyes, grinned at his partner.

"Are you serious? You're the brains of this operation." She smiled at him and then looked at Lucy and Jake. "Speaking of pie…"

"Yes! We have pie. Who would like a piece?" Lydia popped up from her seat. "We can eat pie and drink coffee while we finish the game."

Jake stretched his long arm on the back of the couch. "Sounds good to me. Maybe caffeine and sugar will help us come back."

Lydia covered her mouth and mock-whispered to her partner. "We can only hope."

"I'll make the coffee, you cut the pie." Charly got up and followed Lydia to the kitchen.

"So . . ." Lydia pulled a knife and pie server from the drawer and reached up to remove four dessert plates from the cupboard.

"So what?" Charly was carefully measuring coffee beans into the grinder.

"What do you think about Matthew?" She leaned on the counter, waiting on cutting the pie while the coffee was brewing.

Over the loudness of the grinder, Charly mouthed, "He seems nice."

Lydia grinned. "And he's cute too."

"He is. I'm surprised Jake has such a normal friend." She

laughed. "No, really, he is nice, and cute, in a boy-next-door sort of way."

"Whatever. No, he doesn't have piercing blue eyes and a smile that would launch a thousand ships."

"The reference applies to a woman. Helen of Troy, I think?"

"See? You know stuff! Okay, a thousand Amazonian ships."

"Amazonia doesn't exist."

"No, the Amazonians lived in Themiscyra."

"Themis-what?" Charly stared at her for a second.

"Uh, have you heard of Wonder Woman?" Lydia gave her a look that brooked no argument.

Charly nodded. "Noted. He's a very nice-looking man, and any woman would be proud to have him by her side. But maybe I'm not any woman."

"Well, true. We'll have to wait and see, won't we? Maybe we could double date?"

"Like you said, we'll have to wait and see." Charly transferred the ground coffee beans into the coffee maker and started the coffee brewing. "Are you going to cut the perfect pie, or not?"

Lydia tilted her head and turned the plate, looking at it from various angles. "It's so pretty, I almost hate to."

"I know. You could always take a picture of it." She laughed when Lydia pulled her phone out of her pocket.

"Hey, it's for posterity."

"And Instagram."

Lydia nodded seriously. "And my mother."

As first date fix-ups went, it hadn't been half bad. Charly considered the difference in her evening with Matthew as opposed to her dates with Rance. It was easy. There wasn't anything hidden from her. He told her his parents had lived north of Myrtle Beach their whole lives, and his grandparents, still living, lived in the suburbs.

She was musing the evening before, still lying in bed and thinking her summer break would be over soon, when her phone rang. She looked at it and saw an unfamiliar Myrtle Beach cell number. Surely it wasn't Matthew already. She had Jake's number, unless they were together, and he needed something.

"Hello?" She was cautious. Most of the time if it was an unknown number, it was a telemarketer. She usually ignored them.

"Charly? This is Matthew. I didn't call too early, did I?"

A laugh bubbled up. "No, I was up." Well, it was partly true. She was at least fully awake, thank goodness.

"Good. I'm heading to a conference in Atlanta and had to leave early, so I've been up for hours."

"Sounds like fun. What kind of conference?"

"Technology. I know. Boring. I'm presenting a session, and there's equipment I want to check out, and the vendor is going to be there."

"I understand. Still, Atlanta is fun. Hope it goes well."

"Thanks. Hey, I was wondering if you had any plans for Saturday night? Would you like to go out? Unless you have a wedding to work. I heard you say you were working for a wedding planner?"

"I am, and no, I don't have a wedding this weekend, finally. After last weekend, we're getting a couple of weekends off. I think I'd like that."

"Great. Can I pick you up around seven? It should have cooled off by then."

"Sure. Let me know what I need to wear."

"Casual. I thought we'd go mini-golfing and grab a bite, if that sounds okay to you?"

"Sounds like fun. Would you like me to meet you? Save you the drive down?"

"No, I thought I'd like to try Runaway Bay there in Murrells Inlet."

"You do realize I'll have the home course advantage."

"Ah. Well, I'm a champ at my own course. I think I'll be ready."

"We'll see."

"Yeah, well, I'd better go. My cell reception is getting spotty."

"Good luck with your session and have fun."

"I'll try." He laughed. "See you Saturday."

"See ya."

Charly stared at the phone as the call ended from his end. Matthew was fun, but she didn't know if she was ready for a new relationship. She didn't know if she was done with the old one yet.

CHAPTER TWENTY-NINE

Lydia was more excited about the date than Charly. When Matthew picked her up, she was the one jumping at the sound of the doorbell.

"Chill, Lyd. I've got this."

"I know. I want this to be a successful fix-up." Lydia twisted her lips a little when Jake guffawed from the living room. "I'm making this about me, aren't I?"

"A little bit. We'll have a good time. I have no doubt. I'm not looking for a husband, simply a nice outing. Got it?" She stared at her best friend, hoping the message got through.

"Got it."

The pinky-swear sealed the deal.

Charly let Matthew in and was impressed by his casual yet stylish attire. She had chosen her outfit carefully, too, knowing that playing mini-golf, even in the evening, you got hot.

"Hi, Charly. Oh, hey, Jake, Lydia."

Okay, so he was as nervous as Lydia. Why was she the only one not nervous?

"I'm ready. Let me get my purse, and we can be on our way."

He rubbed his hands together. "I've made reservations for supper at Bisqit there by the Hammock Shop."

"Wonderful! I love the place, and I won't feel underdressed." She put her purse on her shoulder. "I'm ready and hungry."

"Good. See you later, Lydia."

"Jake and I may not be here when you get back. I think we're going to try to catch a movie up the road."

"I thought you didn't like movie dates."

"I don't like movie first dates. When you're not sure you want a stranger to put his arm around you, it's not fun, but when you've decided you definitely want said stranger to put his arm around you, it's lots of fun." Lydia's face turned pink as Jake walked over and looped his arm around her shoulders.

"I agree. Let's get out of here before we miss the previews." Jake hugged her to him for a second and then went to the door, opening it for everyone. "I hope they have the preview for the new *Star Wars* movie."

"Hmmm. They may preview the new Nicolas Sparks movie too."

"Bite your tongue, woman." Jake looked at her in horror.

Lydia giggled. "Just kidding. You kids have fun."

"Thanks, you too."

Matthew opened Charly's door for her, and as he went around the front of the car, she looked around at the late-model Ford sedan. It was a top-of-the-line Fusion, with leather interior. It was very nice, but she couldn't help comparing it to Rance's Jaguar.

When they turned south on Highway 17, Charly turned toward him. "You know, I don't remember asking what you teach?"

"Jake and Lydia kind of maintained the conversation the other night." He laughed. "That's one reason I like to hang out with Jake. I don't feel the need to contribute as much to the conversation."

"I know what you mean. Lydia has always been the one who pushed or pulled me into things, including conversations. She has no mercy."

"Oh, and I teach high school biology and chemistry." He turned to her with a smile.

"This explains so much. No wonder you're a whiz at Trivial Pursuit. The very areas I stink at are the ones you have a degree in." She shook her head with a smile. "Did you always want to teach?"

He paused, looking pensive. "No, originally I wanted to be a doctor."

The information hit her straight in the gut. Great. Another one. "What changed your mind?"

He grinned slightly. "Undergrad clinicals. I found out I don't have the personality for it."

"Seriously? I would go to a doctor like you. Talkative doctors are annoying to quiet people, like me."

"True. I've thought about going back, after I've saved up money for grad school, but it hasn't happened. In the meantime, I found out I love kids. Amazingly, I can be a clown in front of a group of kids, when I clam up like—"

"A clam?" Charly laughed.

"Exactly. See? I get tongue-tied one on one."

"Excuses, excuses."

"Yeah. I've been teaching three years now, and I love it."

"Then that's what you should do. I love it too. Originally, I wanted to be in broadcast journalism."

"Well, you have the looks for it."

"Thank you, kind sir. I decided I didn't want to live that kind of life." She shrugged. "Then my mom went blind, and I knew I was interested in helping people with disabilities. It became my passion."

They drove into the area of little shops that make up Pawley's Island Hammock Shoppes and found a parking spot. One of these days she would definitely buy one of the handmade hammocks they sold there. They were amazing. Tonight, their destination was Bisqit.

Their order in, they found a table on the outside screened-in eating area.

"I love this place." Charly sipped on her RC cola and nodded toward his glass bottle. "I've never tried Mexican Coke. What's different about it?"

"I like it. The scientific answer is that it's made with cane sugar instead of corn syrup. The foodie answer is that it has a hint of root beer flavor I like."

"Forget it. I can't stand root beer. Or regular beer either."

He smiled. "Don't develop a taste for it then. Unfortunately, I liked it too much during college."

She looked at him over her straw then set her bottle down and crossed her arms on the table. "I guess everyone has their vice."

"I can't imagine you have much of one."

She smiled then sobered. It was so easy to fool people. "You'd be surprised."

"One of those hidden ones, huh? I get it. I hid alcoholism for a long time, until I found myself walking to class with beer in my water bottle at eight in the morning."

"Really?" She stared at him.

"Not something I'm proud of. It lost me my scholarship and the confidence to go to medical school."

"Wow. I had no idea." She pondered this as she traced the letters on the dewy bottle on the table. "I was always the 'good girl' who never got in trouble, but I've always struggled with feeling like I was an imposter, you know?"

"I know."

Their food came and with it a flurry of excitement. Charly's

Lobster BLT and Matthew's American Beauty Burger brought with them smells that would dismantle the strictest of diets.

The waitress stood back, checking their order before she left. "Can I get you anything else? More to drink?"

"I think we're doing great, thank you." Matthew smiled and winked at Charly.

"Definitely. This looks amazing." Charly was waiting for her to leave so she could dig in.

"The Lobster BLT is my favorite. You won't be disappointed."

"I know. I've had it before and love it."

"Locals, then?"

"Yes, up the road at Murrells Inlet, and he's from Myrtle Beach."

"Good deal. Listen, if you need anything, holler. My name is Wendy."

She smiled and walked away.

Matthew held out his hand. "Can we say a quick blessing?"

"Yes, because I'm starving, and this smells so good." She took his hand lightly and bowed her head as he prayed.

"Lord, thank you for this food you've provided, and for the company of Charly. Bless us, keep us safe, and help us to be a light for others to see You."

Charly looked up. "Thank you." She felt a lump in her throat. It had been a long time since she prayed on a date. She took a sip of RC and then picked up her sandwich.

"How did your session go, at the conference?"

He laughed. "It was fine. They gave me half a ballroom, and I had about ten people come to the session. The few who were there seemed to enjoy it." He took a bite and savored it. "Oh, and I got to see the vendor I wanted to talk to about lab technology. He's supposed to contact my principal next week, so here's hoping."

"I'm glad it was worthwhile. Nothing worse than going to a

big, expensive conference and not getting the info you need or can use."

Halfway through the first half of her sandwich, she felt a touch on her shoulder, and she looked up.

Rance.

"Um, hi, Rance."

"Hi, Charly. How have you been?"

"I'm fine. Matthew, this is Rance Butler. Rance, Matthew Graves."

Matthew stood and shook hands with Rance, nodding cordially.

"Lucy said she saw you a few days ago."

"Yes, she nearly mowed me down with the twins, but I lived to tell the tale." His charming half-smile threatened to undo her.

"When will the surgery be?"

"In about two weeks, unless they move it up. It'll depend on the condition of my father. He's getting weaker."

"I'm sorry."

"I've almost called you several times, to tell you." He glanced over at Matthew, then at her, his jaw working. "I know you've been busy. With your class and all."

Was he jealous? She looked up at him, her mouth set. "I have been busy. Class is over, and now I'm getting ready for school to start."

"Right." Rance cleared his throat. "I won't keep you. I wanted to say hello." His phone buzzed in his pocket, and he pulled it out. She thought he paled a little when he read what was on the screen. He closed it, put his phone away, then glanced at Matthew again and smiled. "Have a good evening." He looked back at Charly, and she could see the lines of worry around his eyes.

When he walked away, she closed her eyes for a second to close out the rest of the world. It must have been longer than she thought because she felt a touch on her hand and heard a concerned voice saying, "Are you okay?"

She opened her eyes. "I'm fine. When does your school start?"

RANCE GOT out of his car, grabbed his gear, and ran into the hospital at a dead run.

Plans had changed. The timetable for the transplant had been moved up to now.

Rance could tell his heart rate was up, but it was from the text, not the run from the parking lot. He reached the surgical wing in time to see the doors swing open. "What's going on?"

"Your father has been having chest pains, and the dialysis has had to be upped to every day. He can't wait any longer." Dr. Hobgood was dressing in his surgical gown. He glanced up at Rance while tying his scrubs. "How long since your last meal?"

"Lunch. I was about to get supper when you sent me the message."

"Good. Any meds, alcohol, I need to know about?"

"Not recently."

"Even better." He looked up at the surgical nurse coming through the door. "Pam, take Rance and get him prepped for surgery."

"Yes, doctor. Mr. Watson is already in the prep room."

"Can I see my dad before the surgery?"

Pam looked at Dr. Hobgood, who nodded, then said, "Follow me."

He wound through the corridors into a surgical prep room where nurses and the anesthesiologist were working on his father. Clifton's eyes lit up when he saw Rance.

"Son, I'm sorry they had to move it up."

"Hey, don't worry about me. I'll be up and around when it comes time to pick up Sam."

"Maybe we can both pick him up."

Rance gave him a big smile. "That would be optimal." He took his father's hand and squeezed it. "You'll do great. I know it."

Clifton pointed up. "It's all Him now." He gazed into his son's eyes. "What about you? Do you know Him? Do you know what He did for you?"

Rance looked down for a moment and then up at his father. "Yes sir, I do."

"When?"

Rance smiled, a little embarrassed he hadn't told anyone. "A few days after I got home from Nashville. I went to see Sam that day, and on the way out, Tom Livingston was coming in, and we talked. He told me I was making it too hard. Took me a little more time to settle it, but it's settled."

"Trusting God is the easiest, and the hardest, thing you'll ever do, Son."

"I agree. I've been working through stuff and seeing a lot of things come together."

"Have you seen Charly?"

Rance sobered, looking down. Clifton squeezed his hand. "I saw her before I came."

"Have you told her you're a Christ follower?"

He shook his head. "Not yet. She was on a date, so I didn't get to talk to her."

"I'm sorry." Clifton narrowed his eyes in sympathy. "You're gonna have to settle things with her, Son. I can tell you have pretty strong feelings for her."

He let out a humorless laugh. "Strong feelings don't begin to describe it. I want to get this family situation settled before I start thinking long-term."

"She might be the key to helping you figure things out."

Pam opened the curtain. "Dr. Butler, we need to get you prepped, and the anesthesiologist needs to start getting Mr. Watson off to sleepy town." She grinned when Clifton laughed.

"Best part of surgery. Free nap." He held his arms out, and Rance hugged him. "Get going. Pray. It's the only thing you can do right now, and we'll both have plenty of time to do it."

"I will. Thanks, Dad."

Clifton grinned. "That's the first time you've called me Dad."

Rance noticed the mist of tears in his father's eyes. "Won't be the last, I promise." He winked at his dad and then followed Nurse Pam to a nearby cubicle.

WHAT HAD STARTED out as a great evening with Matthew had turned to dust, at least inwardly, after the encounter with Rance.

"I can't believe I got the hole-in-one prize." Charly smiled at Matthew as he handed her the teddy bear and coupon for a free game.

"You're good."

"I did grow up on the Grand Strand, after all." Charly hugged the teddy bear.

"As did I. With fifty mini golf courses in twenty miles, there always seemed to be a new one to try." He opened her car door for her. "Fun fact. Did you know they have pro mini golf players? The Master's Tournament was at Hawaiian Rumble and Aloha Mini Golf in Myrtle Beach this year."

"I was aware. I had friends who played in the charity tournament one year. It was pretty cool to watch. One of the courses actually has bleachers outside the fence so you can watch." She grinned. "Someday maybe I'll get a team together and play."

"Sounds like fun." He looked at her as she fiddled with the bear. "Is everything okay?"

She looked up in surprise. "Of course. Why wouldn't it be?" Had she dropped her guard? Let him see she was bothered?

"You've been a little, I don't know, quiet since supper." He pulled out of the parking lot and headed toward her house.

"Long week." She smiled brightly. She hoped he would accept her explanation.

"I get that." When they pulled into the drive of the house, he turned toward her. "I had a great time tonight, but I have a feeling you're torn."

Jake must have told him about Rance. Not all the details, just that she was between relationships. Or was she?

"It's a little confusing right now. I had a great time, too, and I'm sorry if I was a little 'off' after seeing Rance. We met when the twins were born and dated for a little while. Some things happened, and we decided to cool it." She shrugged. "That's all."

It wasn't all, but it was all she was willing to share.

RANCE HEARD CLICKING and clanking sounds and muffled voices. It was as if only one layer of sound came through at a time, and from a distance. By the time he realized what was going on, he had opened his eyes to see a nurse hovering, talking to him.

"Mr. Butler, can you hear me?"

His mouth felt like there had been cotton in it. Probably because up until a few minutes ago, there had been a tube down his throat.

"I can hear you. Is the surgery over?"

"It is, and you did fine." Nurse Pam was covering him with more blankets, preparing him for the trip to recovery.

"How's my dad?"

"Mr. Watson? He's doing admirably as well. His surgery is taking a little longer, as expected. He's a trooper."

He cleared his throat to get some sense of normalcy back. "When can I see him?"

"We'll put you in adjoining cubicles in recovery 'til we take him to ICU. How's that for service?" She chuckled as she checked the monitors before she unhooked them for the trip down the hall. "I'll be moving you in a minute."

"Thanks, Pam."

She left to go into the next operating room, probably where his father was still in surgery.

Before he drifted off again, he prayed. "Be with my dad, God. He loves You, and I know You love him."

CHAPTER THIRTY

Charly didn't always check the news on a Monday morning. There was a story on Facebook that she clicked through, leading her to the online presence of the South Strand News. The first headline caught her attention immediately.

"Local Businessman Clifton Watson on the Mend"

"Lydia, come here."

Her roommate came out of the bathroom, half-dressed and with a toothbrush sticking out of her mouth.

"Wat?" The toothbrush impeded her speech.

"Look at this."

Lydia ran to the sink to spit and rinse then came back, toothbrush in hand. "Who's Clifton Watson?"

Charly looked up at her friend. "Rance's biological father."

Lydia's eyes widened. "He had the surgery."

"He told me it was going to be in three weeks unless his dad worsened."

"Wow. That's big." Lydia looked at Charly intensely. "Does it say where it happened?"

"Georgetown General, which surprises me. I would think

anyone with his connections would be in Charleston or somewhere even bigger."

"Unless the doctor he likes is here." Lydia shrugged.

"True. When I saw Rance the other night, he got a text while we were talking. I wonder . . . ." Charly took a deep breath. "He seemed out of sorts and hurried away."

Lydia read the article over Charly's shoulder. "It says here it was an emergency surgery, and the donor had agreed to waive the waiting time and have it done immediately. Doesn't mention a name though."

"It's Rance." Charly closed her eyes. "I need to find out if he's okay."

"I know."

"I'm not saying there is anything between us, but I do care about him as a friend." Charly felt the heat on her face even as she tried to convince herself more than Lydia.

"Right." Lydia arched an eyebrow and said nothing more. She walked away and went back to prepare for her work day.

She read the article again, reading also the background material they wrote about Clifton Watson. It was a name she had heard of as a lifelong resident of the county, not anyone with which she ever thought to have any connection. And this was Rance's father.

Lydia came back to her, fully dressed in her distressed jeans and coffee shop uniform top. "I can check on him for you, if you'd like."

She looked up at her and saw her smock in her hand. "Thanks, Lyd."

Should she go and see him? Or not. She wasn't sure how it worked with transplant surgeries. Was the donor in as much danger as the one receiving the organ?

"Gotta go."

"Right. Have a good day."

"You, too, and don't worry. I'm sure he's fine." She gathered her purse and keys, ready to go out the door. She stopped and turned back to Charly. "Listen, I know Rance is uppermost in your mind right now, but don't lead Matthew on."

"I wouldn't dream of it. We had a nice time, and even he knew I wasn't over Rance."

"He's been hurt too. Just wanted to give you a heads up."

"He didn't say anything." She paused. "It was our first date, and how many people spill their guts on a first date? I know I didn't."

"Exactly. Be careful, for both your sakes. He's too nice a guy to get involved if you're not interested." She walked to the door. "I'll be home to change. Jake and I are going to the beach this afternoon. Wanna come?"

"No, I'm meeting with Emma and Lucy at two, so I'll probably miss you. You two have fun."

"You too. I'll text you if I find anything out."

Charly walked over and hugged her. "Thank you. And thank you for being the voice of reason. Would you believe Rance called me his voice of reason?" She laughed.

Lydia looked at her soberly. "Most of the time, you are. This is different, isn't it?"

Charly nodded. "Is it normal to be so out of sorts?"

Lydia smiled. "It is when you're in love."

"Mom, I'm fine."

Rance wished he hadn't left his mother on his next-of-kin list. If he had changed it, she might not be hovering over him like she had been since the surgery was over.

Anna Butler took a step back and waited until he rose from the bed unaided. "I'm only trying to help. They said you might be shaky for a week or so."

"I've got to get used to doing things on my own. I don't mind you being here, but you need to let me do this." The pain in his left side almost took his breath away, but he wasn't going to admit it. He also wasn't going to admit to the slight vertigo he experienced when he first stood up.

She simply watched as he stood quietly, slowly stretching the muscles that weren't used to being in bed. Maybe if he showed her he was fine, she would leave him alone for a while.

"I need to go and check on Dad." He watched her as he called Clifton Watson Dad. She flinched. It wasn't his intention to hurt her, but even as a new child of God, he wondered how she could have kept his own father from him.

"I'll go with you." She turned and pulled a tissue from the box next to the hospital bed, dabbed her eyes, and blew her nose.

"I'm sorry, Mom." He sat down on the side of the bed. His emotions had been all over the place since the surgery, and he knew it was to be expected.

How did God make people to be so complicated? He was told he would experience a sense of loss and have days of being blue. How do you feel a loss of a body part you spent zero time considering on a daily basis?

Rance reached for his mother's hand, and she came to him. "I guess I'm a bad patient. You know they say doctors make the worst ones."

She smiled. The first genuine smile he'd seen from her since all this started.

"You never were a good patient, even before you were a doctor."

"True, that." He winked at her and grinned. "Let's go see how he is. Does it bother you for me to call him Dad?"

"A little. I'll try to get used to it." They walked to the door, and she paused, her hand on his arm. "What about Ashton? He raised you, and you've considered him your father all your life."

"I'm still working on it, Mom. I love him. He's the only dad I ever knew, but there was always a distance between us I couldn't understand."

She looked down. "I know. I felt it. I think it was the real reason why I was afraid to give him a child of his own. I was afraid of the difference he would make, even unintentionally."

He nodded. "I get it. At least now, I do." He shrugged. "I guess, for now I have two men I call Dad."

She grinned. "I can't think of two men I'd rather you call by that name. Clifton is different now. I can see it."

"I'm glad."

"I didn't tell you, but I saw Sam last week, right before your surgery."

This was unexpected. She had been so fearful for so long and now she was definitely stepping out of her comfort zone. "How did it go?"

"It was awkward, at first. I wouldn't let Ashton come in with me."

Rance snorted. "Good call."

She looked at him over her glasses. "We talked. He told me he forgave me a long time ago." She wiped her nose again. "I was thankful, but it still hurt. I asked him, what kind of mother did such a thing to her son?"

He put his arm around her shoulder. "What did he say?"

"He said, a mother who was desperate and who didn't know God." She blew her nose, then straightened her spine and took a deep breath. "Then he told me about his experience there in prison, and with Tom Livingston. I never knew about his part with the girl who died in the car accident."

Rance nodded. "He told me."

"I've hidden my head in the sand too long. Starting now, or rather starting last week, no more secrets. Deal?"

He smiled. "Deal. Now can I have a real hug? But not on my left side."

"Noted." Anna hugged her son with genuine love and confidence.

GOOD GRIEF. How could a guy recovering from surgery look so good? Lydia was surprised to see Rance show up in her line at the hospital coffee shop, Cafe George.

"Rance! How are you?" Lydia knew she was turning red on Charly's behalf, but that's what you do when you need to interrogate your best friend's ex-boyfriend.

"I'm doing well, and they tell me I can have coffee now. Can I get my usual?" He smiled and looked a little nervous. As well he should.

"Double shot espresso on ice, with a shot of syrup?"

He pointed to her and said, "Bingo. By the way, how's Charly?"

She twisted her lips and paused. "She's okay." She looked up into his eyes after giving him his change. "Worried about you."

His eyes brightened. "Is she?" He coughed and looked back at the lobby where his mother was waiting. "Tell her I'm okay."

"Tell her yourself. You have her number." These kids were going to have to figure stuff out, because she was done being the matchmaker and intermediary to relationships.

He paused. "I will. Thanks, Lydia."

"You're welcome." He started to walk away, but she stopped him with her voice. "How is Mr. Watson?"

"He's recovering well. They expect to move him to a regular room today, and I'm supposed to go home tomorrow."

She tilted her head, hoping to soften what she had said earlier. "I've been praying for you guys."

He gave her his killer smile. "Thanks. We need it."

She nodded and watched as he went to the next counter to pick up his drink, then smiled brightly at her next customer.

When there was a small lull, she looked up to see the one customer she always wanted to see.

"Jake, what are you doing here?" There was no doubt she was red-faced this time.

"Came to check up on a certain purple-haired pixie, only to find her talking to this good-looking patient."

She waved her hand in dismissal. "It was just Rance."

"Rance? *The* Rance? Ra-ance?" He dragged the name out dramatically, in whisper-mode.

"Shh. Somebody will hear you. He's been here for three years, and people know him."

"Humph. When do you get a break?"

She looked over at her shift manager, who nodded. "Right now, mister. What can I get you?"

He gave her his order, and while the barista was making his white chocolate caramel macchiato, she made her own mocha with extra espresso, then carried both with her to a table in the lobby, secluded by a couple of planters full of palms.

"I feel like we're having a secret rendezvous or something." She settled into her seat and took the lid off her mocha to let it cool down.

"No, just trying to get out of the fray." He took a sip of his drink. "This is great." He took another sip then blew on it and stirred it with a spoon. "So, that was Rance."

"That was Rance."

"What did you find out?"

"He's doing fine, his father is doing fine, and I basically told him if he wanted Charly to know he was fine, he would have to contact her himself."

"Harsh."

She frowned. "I know. I lightened it up by telling him I'd been praying for them."

Jake laughed. "Did you tell him you'd been praying he'd get his act together and make up with your best friend?"

"Not exactly. That would be rude." She took a sip of cooled mocha and sighed with pleasure. "This is so good, if I say so myself. How was your morning?"

"Good. I had a meeting at the high school with the new special ed director. I guess Charly will have the same meeting tomorrow."

"Probably. She's meeting with Emma and Lucy this afternoon. Wedding stuff, I assume."

"I talked to Matt this morning." Jake swirled his cup to mix the contents of the bottom.

Lydia leaned toward him across the table. "Did he say anything about the date?"

"Only that they had a good time, but Charly wasn't ready for another relationship, if she was even done with the last one."

"I thought so. Is he okay?"

"I think so. You know Matt. He's pretty low-key."

Lydia grinned. "You're trying to say, 'unlike us,' aren't you?"

He laughed. "Actually, I feel like since I met you, I've been more low-key."

"It's because you can't compete with my effervescence."

"Oh?" He raised his eyebrows and leaned toward her, his tall frame having no trouble meeting her in the middle, settling a lingering kiss on her lips. "If you say so."

She smiled and put her chin in her hand, eyeing him closely. "I'll say it again if you'll do that again."

"I'VE ALWAYS HEARD it was better to give than receive. The way I feel right now, I think I got the best end of the deal." Clifton laughed as Rance and Anna came to his bedside. "How are you feeling?

"I'm doing great. Still a few twinges." More than a few, but he would get over it. "What about you?"

"Things are starting to work. Actually, started as soon as the surgery was over to hear the doctor brag about it."

"Clifton, I'm so glad." Anna put her hands on the side rail of the hospital bed, and Clifton put his hand on hers.

"Thanks, Anna. I appreciate you being here with Rance." He grinned sheepishly. "If I hadn't messed up years ago, you'd have been seeing after both of us."

"We both messed up, so hush about that. It's a new day."

"It surely is."

Rance looked at his parents. What would their lives have been like? If the things that seemed so bad hadn't happened, would they have found God? The thought astounded him. He supposed there was a reason for all they'd gone through.

"Hey, when are they going to get you out of ICU?" Rance decided they needed to refocus.

"This afternoon, hopefully. Hobgood said there was a bed opening up, and as soon as they had it ready, they'd move me to the fourth floor."

"Good. That's where I am. They're planning to send me home tomorrow. You might be my new roomie. The guy in the second bed is getting ready to go home."

"I hope so. Have you been walking much?" Clifton looked concerned.

"Yeah, up and down the hall. This has been my longest trip. It's getting in and out of bed that gets me, and I have a feeling I'll have a backache until I can get a little real rest in my own bed." Rance grinned. "Mom says I'm a bad patient."

"If they move me in with you tonight, we'll show her what a double-dose of bad patient looks like."

Anna laughed, and looked more relaxed than she had in a long time. "I think I can handle it." She sobered then looked at Clifton. "I saw Sam last week. We had a good visit."

"I'm glad. He called me this morning and told me he'd seen

you. There's a lot of forgiveness needs to be done in this family. I hope we can hang on to it."

"I think we can, Dad."

Clifton smiled tenderly at his son. "I appreciate it, Son. I've had a lot of time to pray, and a lot of that prayer has been for you."

"I don't think you're the only one."

"Have you talked to your young lady yet?"

"Young lady? Why am I the last to know everything?" Anna swatted Rance's arm gently.

He flinched. "Watch the left side, Mom."

"That was your right arm. Now what young lady?"

He sighed. "Charlotte Livingston. And no, I haven't talked to her."

Clifton shook his head. "No time like the present. We're not promised tomorrow, you know."

"I know."

Anna pondered. "Livingston. I used to know some Livingstons. North Litchfield Beach area?"

"Yes. Her dad, Hayden, is dead, and her mother is Mary Ann Livingston. Did you know them?" He was still getting used to the fact that his mother knew people up here.

Recognition dawned on Anna's face. "Slightly. They were a little older than me, but we were in school at the same time. Mary Ann was the president of the Future Homemakers of America her senior year, and I was a freshman. She seemed nice. She got engaged to Hayden Livingston at their senior prom, I believe."

"She's still a great lady. Her daughter takes after her."

"Then she's a beauty." She smiled tenderly at her son. "I'm sorry things have been so crazy I didn't even know you'd been seeing someone. It's been a while since you have, hasn't it?"

"I've been too busy."

"No, you hadn't met the right girl."

"Your mother's right." Clifton spoke up. "When you find the right girl, don't mess it up like I did. Don't let her go, and don't neglect her. That's the kiss of death to a relationship."

Rance smiled. "Thank for the parental advice."

Anna and Clifton smiled at one another and reddened slightly.

"It's been a long time coming."

CHAPTER THIRTY-ONE

September

"October is looking like a busy month. I hope hurricane season holds off." Lucy sighed as she looked at the calendar, and the list of clients who had booked them for the upcoming fall months.

Emma nodded. "We need to hire extra help. You are somewhat hindered by the fact you now have not one, but three children to look after."

Charly spoke up. "I've already decided I'm not taking any classes this semester. They would have started last week. I'm two classes shy of my master's, and I've decided I don't have to rush it." Charly had the calendar app on her phone up.

"Who are you, and what have you done with my sister-in-law?" Lucy stared at her. "I thought you were on track to get the fastest master's degree on record?"

Charly laughed. "I've started listening to my mother." She cut her eyes at Lucy. "Don't you dare tell. If you do, I'll never hear the end of it."

Lucy nodded. "Noted. Are you saying you'd like to keep working weddings when you can?"

She arched a brow. "I don't seem to have anything else going on, so yes, I'd love to. This way maybe I can save up and pay cash for my classes."

Emma had been quiet during the exchange. She was beginning to need a little more time off, and she didn't quite know how to approach it, business-wise. "Charly, that would be perfect. You're so good with the clients and can easily take my place when I have to be two places at once, or if I have to be out."

"I wouldn't go that far, but it's fun, and I get to try things out with other people I might want to try someday." Charly wrinkled her nose. "Although right now it's looking like I have plenty of time to experiment."

Emma smiled. "It can happen fast."

"I'll say." Lucy put her chin in her hand and leaned her elbow on the table. "So, how are things in your love life, Emma Quince? I've seen almost as much of Rafe Jernigan as I have of you." Lucy waggled her eyebrows comically.

Emma felt heat rush to her face. That redhead complexion. "It's going well. Sophie likes him."

"What about Emma?" Lucy wasn't going to let it go.

"Emma likes him too."

"A lot, if your face is any indication."

Emma put her hands to her face to hide her blush and her smile. She felt a laugh bubble up. "I'm giddy as a schoolgirl."

Lucy and Charly laughed out loud. Lucy finally stopped laughing and said, "Finally!"

"Honestly, I never thought I'd feel this way again. And it was such happenstance we even met."

"No such thing." Lucy shook her head.

"I know. God's in control. It was so random." Emma wiped the tears from her eyes that had come with the bout of laughter.

"You know, now that I think about it, maybe it wasn't random. When you had the twins, it started making me think about how Sophie hadn't had a father influence in her life and hadn't had any brothers or sisters. All of it made me wonder, even at forty, if maybe . . ."

"Maybe you weren't only here to fulfill other people's dreams after all?" Lucy grasped her friend's hand. "Girl, it's not over 'til it's over, and you have so much to give. I'll admit, the first time I met Rafe, five years ago, he scared me a little. He's certainly a different man than the one Sarah met the summer she came to South Carolina."

"He is. At first, I thought I was attracted to him because he knew Daniel. I thought it would be nice for Sophie, and for me, too, to be around someone who could talk to us about the things they had experienced together, but you know, the more I know him, the less Daniel comes up. Sophie asks questions because she has no memories of her dad except in snapshots and home movies, and I'm enjoying getting to know Rafe as himself, not Daniel's friend." Emma shrugged her shoulders and smiled. "He told me the other night he thought he was falling in love with me."

"Get out of town." Lucy's mouth hung open.

"Are you serious?" Charly sat up straight. "What did you say?"

Emma paused. "I told him I thought I might be falling in love with him too."

"CAN I GET YOU ANYTHING, Rance? Tea? Maybe cookies?"

"I'm fine, Mom. I think I'll go upstairs and take a little nap." Rance had been stuck here at his parents' house for two weeks, the length of time before the doctor would consider letting him drive. He was getting stir-crazy. Funny, a year ago he would have been annoyed because she seemed so nervous all the time. Now it was cabin fever.

"Are you sure you're okay? Do you feel feverish?"

"No, Mom. I'm tired and need a little time to myself."

She shook her head and grinned. "I know. You're a big boy, and I'm hovering."

He grinned at her and winked. "You got it. I'm tired. Tomorrow's a big day."

"I'm not sure if you're ready to drive or not." She frowned.

"We'll see what Dr. Hobgood says. If I can drive, I can pick Sam up next week."

"If not, I'll take you." She looked down. "I had a good visit with him the other day. He filled in a lot of blanks for me. I wish I could get over the guilt that wells up from time to time."

"I know. Sam has forgiven you, I have, and Clifton has."

"I think Ashton still has a way to go." Anna wiped a tear from her cheek. "I'm trying. I do love him, Rance. So much."

"I know you do. And he loves you. It's all been a lot to take in. You keep a secret like this so long, and it feels wrong for it to be out in the open. Am I right?"

"You are." She gave him a half-smile. "You go on up and rest. I'll get supper started."

He walked over to his mom and hugged her. "God's got this."

She returned his hug and kissed his cheek. "Love you, Son."

"Love you, too, Mom."

As he walked up the carpeted stairs, barely feeling the twinge that had been a full-on ache a few days before, he thought about the change in his family over the last two weeks.

Charly.

He wanted to talk to her. It had been nagging at him ever since he saw her last. Today he hadn't been able to get her off his mind.

He pulled out his phone and pulled up her name and the

picture that accompanied it. Her clear, hazel eyes, her long blonde hair, and a prim smile on her face that looked both happy and pensive at the same time. She'd been battling things too. He wanted to battle them with her.

As soon as he got to his bedroom, he closed the door, sat cross-legged on the bed, and pushed the call button. He could text, but it wasn't enough. He needed to hear her voice. He needed her to hear his and not in a drunken state.

THE MEETING with Emma and Lucy was breaking up when Charly's phone began to ring. Since it was on the table, Rance's picture came up for all to see. She looked down, and when she saw who it was, she froze.

"Aren't you going to answer it?" Lucy looked at her, her eyes round with anticipation.

"I . . . yes." She swiped the window to answer the phone and walked out of the room, through the front of the shop, and into the parking lot. "Rance?" She got in her car, started it, and rolled down the windows.

"Hi, Charly. Did I catch you at a bad time?" He sounded subdued. Kidney removal surgery would do that to one.

"No, I was finishing up a meeting with Lucy and Emma." She swallowed. "How are you?"

"I'm good. I have an appointment with the doctor tomorrow, and I'm hoping to get my freedom back."

"What kind of freedom?"

"My car. I haven't been able to drive for two weeks." He chuckled.

"That's rough."

"I feel like I'm back in middle school, living with my parents."

"How's . . . Mr. Watson?"

"My dad? He's doing great. He went home a few days ago. He was so weak before he had the surgery they had to build him up before they would let him out of the hospital. He's recovering nicely."

"I'm glad. I guess things have been . . . strange."

"Yes and no. We've actually been able to work through most of the family stuff." Rance paused long enough that she wondered if the call had been dropped. "Charly, I want to see you. We need to talk."

She closed her eyes. She had prayed. Oh, how she had prayed, for him to call. She had tested God. She had prayed that if God wanted them together, she would have a dream they had reunited. She had the dream and then wondered, since she knew something about how dreams worked, if it hadn't happened simply because she had been thinking about him. She didn't know what to say.

"Listen, if I get the all-clear to drive tomorrow, can I see you after school?"

She grimaced. She was helping Sarah with their children's choir musical from four until time for prayer meeting at six, and then choir practice.

"I can't." This was so frustrating.

Nothing. "I understand."

He thought she didn't want to see him. She rushed her answer. "No, you don't. I have children's choir, then prayer meeting, then choir practice, and I'm tied up from about four o'clock to nearly eight o'clock."

"Okay, then I'll come to prayer meeting, and then I'll go wait at your house while you're at choir practice. Please?"

"Are you sure? We can plan for Thursday."

"No, I've already wasted enough time. Like Dad says, we're not promised tomorrow, so we're pushing it as it is."

She could tell he was smiling. His voice sounded different when he did, and it made her smile. "Then tomorrow it is."

"Thanks, Charly."

"I'm glad you called."

"Me too."

Charly watched as the red button went gray when Rance ended the call on his end. He wanted to see her. She felt her lips curl up in a smile she couldn't pull down, and a tune bubbled up from somewhere deep inside. *Amazing grace, how sweet the sound . . .*

CHAPTER THIRTY-TWO

"Young man, you've apparently done everything I've told you to do, or you've had an extra-special nurse for the last week and a half." Dr. Hobgood looked at his chart and then back at him, over his reading glasses. "I suppose you want me to tell you that you can drive and do all the crazy stuff you did before the surgery."

"I'll be happy if I can drive."

"Good, because driving is about all you can do, and that very carefully. No hot-rodding. You can start walking and jogging but absolutely no weight-lifting or strenuous exercise for a few more weeks."

"I understand. I've been reading up on recovery, and it looks like I'm right where I need to be."

"Physician, heal thyself, huh?" The older doctor laughed. "You're learning good practice, as long as you're not self-diagnosing too much. Sometimes we doctors need someone else to point out what's going on. Our minds have a way of convincing us we know our body better than anybody, but our minds can lie to us."

"I hear that."

"Is your mother here?"

"She is. She's taken good care of me."

"Good." He looked down at his desk again. "Saw Clifton yesterday, and he's doing well. I think you may have added another ten years or more to his life."

"I hope more. I told him my goal was to jump out of an airplane with him someday."

Dr. Hobgood laughed. "Oh, don't tell me that. I've put too much work into you two to think about it."

Rance smiled. "I appreciate it, doctor."

"Call me Clay. I'm a friend of the family now, and we're both doctors. Before you leave, the nurse at the front will give you appointments for your re-checks. Will that be a problem? What have you decided as far as your job situation? If I need to refer you to a kidney specialist in another city, I'll be glad to."

"I haven't signed anything, but I'll let you know when I do. I plan to take the next few weeks off to keep healing. I don't want to start a new job in a weakened state."

"I understand." Dr. Hobgood stood and held his hand out, and Rance rose to grasp it. "Take care of yourself. And remember, nothing over ten pounds."

"Got it. Those weights in the corner will have to gather dust for a while."

Rance picked up the list of appointments from the nurse and walked over to his mother. "I've been granted my freedom, with limits."

"You can drive? Are you sure? Do I need to talk to Clay?"

"No, Mom, I'm fine. He said I can drive, to be careful, and to not lift any more than ten pounds for a few more weeks."

"All right. Well, what now?"

"Now, you take me to my car, and you go home."

He could see the sheen of tears in her eyes. "I hate to leave you. Are you sure you won't come back home and stay a few weeks?"

"No, I need to be here."

When they got to his car, still parked in the employee parking lot at the hospital, he turned to her. "I'm going to see Charly tonight, and I want to see Dad."

She put her hand on his cheek tenderly. "I know. Don't forget Ashton."

"I won't, Mom, I promise. We've come to a new understanding in the last few weeks. I think we're closer than we've been in a long time." He smiled and put his hand over hers.

"That makes me happy."

"Good. Now, I have to go." He held his hand up when she started to talk. "Don't worry. I'm fine. I'll take it easy."

"I saw that grimace. I don't think you know how to take it easy."

"I'll figure it out. Just think, this will make me a better doctor."

He kissed her quickly and opened the car door. "Thanks, Mom."

GETTING in and out of a low-slung Jaguar wasn't as easy as he thought it would be. It reminded him of the pain he felt getting in and out of bed when the surgery was fresh. He wouldn't complain. He had his wheels, and he was going to see Charly tonight.

He drove down Highway 17 toward Calvary Church, his still-tender incision feeling every bump in the road. He was trying to ignore it. Pulling in, he saw Charly and Mary Ann Livingston getting out of their car.

It took him longer to get out of the car than he was comfortable with, but Charly and her mother waited patiently.

"You made it." Charly's smile made him feel good all over.

"I said I would." He limped a bit as he walked over to them. "Mrs. Livingston, how are you?"

"I'm fine, Rance. It's I who should be asking you."

"I'm recovering. Still a few twinges. Nothing major. I was released to drive today."

"Well, don't overdo it."

Rance chuckled. "I got the same advice from my mother a few hours ago."

"It probably bears repeating."

Music began to play, and Rance walked in behind the two ladies and found their pew. Sitting by Charly was all he had thought about since he talked to her the day before.

Sharing a hymnal with her, he tried to keep up. He was unfamiliar with most hymns, so he mostly enjoyed reading the words and listening to Charly's soprano and her mother's sweet alto voice. Mrs. Livingston never missed a word.

During the prayer time, he found himself in his own prayer, even here with the other people. "God, thank You for bringing me to this point. Be with Charly and me as we talk. Help us to get it right this time and not depend on what we do, but what You've done."

It was difficult for Rance to maintain his attention to the message. His mind was full of all the things he wanted to say to Charly. At one point in the message, he stopped thinking and started listening when he heard that word again. Grace.

And He said to me, "My grace is sufficient for you, for My strength is made perfect in weakness." Therefore most gladly I will rather boast in my infirmities, that the power of Christ may rest upon me. [2 Cor. 12:9]

He started smiling. He knew people were looking at him like he was an idiot, but he couldn't help it. He knew God's grace. He glanced around and caught the eye of Tom Livingston, who was watching, nodding, and smiling back at him. He'd been weak the last few weeks, but he felt stronger in many ways than he had the last time he bungeed off a bridge or rode a mountain bike through the Blue Ridge Mountains. It was a strength like no other. It was the power that Christ made perfect, even in the most imperfect.

He glanced down at Charly, who was looking at him, then back at her brother. She was curious.

When the pastor asked Sarah to come to the piano, all Rance could think was that if they "coincidentally" sang the one song that had been in his head and all around him this summer, he would know God was here, and His strength had been made perfect in Rance Butler's weakness.

As soon as the song started, Rance began to smile. He'd never considered singing as anything he would like to do, but right now, right here? He was singing to the Lord.

"SARAH, I'M SKIPPING CHOIR TONIGHT." Charly couldn't stay. She simply had to find out what was going on with Rance. He actually sang the last hymn. And what was going on between him and Tom? Her brother had a few questions to answer. Right now, however, she wanted Rance's answers.

"I had a feeling." Sarah looked over Charly's shoulder at Rance talking to Tom as they stood in the aisle. "No problem. I'll let you know what we're singing. And you let me know what happens, okay?" Sarah winked at her and then pulled her into a hug. She whispered in Charly's ear, "I've been praying for you today. You were on my mind, and now I know why."

Charly hugged her back. "Thank you." She took a deep breath and then smiled. "Here goes nothin'."

"Or maybe somethin'." Sarah smiled and waved at Jared before disappearing through the back door of the sanctuary and to the choir room.

When she got to Rance, Jared, Tom, and their mother, she smiled.

Tom spoke first. "I'm going to run Mom home. Lucy's staying for a decorating committee meeting, so I've got an empty seat."

"Sarah and I drove separate." Jared looked down at his sleeping six-month-old son then looked up, eyes narrowed. "How about I come over with Beau, then the girls can ride to your house together, since you're on the way to our house."

Tom nodded. "Sounds like a plan. Braves game is on."

"That's what I know. Got any ice cream?"

"Yeah, for after we get the kids to bed or to sleep. Hayes can sniff it out." Tom shook his head. "He's just like his mother."

Charly grinned as Hurricane Hayes careened down the aisle to barrel into his dad's legs. She nodded. "Okay, if our logistics are settled . . ." She looked up at Rance. "I'm going to skip choir tonight."

His eyes widened, and he had a grin on his face, just for her.

Jared's eyebrows went up. "Did you have a note for Sarah?"

She dragged her eyes away from Rance's and sighed impatiently. "Don't worry, Sarah cleared my absence."

Jared laughed then stopped, when he saw little Beau begin to wiggle. "Better get this guy back in the car. A car ride is the best way to ensure he'll sleep during the ballgame."

Tom shook his head. "Hey, bud, you know if he sleeps now, he'll be up all night. I've been a dad for a while. I know this stuff." Tom puffed his chest out.

Jared thought a second. He lifted one side of his mouth in a grin. "Sometimes it's worth it."

Tom nodded, lips pursed as he thought. "You know, I think we've got nacho dip too."

"Sweet. Better get out of here. Beau and I will see you on your front porch. Nice to see you, Rance." He shook his hand and waved at the others before hurrying out the door.

"Ready to saddle up, Mama?" He had a baby carrier in each hand, and his mother had Hayes's hand.

"Ready. Hayes is going to help me to the car. You're getting to be such a big boy." Mary Ann smiled, loving the contact with her grandchildren. "Charlotte, have a good evening. You, too, Rance."

After she kissed Charly on the cheek, she walked out with Hayes, leaving Charly and Rance standing on the front stoop of the church.

"Do you want to go to the patio at my house? I think Lydia is working tonight at the hospital."

"I'd like that. See you there."

She watched as he walked carefully to his car, then as he squinted his eyes in pain as he folded himself up into his low-slung car.

RANCE WAS MORE tired than he thought. As soon as he got to Charly's house, pulling in right behind her, he pulled himself up out of the car, shut the door, and stood there a minute.

Charly walked over to him. "Are you okay?"

"I'm fine. It's been a big day." He stood straight, hoping she wouldn't notice the grimace on his face.

"You've driven too much. I saw you getting out of the car at church."

"I'll be okay. Recovery is tough."

She nodded. "All kinds." She gazed into his eyes, and then turned toward the door with her key. "Come on in. Would you like a glass of tea?"

"Is it sweet?"

She looked at him in horror. "Is there any other kind?"

"I've heard of people not sweetening it. Personally, I think it's an urban legend." He grinned as he caught up with her on the porch.

They entered, and Charly put her bag down and went straight to the kitchen. "Do you want to have a seat in here where it's more comfortable?"

"Might not be a bad idea. I wanted to walk on the beach, but I think I've done enough walking today."

She came in carrying his iced tea and put it on a coaster on the coffee table. She hesitated, as if unsure where to sit.

"Sit with me?" He looked up at her, hating the uncertainty in her eyes.

"Okay." She waited. After all he was the one to make first contact, and he was the one who wanted to talk.

"Charly, a lot has happened in the last few months. Most of it you know, and after the fool I made of myself in Nashville, I wouldn't blame you if you asked me to leave."

"I haven't, have I?" She looked at him calmly.

"No, you haven't." He looked into her eyes. He knew, weeks ago, that he loved her. He knew he would do anything for her. She had to know he hadn't turned to God to gain her favor.

"When I went to Nashville, I did a stupid thing. Ever since, God has surrounded me with people pointing me to Him. I can't explain it."

Her eyes widened, and she stopped him. "I can. It was prayer. After that night, the next morning Jake and I prayed for you. We prayed for someone to come by your side and help you." She paused, gazing at him. "Tell me what happened."

"First, it was Phil, the corporate headhunter that got me the interview. He reamed me out and set me straight before I left. Then, when I got home, I saw Sam, who is a Christ-follower now because of your brother and Jared."

"Wow. I never knew. He's been in contact with Sam all this time?"

"Yes. On my way out of the prison, I saw Tom, and he

answered a lot of questions for me. Questions about why God would love somebody like me."

"God's grace."

"And then there was that song. 'Amazing Grace.'" He chuckled and shook his head in amazement. "Would you believe everywhere I've gone, I've heard that song? When I heard it walking down the street in Nashville, coming out of a music venue, I was so angry I found the nearest bar and got drunk."

She nodded, listening intently. "God loves us enough to not let us go."

"I'm discovering that." He took her hand and rubbed the top of it with his other hand. It was so soft, so smooth. "Charly, I don't pretend to know everything about this, but I know I have faith in God and that he loved me enough to die for me."

Charly flung her arms around his neck and held him tightly, sobbing into his shoulder.

"Hey . . ."

She pulled away finally and smiled at him. "I'm sorry. I just . . ." She reached for a nearby tissue and blew her nose. ". . . I'm so happy to hear you talk like this. I was so afraid I'd messed things up."

"Messed things up, how?"

"Oh, I've held a lot of bitterness inside, and it made me angry with God. First, for taking my dad away and then for Mom's blindness. It started out with me going through the motions, doing all the things I was expected to do, and then it got to be a battle of wills. My will against God's, all the while, fooling myself and everyone else. Except I couldn't fool Him."

"No, I don't think we can." He pulled her to him and sat there, holding her.

"I wanted to prove I could do all the stuff without having to depend on God, and it hasn't worked out very well."

"I know. I was doing the same thing, but from a human

standpoint on the other side of faith." He pulled away and looked deeply into her eyes. "Charly, I love you."

She smiled, touching her fingers to his face. "I love you too."

He couldn't stand it anymore. His lips automatically caught hers in a kiss that had to tell her all she needed to know about how much he had missed her.

His kiss seared its way into her heart. She had known for a while her heart had been captured by Rance Butler, and God used so many things to draw them together.

Sitting together on the sofa, arms entwined as they relaxed in their new love, Charly suddenly had a thought, and she sat straight, looking him in the eye.

"Rance, what job did you take, or have you taken one yet?"

He grinned and reached over to kiss her once more. "I have a couple of options. I didn't want to decide until I talked to you."

"What if things hadn't gone the way you wanted?"

"I had a feeling." His lips found hers once more, and he laughed when she pulled away. "Okay, okay, I'll tell you. I've had two offers. One is with Dr. Hobgood, who did my surgery, and one is with a family practice on Pawley's Island."

"Seriously? Both of them are here? What about Nashville?"

He twisted his lips. "Honestly, after that night, I kinda lost interest. It would be a great gig, but I don't want to be so far from my family. Sam gets out next week, and Dad's not getting any younger, and then there are my parents." He shrugged. "I've found home. Do you know the main reason? I don't think I could leave you again."

She smiled. "I like your reasons, especially the last one. Although, I don't think you could have gotten rid of me so easily."

CHAPTER THIRTY-THREE

February

Rance pulled Charly into the pantry of Pilot Oaks after making sure there were no onlookers then proceeded to kiss her senseless. "I've wanted to do this all day."

She swatted his arm. "You're incorrigible."

He pulled her closer and leaned his forehead on hers. "And you love it."

"I do." She grinned, knowing from experience she was turning several shades of red.

"And you'll be saying those words to me soon. How soon?"

"We haven't even told our families yet." She snuggled into his arms and played with his tie, then the sparkling ring on her left hand, third finger.

"Well, you didn't want to steal Emma and Rafe's thunder." He bent down to kiss the little bit of shoulder he could access with the wide neck of her dress, making her shiver, which made him chuckle.

"I guess I should take my ring off until we announce it."

"Leave it on. See if anybody notices."

She nodded. "We'll announce it tomorrow. How's that?"

"I guess it will have to do. Unless somebody notices, and then all bets are off. Then can we set the date? And by set the date, I mean, how soon can we possibly get married?"

Her arms snaked up and around his neck, pulling closer to him. "Less than a year."

"A year? Are you kidding me? There's no way we're waiting a year to get married."

"I said less than."

"Not good enough."

She felt the giggle bubble up as his hand clutched her sides tighter. He knew she was ticklish, and he knew exactly how to use the hard-won information. "Stop tickling me, or I'll start planning for a destination wedding in Hawaii two years from now."

"I can think of worse places, actually. I figured you wanted to get married here."

"I do." She sighed. "I want to get married at the church and have the reception here."

"Me too. And, since we kind of have an 'in' with a local wedding planner, as well as the venues, don't you think we could throw something together for, say, June?"

"Rance Elliot Butler, it'll take longer than four months to get my dress."

His face fell a little.

"I can see we're going to have to start watching *Say Yes to the Dress* together, so you'll get the idea." She shook her head. "Poor thing, you have no idea, do you?"

He gazed into her eyes. "However long we have to wait, it will be worth it."

"It will. And by the way, I'm not any happier about it than you are."

"Good. Maybe that will speed things along."

When the pantry door opened, Prudie, the housekeeper, gave

them a pointed look. "What are you two young-uns doin' in here?"

Their eyes met, and then both of them said, "Um . . ."

Prudie laughed. "I wasn't born yesterday, and there's been more than one courtship going on around here, looks to me like. So, when's the wedding?"

They simply stared at her.

"I noticed a little more sparkle in my pantry than usual." She pointed to the ring on Charly's hand still draped over Rance's shoulder.

"Don't tell anybody. We don't want to spoil things for Emma and Rafe." Charly whispered. "It happened last night, and we're going to tell everyone tomorrow."

Prudie waved her hand and laughed. "You'll never be able to keep it to yourself. Trust me. Remember when Lucy and Tom got engaged? It was at Sarah and Jared's reception. Everybody was thrilled, and nobody thought of it as stealing anybody else's thunder. Instead, they were glad it finally happened." She chuckled. "They sure did beat around the bush, those two."

"Tell me about it." Charly looked up at Rance. "What do you think?"

"I think we wait and see what happens."

"Okay, it's the non-plan, then." She gave him her most brilliant smile.

"I know one thing that would help Emma and Rafe."

"What?"

"If you two would get out of the pantry and set those tables up in the dining room like you were supposed to be doing." Prudie gave them the stink eye and then softened it with a wink and a grin.

"Yes, ma'am." Rance saluted and followed Charly, who was pulling him by the hand into the dining room.

VALENTINE'S DAY weddings were popular, and Quince Wedding Designs had already put on an afternoon wedding. But the one this evening was special.

Charly and Rance arranged and set the tables in the large dining room with cloths, fine china, silver, and beautiful peonies imported from South America. It was a truly elegant Southern wedding at Pilot Oaks. Lucy was discussing logistics with the caterers and Prudie in the kitchen, Lydia was putting the flowers together with her artistic flair, and Sarah was in the parlor getting her music ready for the ceremony.

Emma came into the dining room two hours before the ceremony to check on things.

"What are you doing here? Aren't you supposed to be upstairs resting and getting beautiful for your own wedding?" Charly shook her head in despair. "You're the bride, for goodness sake!"

Emma turned pink. "I know. I guess I'm not used to not being in charge."

"Well, you'd better get used to it, because Lucy and I have things under control for the next month."

Lucy came in when she heard Emma's voice. "Yes, ma'am, we do, and we might want you to be slightly surprised and a little awestruck like our regular brides."

Emma smiled. "You two. What would I do without you?"

Lucy put her hands on her slender hips and shook her head. "You probably would still be planning other people's weddings instead of your own."

She laughed and hugged her business partner. "You're a peach, Luce. All right, I'll leave you to it, and I won't peek until after the ceremony."

"When your mom and dad get here, I'll take them up to you, so don't worry about a thing, please? Where's Sophie?"

"She forgot her shoes, so she went home to pick them up. I

can't believe my baby is driving. I think I'm more nervous about her driving than I am about marrying Rafe."

Sarah came in to the dining room, phone in hand. "Sophie called, and she's on her way back. Said you weren't answering your phone, and she knew you would be worried." She grinned. "Boy, does she have you pegged."

"Fine with me, as long as she keeps me in the loop." She paused and looked at them in horror. "Good grief, one of these days it'll be Sophie getting married."

"She'll have to date first." Lucy was quick. "You know, Hayes has always been in love with her. Maybe you should hold off on letting her date for another twenty years or so?" She shrugged.

Emma laughed, her nervousness dissipating. "That would be all right with me."

Charly went back to setting up, figuring she could be part of the conversation and work at the same time. She smoothed the table cloth with her hands as Rance put cloths on the other tables. "When will Ginger be here to do hair and makeup?"

"In about a half hour, but when were you going to tell us about the sparkling rock on your hand?" Lucy grabbed her hand and looked up at her with her mouth hanging open.

"The jig is up." Rance laughed, and Charly gave him a look.

"We wanted to wait until after the wedding to announce it."

Lucy squealed and pulled Charly into a hug. "Give, girl. When did this happen? Does Mom know?" She looked at Rance. "Do your parents know?" Lucy was tongue tied with all her questions.

"My parents, all three of them, know, and Mrs. Livingston knows. That's the extent of it." Rance put his arm around Charly and pulled her close.

"And Lydia." Charly felt her face heat.

"Lydia? I thought we were keeping it to the parents?"

"She's my best friend. I had to tell her. She practically guessed, anyway. As for the other question, he asked me last night." The room didn't need the candles that were being carefully placed on the tables. Charly's smile was bright enough to light the way.

"Uh, what did you say?" Lucy giggled. "I'm assuming yes?"

"Definitely." She looked up at her fiancé of a day. "I guess it seems quick to most people, but it's been a long eleven months."

"And we wasted most of it. I was determined not to waste any more."

Emma had tears in her eyes and hugged the couple. "I'm so happy for you, and to find this out on my wedding day. It makes it much more special to me."

"You might even get a deal on wedding planning." Lucy winked at her sister-in-law as she went to hug Rance. "I'm so excited!"

Sarah oohed and ahhed over the ring. "Lucy got engaged at my wedding, and now yours is right here on Emma's. I think it's a nice tradition, don't you?"

Charly grinned. "I guess as many weddings as we've been a part of, it isn't too much of a stretch."

EMMA AND RAFE stood in front of the ornate fireplace in the front parlor of Pilot Oaks. Sophie stood next to Emma, and Rafe's father stood next to him. Charly looked at the intimate group of people assembled, wondering at the relationships that had begun, changed, and thrived over the years she had known these people.

Rance put his arm around her and then pulled her left hand in his, playing with the ring he had placed on her finger the night before. She smiled. The ceremony was small but beautiful. God was there.

Emma's dress was a shimmering ivory gown with sleeves

coming down to a point at her wrists and a simple column shape that suited her slender figure. Her auburn hair had been arranged in a sleek French twist, a style she often wore, so it was perfect for the day.

Rafe was handsome in a charcoal grey suit and a red tie, homage to the date, which was Valentine's Day. As beautiful as Emma was, it was Rafe Charly couldn't stop watching. From his first glimpse of Emma, there had been tears in his eyes and a smile on his face. The love flowing from him to his bride was so evident it couldn't help but bring a tear to her eye. To have a man look at one in such a way? It was too good to be true. But it was true.

Charly sighed, and Rance pulled her closer. It was perfect. Since it got dark so early, there were candles all around, out of reach of the little ones in attendance. There were three crawlers in the room, and Hayes, who had acted as the ring-bearer.

Her attention was drawn to the pastor as he began to read scripture from the Song of Songs 8:6-7.

"Place me like a seal over your heart, like a seal on your arm.

For love is as strong as death, its jealousy as enduring as the grave.

Love flashes like fire, the brightest kind of flame.

Many waters cannot quench love, nor can rivers drown it.

If a man tried to buy love with all his wealth, his offer would be utterly scorned."

Love. You can't buy it. It's a gift. Like being a follower of Jesus. It's all about grace, something you can't buy, and you don't deserve.

Charly turned her hand in Rance's and linked her fingers with his, watching as Emma and Rafe, who had been hurt so many times, made a commitment to one another to love, honor, and cherish one another until death parts them.

ONCE THE CATERERS TOOK OVER, Charly was free to enjoy the reception. Word of the engagement had gotten out, so she was getting used to people coming up to her and grabbing her hand to gawk at her diamond.

Rance had done a good job. She had known he was the one since October, but she hadn't expected a marriage proposal so soon. God was good.

Rance had gone to have their punch cups refilled. She was sitting at a table as the crowd began to disperse when Tom and Jared sat down on either side of her, elbows on the table.

"All right, little sister, time to give your brothers the scoop." Tom gave Rance a mock-glare across the room.

Jared gave him the "I'm watching you" signal.

"Don't be mean to my future husband."

"We won't be any meaner to him than we have been to you, I promise." Tom grinned and put his arm around her to give her a hug. "I'm glad you're getting an earlier start than me."

Jared glared at Tom. "Hey, you're just glad the pressure might be off to produce more grandkids. I mean, once you get started, the questions never quit coming about when you're gonna have another one." Jared shook his head.

Tom nodded and grinned. "That might be part of it, now that you mention it."

"You two are impossible."

"Are these gentlemen bothering you, miss?" Rance came up behind her and put his hands on her shoulders.

"What are you, the bouncer?"

Rance smiled. "Only if needed."

"Sit down here with us." Tom pulled out a chair. "If you're going to be in this family, and I'm including Jared and Sarah in this, you better get used to a few things."

"Such as?" Rance looked curious.

"Getting teased, pranked, beaten at sports, watching sports, and doing whatever your wife tells you to do." Tom ticked the items off, one finger at a time.

"I think that's doable. Except for the getting beaten at sports. I have the advantage there." Rance looked at the two men with an arched brow and a serious look on his face.

"And what advantage might that be?"

He coughed. "About six years and an actual set of abs."

Charly laughed. Rance was going to be a great addition to their little family.

Tom looked at Jared and shook his head. "A bit harsh, don't you think?"

"Harsh, but true." Jared looked down at his stomach. "We're going to have to get busy before we end up with a Dad-bod."

Tom picked up his water goblet. "I'll drink more water. Works every time."

"Okay, tell me I didn't walk over here only to hear Tom and Jared talking about their famous water diet." Lucy shook her head in disgust. Lucy and Sarah had joined them, one baby each, MariAnne and Beau.

Sophie was entertaining Hayes, and Lydia was bouncing around with Evan, Jake hovering over them as if afraid she was going to drop him. If only he knew how tough that kid was. He climbed on everything, which meant he fell off of everything.

"You did, but I think it'll work out. They're giving Rance the family manhood orientation."

Sarah laughed and handed Beau down to Jared when the baby tipped himself over, in utter trust, to reach for his dad. "You'll be okay. They needed a little competition." She pulled two chairs over, one for herself and one for Lucy.

"When do we get to start planning your wedding?" Lucy sat, baby in lap, her eyes glittering in the candlelight.

Charly looked at Rance, who answered. "As quickly as possible."

"Well, you know, I am the queen of getting a wedding together quickly." Lucy batted her eyes.

Tom nodded. "She is. We were engaged, what, two months?"

Rance jumped on it. "Seriously? Charly's been saying less than a year, but I say let's get this show on the road."

"We'll see. I don't even have any Pinterest boards for weddings yet. Well, not for mine anyway."

Lucy waved her hand. "No problem." She pulled out her phone, holding it out of reach of MariAnne, and tapped away. "I added you to my secret board, 'Charly's Wedding.'"

"You have a Pinterest board for my wedding?"

Lucy snorted and frowned as she glanced at a few "pins" before looking up. "Of course I do. I'm a wedding planner, and MariAnne won't need my services for several years, so you are my next target." She gave her a cheesy smile.

Sarah nodded. "She can do it. She honed her skills on me and then went into business with Emma."

"Thank you?" She looked at Rance. "Looks like we're going to be planning a wedding. And quickly."

He gave a fist pump. "Yes."

Charly laid her hand on his arm to temper his enthusiasm. "But not too quickly. I want to enjoy planning my own wedding. Tell you what. If I find a dress, I'll let the dress determine the timeline. How's that?"

Rance nodded. "I can go along with that."

They linked pinkies.

"Is it too cold to walk down to the beach?" Rance pulled on her hand as they got ready to leave.

"I don't think so. It got up to a record eighty degrees today, but I'll grab my jacket."

"I'll be glad to keep you warm." He wiggled his eyebrows at her and grinned.

She smiled back but put her jacket on anyway. "I'll hold you to it."

They made their way down the path to the beach, when another thought came to her. "Let's go to the swing instead, okay?"

"Sure. I wanted to get you away from prying eyes."

They changed direction, instead following the landscape lights to the swing overlooking the marsh. "We may wish we'd brought a blanket." The wind had shifted, coming in off the water.

"We won't stay long."

They found their way to the swing, Rance putting his arm around her as they sat, Charly curling her feet up under her, cuddling up to him as he moved the swing gently with one foot. "It's so quiet."

"It's nice." He nuzzled her until she lifted her lips to his.

After a moment, she pulled away and smiled. "I love you, Rance." She splayed her hand on his chest, her ring sparkling in the bright moonlight. "I think my ring is brighter than the stars."

"Your eyes are brighter to me. I love you, too, Charlotte Anne." He chuckled. "It hit me that your middle name is the same as my mom's name."

"Then we shall name a daughter 'Anne.'"

"With an 'E?'"

She grinned. "Of course."

She looked up at him, glad the moonlight let her see his face. "Do you think we're getting too many blessings, too soon?"

He shook his head. "No. I don't think we deserve it either. I think God likes to bless His children."

"I'm glad."

"I am too." He tightened his arms around her.

"Have you told Sam?" She grinned.

He nodded sheepishly. "Sorry I gave you a hard time for telling Lydia. This is the first time I've had a brother to share things with."

"They're pretty great, you know. If you tell Tom I said it, I'll deny it!" She shook her finger in his face and laughed.

"I see how it is. I'm looking forward to spending time with Tom and Jared. I think I can learn a lot from them."

"And Sam."

"Yes, and Sam. I think he's going to stay in Charleston for a while, until he figures out what he's going to do next." He nodded. "He wants to get to know Mom again."

"That's good. How does your dad, Ashton, feel about all of this?"

"I think he wants to help Sam, and he's in a position to do it. He told Sam he wished Mom had brought him along when she left."

"That's progress." Charly nodded and looked out over the marsh, trying to make out a light in the distance.

"It's prayer." He turned toward her. "Thanks for introducing me to 'Amazing Grace'."

She laughed. "It's been around a long time. I don't think I can get the credit for it."

"Okay, thanks for being so enticing I was willing to go to church to spend time with you." He kissed her and then held her for a minute.

"Thank you for not making me choose."

"Choose what?"

"You, or my relationship with Jesus." She gazed into his eyes, shaking her head slowly.

He took his arm from around her and put his hands on her cheeks. "I never want to do that. Even before I knew God, I knew it wasn't right. We're in this together, and I'm determined to be the man you need, and I hope I can make you laugh every day of your life."

"And I'm determined to be the woman you need, and I hope I can make you smile every day of your life."

"Then I think we should get married. What do you think?" He grinned and winked at her.

She put her hands on top of his, her eyes sparkling in the moonlight. "I would say yes to you every day for the rest of my life."

Thank you for reading Carolina Grace and the Southern Breeze Series! I hope you've enjoyed your trip to South Carolina in each one. While I do not live in South Carolina, I've been there, and as I've said many times, fell in love with the area. Many of the places in these books are real, but a few, like Pilot Oaks, Crawford and Benton Real Estate, Calvary Church, and others, are purely figments of my imagination. I tried to remain true to the area with restaurants and historical districts, though.

While I've loved writing about SC, I thought it was time to set some stories in Kentucky! Keep an eye out for my new Reno-Vations series! More info to come!

Thanks again and drop me a line! You can find me on Facebook, Twitter, and Instagram, as well as on my website at www. reginaruddmerrick.com. I love to hear from my readers!

Regina Rudd Merrick

ABOUT THE AUTHOR

Regina Merrick began reading romance and thinking of book ideas as early as her teenage years when she attempted a happily-ever-after sequel to "Gone With the Wind." That love of fiction parlayed into a career as both a school and public librarian, and more recently, as a full-time author. Married for nearly 35 years and active in their local church, Regina and her retired-teacher husband have two grown daughters who share her love of music, writing, and the arts. She resides in a 100-year-old house in Marion, KY with her husband and their dog, Cedric, whose late litter-mate, Oliver, was the model for Sarah's Schnauzer-mix.

An unexpected inheritance in South Carolina comes at the perfect time for Sarah Crawford. But will a dream about an antebellum mansion, many rooms to be explored, and a man with dark brown eyes give her the confidence to take a leap of faith, leaving friends, family, and her job behind?

Carolina Dream by Regina Rudd Merrick.

She's always gotten everything she's wanted. He thinks he has to give up everything. Her best friend's wedding is foremost on Lucy Dixon's radar. Her biggest concern is once again meeting Tom Livingston, who has ignored her since an idyllic date on the boardwalk of Myrtle Beach the previous summer. At least, it is her biggest concern until tragedy strikes. Where is her loving, merciful God, now? When Tom Livingston meets Lucy, the attraction is instant. Soon after, his mother is diagnosed with an untreatable illness, and his personal life is pushed aside. His work with the sheriff's department, his family–they are more important. He knows about the love of God, but circumstances make him feel as if God's mercy is for everyone else, not him. Can a wedding and a hurricane–blessing and tragedy–bring them together?

Carolina Mercy by Regina Rudd Merrick

Prairie Sky Series – Book Three

She had her life planned out ~ until he rode in

Illinois prairie ~ 1859

After four long years away, Esther Stanton returns to the prairie to care for her sister Charlotte's family following the birth of her second child. The month-long stay seems much too short as Esther becomes acquainted with her brother-in-law's new ranch hand, Stewart Brant. When obligations compel her to return to Cincinnati and to the man her overbearing mother intends her to wed, she loses hope of ever knowing true happiness.

Still reeling from a hurtful relationship, Stew is reluctant to open his heart to Esther. But when he faces a life-threatening injury with Esther tending him, their bond deepens. Heartbroken when she leaves, he sets out after her and inadvertently stumbles across an illegal slave-trade operation, the knowledge of which puts him, as well as Esther and her family, in jeopardy.

Under Moonlit Skies is a 2020 Selah Awards finalist in the Western category.

Under Moonlit Skies by Cynthia Roemer.

Hope needs more hope. Faith needs more faith. They both need a whole lot of love.

Two sisters. One summer. Multiple problems.

Younger sister Hope has lost her job, her car, and her boyfriend all in one day. Her well-laid plans for life have gone sideways, as has her hope in God.

Older sister Faith is finally getting her dream-come-true after years of struggles and prayers. But when her mom talks her into letting Hope move in for the summer, will the stress turn her dream into a nightmare? Is her faith in God strong enough to handle everything?

For two sisters who haven't gotten along in years, this summer together could be a disaster, or it could lead them to a closer relationship with each other and God. Can they overcome all life is throwing at them? Or is this going to destroy their relationship for good?

Faith and Hope by Amy Anguish.

After almost three years of living under a fog of grief, Ellen Shepherd is ready for the next chapter in her life. Perhaps she'll find adventure during a visit to Galway. Her idea of excitement consists of exploring Ireland for yarn to feature in her shop back home, but the adventure awaiting her includes an edgy stranger who disrupts her tea time, challenges her belief system, and stirs up feelings she thought she'd buried with her husband.

After years of ignoring God, nursing anger, and stifling his grief, Payne Anderson isn't ready for the feelings a chance encounter with an enchanting stranger evokes. Though avoiding women and small talk has been his pattern, something about Ellen makes him want to seek her —and God again.

Can Ellen accept a new life different than the one she planned? Can Payne release his guilt and accept the peace he's longed for? Can they surrender their past pain and embrace healing together, or will fear and doubt ruin their second chance at happiness?

Irish Encounter by Hope Toler Dougherty.

www.ingramcontent.com/pod-product-compliance
Lightning Source LLC
Chambersburg PA
CBHW060625100726
47907CB00006B/1771